As Others See Us

A novella of Sewanee
and other stories of the Old South

Sarah Barnwell Elliott

Sarah Barnwell Elliott.

DEDICATED
TO
MY BROTHER
John Gibbes Barnwell Elliott, M. D.
OF
NEW ORLEANS, LOUISIANA.

Current edition by Low Country Press, Savannah Georgia, 2012
www.lowcountrypress.net
Preface © 2012 Low Country Press

Low Country Press Trade Paperback ISBN
978-0-9883044-1-3

Praise for the first edition of *The Durket Sperret*

"Hannah Warren moves before us, a homespun heroine, in whose possibility one is glad to believe....The author writes of her mountaineers with discrimination born of intimate knowledge." —*The Nation*

"A refreshing departure. In 'The Durket Sperret' we have found the vigorous drawing of character and the knack of beguiling narrative that must combine to make a book worth reading a second time." —*New York Tribune*

"Strengthens Miss Elliott's reputation as a novelist. . . Each character is sustained and vigorous. . . We find ourselves pondering over each individual mentioned, thinking how perfectly he was made to do his part." —*New York Commercial Advertiser*

"The story is one that would attract attention anywhere, with its racy wit and its sketch of a high-minded, brave, unselfish mountain girl. . . An unusually satisfactory novel." —*Buffalo Express*

"*The Durket Sperret* is an extremely well-written book, and notwithstanding the ambiguity of its title, does not lead one into the labyrinth of dialect one is led at the outset to expect. The realism of the story, and the absolute understanding of the inner nature of the mountain folk it deals with, are remarkable." —*The Overland Monthy*

Praise for other novels by Sarah Elliott

John Paget

"A story far above the ordinary." —*Buffalo Commercial*

"Is vivacious and humorous, and its scenes are evidently drawn from life." —*The Churchman*

Jerry

"Open up on a plane of deep emotional force, and never for a chapter does it sink below that level." —*Life*

Also by Sarah Barnwell Elliott

Novels

The Felmeres

A Simple Heart

Jerry

John Paget

The Making of Jane

Short Story Collection

An Incident and Other Happenings

Non-fiction

Sam Houston

Play

His Majesty's Servant

Table of Contents

PREFACE

As *Others See Us* was the title that Sarah Barnwell Elliott (November 29, 1848 - August 30, 1928) gave to the novella that her publisher printed as *The Durket Sperret*. The odd title the publisher gave the work comes from the Tennessee mountain dialect in which Elliott wrote. At the time, "sperret" was how the word "spirit" was pronounced. The Durket family, headed by the matriarch, Grandmother Warren, had plenty of that spirit, which was heavily tinted with a dark shade of hubris.

The title, "As Others See Us," is given to this current collection as those words capture much of the local color infused into the work of Sewanee's first person of letters. Sarah Elliott. who preferred to be called "Sada," aspired to be an author. Her first book, *The Felmeres*, brought moderate success. A chance meeting in Italy in 1887 set Sada on the path for the type of work for which she is remembered.

She had travelled to the Holy Land with her brother Robert, the Missionary Bishop of West Texas. Robert was ill and the trip was intended to be restorative. While in the Holy Land, however, it became clear that his condition was worsening. He returned home, and Sada continued her travels on her own, journeying next to Italy. There she met Constance Fenimore Woolson (1840-1894). The grandniece of James Fenimore Cooper was already known for regional writing about both the Great Lakes Region and the South. Woolson's work was regularly featured in *Harper's Magazine* and *The Atlantic Monthly*. She was known, as well, for her "local color" writings and encouraged Sada to write what she knew best. Prior to this point, Sada's work, other than *The Felmeres,* had no particular setting. That work, though in the South, did not deal with particularly Southern concerns.

Sada returned from her trip after learning of her brother Robert's death. She would follow Woolson's advice and soon a steady stream of local color writings supported Sada adequately for her to pursue the sort of life to which her characters would aspire—an independent woman who could provide for herself from her own work.

Sada also wrote literary criticism and she viewed her own work most harshly, referring to it as "manufactured." At the time *The Durket Sperret* she told *Book News* of the story,

> "It came to me and so I wrote it. Having lived most of my life at Sewanee, the people are well known to me, and no one can know them without being struck by the pride of family which goes down through every grade of life, and consequently, with that conservative self-satisfaction which is the legitimate child of family pride, and which looks on progress as almost a sin, and change of any kind, as extremely pernicious. Also, the contempt for 'service' which obtains in the heart of most Americans, and which is very rife in the old slave owning regions. But truly, the people were interesting to me, and in 'The Durket Sperret,' I hoped to make them interesting to others."

This gives us an unvarnished glimpse into the thoughts of the author. She wrote to support herself and this meant writing what would sell. She claims no more inspiration than "It came to me and I wrote it." As an interest in local color developed, Sada capitalized on that interest by crafting stories that would interest *Scribner's, Harper's Monthly* and the other publications where her work was regularly published. A particular example of this are the eight pieces of short fiction which she wrote for *Youth Companion*. The publication paid its writers well, but lacked prestige. Yet Sada had become determined to make it on her own and was not beyond mercenary motives.

Sarah Bull Barnwell Elliott

Yet, even while laboring under the very unaristocratic burden of writing what would sell, and working with whatever came to her, Sada still forged a particular vision. She would achieve the most noteriety in her own lifetime for the novel *Jerry*, the tragic story of a boy who runs away from an abusive father to become a labor leader and teacher. Jerry goes on to inherit a fortune and become corrupted by wealth. The success of that novel aside, Elliott's legacy is primarily the creation of strong female characters struggling to make their own way in the world. Their journeys are not unlike that of Sada herself who was born to Southern aristocracy during the pre-Civil War South and went on to make her own way in the world, surviving on nothing more than her keen wit and intellect.

She was born the daughter of the first Episcopal Bishop of Georgia in a family that had already produced colonial governors, distinguished doctors, lawyers, and many of the landed rice and cotton plantation owners of coastal South Carolina and Georgia. She was raised in a family where a woman's success was realized through a good marriage, having children, and managing the household. Her father lost the family fortune in 1852, when Sada was just four years old. He had personally guaranteed the debts of the Montpelier Institute, a school he founded in central Georgia. The school's failure took all of his lands and their enslaved workers. The Elliotts would have to survive only on her father's salary as Bishop. Then, when Sada was 18, the Bishop died leaving his wife with no income. Sada and her mother moved to the University of the South at Sewanee, Tennessee. Bishop Elliott had founded the University before the Civil War along with Bishop Polk of Louisiana and Bishop Otey of Tennessee. But at the time of the conflict, only the cornerstone had been laid. Bishop Elliott's good friend, the Rev. Charles Quintard, was elected as the Second Bishop of Tennessee and went on to found Sewanee anew. The Elliott women moved to the Cumberland Plateau in 1870, the year after classes started at the new school. Sada's brother John was a physician and he built a home for his wife, Lucy, his mother and sister. They called it "Saint's Rest," and alongside they built a boarding house for college students, which came to be called "Sinner's Hope." In her mother's time, Saint's Rest held a weekly Open House on Sundays. A 1913 issue of *The Bookman* described Sada Elliott's back garden as the literary meeting place of the University. Sada wrote in a cabin in the back yard named "Jerry" for her most famous character. She had achieved self-reliance.

Beyond providing for herself, Sada played the family "short stop" as she would call it, attending to the needs of others. In 1904, at the age of 54, Sada became a mother to her orphaned nephews. For the next nine years she raised Stephen, Charles and John Puckette. During that time, she wrote much less and published little.

With the boys on their own, Sada turned to the women's suffrage movement. Having written the well-regarded novel of the model new women in 1901's *The Making of Jane*, Sada was a natural choice for leadership. She was twice elected as President for the Tennessee Equal Suffrage Association. In that role, she wrote its "Manifesto" and invited the National American Suffrage Association to meet in Tennessee. Soon after, Tennessee became the critical 26th state to ratify the Nineteenth Ammendment and so make it law.

Sada left a legacy of local color writing that demonstrates the challenges and paradoxes of the South through her eyes. Knowing her native South well, she could describe its patterns of life such as in the funeral in *The Durket Sperret*. She could also critique its traditions from the inside as when she writes of dueling in "Squire Kayley's Conclusions" and "Without the Courts." She challenges how treatment of blacks after emancipation was not followed with opportunity for education in her closing line of "An Incident." Her language, (such as the persistent use of the word "nigger") and her point of view are not always in keeping with contemporary views of a progressive woman, yet she held what were liberal views for her time.

Her greatest legacy, however, was in living the ideal she wrote about, embodying the changes she wished to see in the New South. It is in her life lived in congruity with her writings that we see both how difficult it was for a woman to become her own person, and also an example of how this could be lived without forsaking her native South or even her family responsibilities. Sada Elliott created strong female characters in fiction and then outdid them all in life.

This humorous story of an attorney trying to teach aggrieved persons to rely on the court system for justice originally appeared in the December 1897 issue of *Scribner's Magazine*. It was published in the short story collection *An Incident and Other Happenings* in 1899 by Harper & Brothers.

SQUIRE KAYLEY'S CONCLUSIONS

THERE IS A CERTAIN FAMILY LIKENESS IN ALL SMALL COUNTRY TOWNS that is quite consistent with a wide divergence in manners and customs, and one thing common to all is a "leading citizen." He is generally a good man, for after all it is the upright who best weather the storm and find permanent haven in the faith of their fellowmen.

The town of Greenville, like all her family, was extremely self-important, and when her "leading citizen," Mr. Joshua Kayley, commonly called Squire Kayley, was sent to Congress, Greenville became absolutely sure of the large place she filled in the public eye, and felt glad for the rest of the world that a teacher should go out from such a place as Greenville. In return, Squire Kayley felt deeply grateful for the honor done him, was proud of his town, of his county, and of his State, and went to his post determined to do all possible credit to his native region.

As has been intimated, Squire Kayley was an upright man; he was also a modest and an observant man, honestly desirous of thinking and doing right, and when he reached Washington he found much food for thought. He did not make many remarks during his term of office, but in a quiet way he made many investigations, and arrived at some astonishing conclusions. He found, among other things, that the West and the South were looked on as being uncivilized because of what in those regions were called "difficulties," not to speak of lynchings and other modes of supplementing the law.

He found out, also, that in quieter regions, instead of "a word and a blow," people brought action for "assault and battery," and "alienating affections," and "breach of promise," and the rest of it—delicate matters which in his experience had always been settled by a bullet or a caning. Not being a bloodthirsty man, he pondered much on these things, and determined at last that he would try the experiment of making his native town more law abiding. It was a herculean task, and he had serious doubts as to his success, but he was determined to try, for although Greenville could not boast that every man in her graveyard had died with his boots on, she could nevertheless bring to mind a long list of sons who had begun their march on the "lonely road" well shod.

He was sitting on the hotel piazza with a number of his constituents one afternoon after his return home, and while a negro handed about glasses filled with a topaz-colored mixture, crushed ice, mint, and straws, Squire Kayley told this story:

"A man up yonder," he began, "made some remarks about another man, a stranger from another region of the country; a few days afterwards the man was on the cars when the stranger walked up to him and, taking him by the nose, pulled him all the way down the car."

"Gosh!" exclaimed one listener.

"Did you stay for the funeral?" asked another.

"He didn't shoot," Squire Kayley answered, "he brought in a charge of assault and battery, and got two thousand dollars damages."

His audience groaned.

"You needn't groan," the Squire went on, with a steadiness in his tone and words such as a man puts into his actions when he is about to light a fuse, "that fellow had a level head. He had followed so quick that his nose wasn't hurt, and two thousand dollars is a lots better poultice for a man's honor than a fellowman's blood."

A dead silence followed this remark, and Squire Kayley, tilting his chair back against the wall, pulled gently at the straw in his glass. After a few moments a young fellow sitting on the railing of the piazza asked, "An' you'd sue for damages, Squire?"

"I ain't sure, Nick," Squire Kayley answered, slowly. "I hope I won't be tried, but I think the fellow had a level head."

"An' two thousand dollars is a heap er money," said another young fellow, thoughtfully.

"'Tain't so much the money, Loftus," the Squire answered, "as not shedding blood. They're lots more peaceable up yonder than we are, and they haven't got it by killing each other, either, and they're lots richer, too, and a good deal of it has come through being law abiding."

"Dang my soul, if you ain't changed J," cried an old fellow, jerking his rocking chair round so as to face Squire Kayley. "I'd noticed thet you'd smoothed your words a heap, an' had cut your hair short, an' shaved your face clean, but I hedn't looked for no fu'ther change, an' this is too much when you say you'd let a feller pull yo' nose an' be satisfied with two thousand dollars."

"I'd let you pull it for one, Uncle Adam," Squire Kayley answered, smiling.

There was a general laugh, but not a hearty one, for their leading citizen was announcing doctrines that would have branded any other townsman as a coward.

"There was another man," the Squire went on, "a fellow began to carry on with his wife; we'll suppose that he did what he could to stop it, then, after watching a while and seeing that things were hopeless, he brought action for alienating his wife's affections, and gained his suit and five thousand dollars."

"Damn it, man, you didn't think thet was right?" Uncle Adam cried again, growing very red in the face, while the other listeners looked at the Squire pleadingly, as if imploring him not to commit himself beyond redemption.

"Why not?" the Squire asked, taking another pull at his straw, "nothing could heal the hurt the woman had done him, and a woman as far gone as that didn't deserve to have blood spilled for her, and to leave her on the other fellow's hands, at the same time taking away his money, seems to me the most dismal punishment on the face of the earth."

"But Squire, could you have held yourself?" cried Nick.

"I ain't sure," the Squire answered, again, "and I won't be tried, being a bachelor, but that fellow had a level head."

Loftus did not venture to remark again on the money, and Uncle Adam and the others, having sunk into wondering silence, the Squire went on, "There was a fellow engaged to a girl; first thing she knew he was married to another girl; she sued for breach of promise and got her money."

"Fur God's sake, Joshua Kayley!" Uncle Adam pleaded, for the third time, and now with a tone of despair in his voice, "you wouldn't er let yo' daughter do thet?"

The Squire shook his head. "No," he said, "seeing I'm a bachelor, I wouldn't, but I do draw the line there. I don't know what I'd do to a man who should ill-treat my daughter, if I had one, but she shouldn't do anything; all the same, the girl had a level head. And I'll tell you," he went on, rising to his feet and waving his glass to emphasize his words, "I'll tell you that the people up yonder have got the right end of the stick. You'll not get peace nor honor by killing people, and you'll not make money by paying lawyers to defend you in murder trials, and we don't gain credit nor bring capital to our country by riots and difficulties, and they call us barbarous and uncivilized, they do, and we've got to change, we've got to become law-abiding. I love Greenville, and I love you all, and you've all got to help me change this town. God knows, and you know, that I ain't a coward, and if you could hear them talk about us and our ways, and read their papers about us and our doings, you'd try to help me," and he resumed his seat.

There was a moment's silence, then Uncle Adam brought his hand down sharply on the arm of his chair. "It's no use talkin', Josh," he said, "we ain't been raised that way, an' we ain't a goin' to change into no pulin' complainers to the law, nor patch up our dishonor with money. Why, Josh, even the niggers would scorn such talk, an' for the land's sake, stop it!"

There was a chuckle from the doorway, where the negro waiter had paused to listen.

Squire Kayley turned. "You there, Sam?" he said. "I'm glad of it, you can help me, too, you can go and tell the niggers what I say, and tell 'em I'm right."

The negro bent double over his waiter as if with restrained mirth. "Lawd, Boss," he said, "'tain't no use talkin' to niggers; it's too easy furrum to shoot en run, en dat's w'at a nigger 'll do ev'y time."

"An' the whites 'll shoot an' stan' to it!" cried Uncle Adam, "an' you've gone all wrong, Josh."

Squire Kayley shook his head. "No, Uncle Adam," he answered, "I'm right. People, and 'specially boys, seem to think that there's some kind of glory in defending what they call their honor, and half the time it's bad temper or bad liquor. But there's no glory in a coldblooded lawsuit, and if they knew that they'd have to go into court and have their lives and their characters turned inside out, they'd control themselves a little better."

A tall young woman, very much overdressed, was seen coming down the street on the other side. Nick slipped off the railing on to the pavement, and, stepping across quickly, joined her. The group on the hotel piazza was silent, watching the couple out of sight.

Then Uncle Adam said, "It beats me why Nick Tobin's wife is forever passin' this hotel. To my certain knowledge she's been by three times today."

"Maybe she has business downtown," suggested the Squire.

"Loftus Beesley's smilin' like he knows," was another suggestion.

Uncle Adam nudged Loftus. "Not long ago," he said, "we mighter thought it was 'cause Loftus was a settin' here."

"Well, she's gone," said Squire Kayley, sharply, "and I can't see how it's our business what she's gone for."

Uncle Adam looked at the speaker for a moment, the color mounting to his face. "It seems to me, Joshua Kayley," he answered, "thet you're losin' yo' mind. If I choose to make it my business who passes this hotel, I'm goin to make it my business, an' if I choose to say thet Nick Tobin's wife spen's her life gaddin' roun' these streets, I'm goin' to say it, an' I'll add thet when Nick's in town she does spen' her time on the streets, an' when he's travellin', or with his firm, over in the city, she spen's it at home receivin' the boys. An' fu'thermo' Loftus is one o' them boys, an' I'll instruct you again—Nick suspicions it, an' he leaves the Seelye boys, his own cousins, on guard' when he's gone, 'cause Nick's got no man to help him, an' the girl's own people can't do nothin' with her—now, what do you say?"

"That I'm mighty sorry for Nick," Squire Kayley answered, quietly, "he's a good fellow, a little hasty, but straight, and the least his friends can do is not to trifle with his wife behind his back, nor make her the subject of public comments, and I'll stand by Nick, and I'll stand by her for his sake. We all ought to."

Loftus moved uneasily, then joined Uncle Adam, who had risen, and, with a very much disgusted expression, stood looking down on Squire Kayley.

"I wish yo' new doctrines good luck, Josh," the old man said, sarcastically, "but I'm an ole bottle, an' the preacher says new wine busts ole bottles, an' I'm 'fraid o' bustin' if I takes in any mo', a' then you'd bring a suit for damages, so I'm goin'."

Squire Kayley laughed. "You can't make me mad, Uncle Adam," he said, "and you can say anything you please. Some day you'll see that I'm right."

Of course Squire Kayley's new doctrines were the town's talk in a few hours, and the women with one accord took his part.

Squire Kayley was right, they declared, was always right, and if he had broken up that hotbed of scandal that collected every afternoon on the hotel piazza he had done a good work. Women scarcely liked to pass the hotel, and although Letty Tobin deserved to be talked about because of her scandalous behavior with Loftus Beesley, still they were glad that the Squire had spoken plainly, even if in so doing he had taken Letty's part. Further, if he could persuade their sons and husbands to stop bullying each other, they would look on him as their deliverer from many anxieties and evils, and they would try to help him.

The next thing Greenville knew, an action for assault and battery was brought by Sam, the waiter at the hotel, against Uncle Adam Dozier, the autocrat of the hotel piazza.

The excitement was intense.

Of course Sam had come at once to Squire Kayley, and of course Squire Kayley could not refuse the case. He did his best to persuade Sam from it, for Uncle Adam had often before whacked Sam with his walking stick, but though perfectly amiable, Sam stood to his point.

The town was in a fume. Squire Kayley's popularity wasted like snow under a July sun, and there were no words capable of expressing Uncle Adam's sensations, nor any reputable printer who would have put his language into type.

The women, hitherto solid for Squire Kayley as the man in town who stood next to the clergy in the matter of uprightness, were divided, for though they detested Uncle Adam as an old reprobate with an unscrupulous tongue, still, the case was a negro against a white man, which brought many feelings other than justice into full play.

However, through it all, Squire Kayley was "quiet and peaceable and full of compassion," and he gained his case, and Sam his money, and Uncle Adam, having exhausted his vocabulary, took out his vengeance in an ostentatious and belligerent avoidance of the Squire.

But time, humanity's one patent medicine that really cures all, soothed Uncle Adam, and as Sam had discreetly disappeared, the old man resumed his position on the hotel piazza, where each day he used Squire Kayley's new doctrines as a peg on which to hang an ever-enlarging book of lamentations over the old times, and declared that since Sam's victory "every nigger in town was tryin' to git licked, which would be mighty good for them but for the money which the Squire hed attached. For everybody knew that a thrashin' was a nigger's bes' frien', while money was a pitfall of danger," but that "the nex' time he hit, he'd hit to kill, then Josh Kayley could have the pleasure of puttin' him in the penitentiary." Furthermore he said that he hoped "thet no other Greenville man would ever go to Washington if it was goin' to ruin him like it had ruined Josh. Josh had gone away an ole-time gen'leman, but only the omniscient Almighty knew what he had changed into 'fore he got back."

The occurrence had its effect, however, as object lessons always do, and, as the Squire observed, "Uncle Adam had ceased his gentle play with his walking stick."

Greenville resumed its deadly stillness after this, until the first cold snap in the autumn waked up the young people to a sense of the beauty of dances and candy-pullings, causing them to drive long distances to country places or to neighboring settlements to find a sufficient amount of amusement.

Of course Mrs. Grundy waked up, too, and while allowing them to have the most unquestioned freedom, the gossips kept a viciously strict account of the young people's fallings from grace, and especially were their eyes fixed on Letty Tobin, Nick's wife.

That Letty was beautiful no one denied, and her marriage to Nick Tobin had been an astonishment to all who knew her. Nick himself had been somewhat surprised, for up to the moment of her acceptance she had treated his loyal service as something of a joke, giving all her favors to other young men, especially to Loftus Beesley, who, for Greenville, was rich.

Nobody understood this sudden change of front, and all prophesied that the marriage would never take place. But it did, and in his love and gratitude Nick swore that if love and devotion could make Letty happy she should never have cause to repent her choice. And work he did, even Letty's mother declaring that he "spoiled the girl to death."

As Nick "travelled" for a firm in a neighboring city, he could be very little at home, which was declared to be "unfortunate," especially as Letty lived alone, declining even the company of her own sisters, who, doomed to the country, would have been very glad of a change to town.

Nick's comings and goings were uncertain also, but he came home as often and stayed as long as possible, meanwhile leaving to his cousins, Ben and Reub Seelye, the care of his wife and his home.

They had been married for a year now, and Nick had not yet entirely recovered from his surprise at his luck, for, besides being a modest fellow, his mind was as slow as his temper was quick. But when this first cold snap came, and all the young people of the town waked up to the delights of this weather that was so ideal for merrymaking, Nick was away, and Ben Seelye found himself very unhappy about his cousin's wife and about the talk that was so rife concerning her.

There was nothing that he could have proved, and yet he knew, and every one else knew, that things were not as they should be, and that Loftus Beesley was the man.

One morning Ben walked into Squire Kayley's office, pale, and somewhat breathless.

"What's up?" the Squire asked, at once, not even suggesting that his visitor should be seated.

Ben held out a telegram. "Nick's coming," he said, "and Letty's not here."

"Where is she?"

"We all drove over to Pinehollow last night to a candy-pulling," Ben explained, "and some of us stayed over all night at Colonel Bolles's, but this morning when I reached town I found that Letty had not come. She and Loftus left Bolles's a little ahead of me, and took the road home, so that I felt safe, but John Brewin says that she and Loftus turned off on the Valley Creek pike, and told him to tell me they'd be back by five o'clock and . . . and Nick is most here now!"

"Well?" queried the Squire.

"Well, it'll be death to somebody," Ben answered.

The Squire walked about a little bit with his hands in his pockets, then paused to look out of the window. "It shall not come to that," he said, at last, "there's no harm in the girl's going to a picnic, and if you'll meet Nick and tell him about it quietly, it'll be all right."

"If it was any other fellow but Loftus," Ben answered.

"Is Nick jealous of Loftus?"

"I don't know, but Loftus is so careful when Nick's at home that it makes a fellow think, an' when Nick's away, not a day passes but he sees Letty."

"And I've known that girl since she was a child," the Squire said, as if to himself, again pausing to look out of the window. After a moment he turned, "If she comes at five," he continued, "we can smooth it, but a girl who deceives her husband systematically may not come home at five."

Ben groaned.

The Squire sat down again, and there was silence in the little office until the Squire roused himself with a deep sigh.

"Well," he said, "you go and meet Nick and explain things as lightly as you can, and if she does not come at five you bring Nick here; I'll be here late this evening." And Ben went off.

Five o'clock found Nick and Ben waiting patiently at Nick's house; at six o'clock Reub Seelye joined them; at seven, Nick was lying on his bed, tied, with Ben seated beside him, while Reub went for Squire Kayley.

"He tried to kill himself," Reub said, "an' we had to tie him."

When Squire Kayley entered the room Nick was attaching every oath he had ever heard to Loftus Beesley's name, and doing it with a deliberate, monotonous carefulness that was almost rhythmical and truly awful.

"That's no good," the Squire said, quietly, standing over him with his hands in his pockets, "and I'm ashamed to see you lying here tied like a beast. Untie him, boys."

Nick got up and shook himself.

"You've got no right to behave as if your wife had sinned," the Squire went on, "any accident might have kept them; if you loved her you'd not treat her with this dishonor."

"She's been two days, an' this 'll be two nights, with Loftus Beesley!" Nick cried.

"True, but last night she was with all the party at Colonel Bolles's, perfectly respectable and legitimate, and now she may come in at any moment and give a perfectly clear account of herself, and even if she does not come until morning, she may be stopping with some friend . . ."

Nick struck his hands together.

"Then she'll have to stop away altogether!"

"Not at all," the Squire returned, "you must give her every chance to clear herself; she's young, and beautiful, and fond of admiration and gaiety, and that kind of woman has a thousand temptations that a quieter kind never dreams of. She had the choice of every unmarried man in this town," the Squire hesitated a moment, then added, "even of your humble servant, and out of all she selected you."

Nick turned quickly, "You, too, Squire?" he asked.

The Squire nodded. "And I love her enough still," he added, "to insist that justice be done her."

The evening wore on. The town clock struck nine, then ten, then the Squire sent Reub Seelye out to the house of Letty's mother, to see if she was there.

It was a long ride, and until Reub returned, after midnight, the Squire managed to keep Nick quiet, but when a negative answer came Nick was almost beside himself, and Squire Kayley had to compromise, giving up the point that Nick must let his wife come home, and advising, instead, that he should pack all Letty's belongings, and in the morning send them to her mother's house and, leaving Ben Seelye to meet the couple, come to Squire Kayley's place outside the town. For, at any cost, Nick and Loftus must be kept apart.

"Don't receive her," he said, "but give her a chance to clear herself."

"And Loftus?" Nick snarled between his teeth.

"What's Loftus done?" the Squire asked, "Letty's not the kind to be led nor driven."

"If Loftus blames her I'll kill him."

"No, we are not going to have any bloodshed," the Squire went on, "if you can't hold yourself, I'll hold you. If I can't do any better I'll put you in jail."

Nick laughed long and loud, then burst into tears, "I love her so!" he cried, "I love her so!"

"Of course you do," his mentor answered. "And first thing you know it'll be all right."

Daylight found Reub Seelye, with Letty's trunks, being driven out to Mrs. Purdy's, Squire Kayley and Nick on their way to the country, and Ben Seelye, with a note in his pocket, and the key of Nick's house, on his way home to breakfast.

But, alas, as the day wore on and Ben did not come with news of Letty's arrival, Nick became almost wild, then the Squire tried to soothe him into quiet with talk of a divorce.

"You think she's too far gone to shed blood for," Nick said, at last, his voice grown low and weak from weariness, "that's what you said about that other woman at the North; you want me to sue Loftus for his money, and let him have Letty? Great God!"

"Do you want her?"

"But Loftus," Nick reiterated, "leave her to Loftus?"

"Humanity's strange," the Squire began, slowly, "let 'em have what they want, and ten to one they don't want it. Letty belongs to you, and that makes her the one thing on earth that Loftus wants. You belong to Letty, and that cheapens you in her sight. Let her go—that minute your value will double, and, like Esau, she'll shed many and bitter tears for what she threw away. Let her go, and Loftus will wonder what it was that made him so crazy. There's nothing makes a man feel so Godforsaken as to be left to follow his own evil courses, as to say to him, 'You've hurt me beyond help. Take what you've been striving for and go your way,' and right then and there the tiptop apple on the tree that he's been fighting for turns to dust and ashes in his mouth, and he can never, never, never get you and your maimed life out of his heart. But just lift one finger to revenge yourself, and you lift the burden from his heart on to your own. Let 'em go, boy, wash your hands clean of 'em, and after a while peace will come to you, peace such as you've never dreamed of. But not to them, they'll have entered on a new lease of tribulation, for 'what ye mete, it shall be measured to you again.' I'm not much of a preaching Christian," he went on, in a lower tone, "but there's one thing I've read in Scripture, just a few words, 'Are not all these things written in Thy book?'"

Nick sat silent, his arms crossed on the table and his head bowed on them. No food had passed his lips, and he was faint and weary, and for a little while he seemed to see as Squire Kayley saw, and so he fell into the deep sleep of exhaustion.

Just as the sun was setting Ben Seelye rode slowly into the yard and around to the stable, and the Squire stepped out very carefully, so as not to waken Nick.

"She's come," Ben said, "an' when she read the note she laughed a little, then she turned right white, and gave it to Loftus."

"And Loftus?"

"He looked like a rooster with his tail feathers pulled out, an' said he thought he'd better leave town for a while, and then he looked at me and sorter straightened up, and asked Letty, 'What do you want me to do?' an' she said, 'Leave town,' then he turned to get into his buggy, an' I told him he'd better drive Letty out to her mother's, 'cause the servants were gone an' the house locked up, an' all Letty's things were out there waitin' for her. It was pretty bad, but they did what I said, an' I rode my horse right behind 'em through the town, an' everybody stared, an' nobody spoke, not even Uncle Adam Dozier. It was bad. Loftus leaves at seven o'clock, if Nick 'll only sleep till then."

Never in the annals of Greenville had there been such excitement as when Nick Tobin sued Loftus Beesley for alienating his wife's affections.

The whole town and county, men, women, and children, rose in a solid, clamoring body against Squire Kayley. Women who had often torn poor Letty's character into ribbons now rallied around her, declaring that to bring a woman into such unheard-of publicity, into court, subjecting her even to the evidence of her negro servants, was to destroy not only all the old and time-honored customs, but to subvert society.

Uncle Adam proclaimed that any man in Nick's position who did not shoot his rival was a coward, and that if Squire Kayley had not meddled, it would all have been arranged as of old; Loftus decently buried and his money left to his family, Nick could have come back, and everybody would have been his friend, and Letty, well, Letty would have been a "grass widder" with a bad name. Now Squire Kayley's methods had turned the two sinners into hero and heroine, and the injured man had become an object of pity and contempt, who deserved all he got.

Every sort of compromise was suggested, but Squire Kayley was determined to teach a lesson once and for all to his native town, and he did it, an awful, searching, withering lesson that revealed to mothers, and fathers, and brothers the perilousness of the liberty which they accorded their young daughters and sisters, which revealed to the women the views of themselves as given in the talk of the men who formed their society, which revealed to the men their own unloveliness as seen by purer eyes and an unanswerable logic, an awful, withering lesson that was as if the whole town had been driven into the Palace of Truth, there to endure a day of terrible judgment.

Through it all Squire Kayley kept Nick away, travelling, as usual, for the firm that employed him, while Loftus met the public eye only when the dreadful engine of the law dragged him into view, showing him in all sorts of false and pitiful guises. The Squire was virtually ostracized, but he had the courage of his convictions and the spirit of the martyr, which every man should have who undertakes the work of reform.

At last it was over. Loftus had to sell most of his possessions to pay costs and damages; Letty hid herself in her mother's house, while Nick, travelling incessantly, did not hear the half that was said, and paid no heed whatever to the money that was now to his credit in the Greenville bank. The town subsided, having become "sadder and wiser," and Squire Kayley's reward, for he had declined all fees, was to see that when expeditions were organized, at least one mother went to look after the young people, and that brothers and fathers took some heed as to who escorted their sisters and daughters, further, the girls themselves were seen less often on the streets, and it became a great breach of social observance for any woman to pass the hotel.

All this soberness was gall and wormwood to Uncle Adam Dozier, who having, through the fall of Squire Kayley, regained the position he had lost because of his defeat by Sam, bloomed once more into the hotel piazza orator of happier days, and from this altitude he made one declaration which raised a puzzling question for the people of Greenville.

"Josh Kayley is the most immoral man in this town," he declared, boldly, "he is attempting to reduce everything to a money value, an' says thet even our mos' sacred affections kin be paid fur. It's wrong, it's damned wrong, an' I say thet the man who kin spen' the money gained through the ruin of his wife is a poltroon an' a sneak! But Josh Kayley ner no other man kin bring us to sich er pass, no, sir, I tell you the end is not yet, an' you'll see I'm right, wait, an' you'll see!"

So Greenville, a little at a loss between the practical ills as exemplified by Uncle Adam, and the theoretical ills as exemplified by the Squire, waited.

In a convict-worked coalmine two prisoners labored side by side, a negro and a white man. In the dim light cast on each by the other's lamp the negro showed a contented, rather cheerful face, and worked skilfully, while the white man, young and comely, was haggard and hopeless, and worked clumsily. The negro watched him furtively, but a guard stood near, for the white man was a new prisoner, and the negro did not speak. After a while sounds of laughter came from a group nearer the opening, and the guard moved on, then the negro said, "Fur Gawd's sake, Marse Nick, whar's you come from?"

For the first time the white man looked at his companion. "Sam," he said, "you here?"

"Yassir, Marse Nick, I git yer kase o' dat money what Marse Josh got fumme f'um ole Marse Adam Dozier. Over to Duserville a gal fool me kase o' dat money, en her mammy had er funerl to perwide, an' I come yer—yassir. An' you, Marse Nick, you got yo' money, too, sir?"

"Yes, I got my money, too, Sam," the young man answered, wielding his pick deliberately, "an' I gave it all to your Miss Letty; she never had worked, an' I wasn't satisfied to think about her workin'."

"Yassir, Marse Nick, en den, sir?"

"An' then I heard 'bout the things your Marse Loftus had said 'bout her on the trial, an' so I killed him, for I thought the trial was 'tween me an' him, not her, an' while I was killin' him I told him why I did it; not 'cause he'd hurt me, but 'cause of what he'd said 'bout my wife on the trial. I told him so, I got him by himself, an' I told him; then I killed him, killed him slow, him, my old friend."

"An' Marse Josh?" the negro was breathless.

"I told the Squire that I'd tried my best to do his way, but no man could say the things Loftus had said about my wife on that trial an' live. I was sorry to disappoint the Squire, for he's right in the main, but my case was diff'runt."

"An' Marse Adam Dozier?"

"He said I was right, an' a gentleman, but I told him no, that the Squire was right, but my case was diff'runt."

This story of the aftermath of a duel
originally appeared in the March 1899
issue of *Harper's Magazine*. It was published
in the short story collection *An Incident and
Other Happenings* later that same year by
Harper & Brothers.

WITHOUT THE COURTS

IT WAS A WIDE MARSH, with a dim blue shore on the other side. Away down to the right the horizon was clear, for there was the sea into which the tidewater river emptied itself. To the left the river showed more definitely and in longer reaches, though still shored by the marsh. The low sand bluff that bounded the marsh on the south was fringed with saw palmettos and bunches of wild myrtle, with here and there a solemn pine rising to lonely heights, and here and there wide-spreading, moss-draped oaks making dense shadows.

Where the trees were thickest, a plantation house, built very much on the plan of the oaks, low and wide-spreading, stood looking out through its old-fashioned, small-paned windows, as it had looked for many, many changing years over the desolate marsh and sinuous river. So many had lived and loved, had come and gone, in that plain, heavily timbered old house, that at last it seemed almost to have acquired personality and the cheerful expression of a serene old age, which could look back on a simple, honorable, kindly past, and forward to a safe future.

Today its outlook was misty, for a fine white film was stretched across the sky that dimmed the sunshine a little, and blurred the outline of the far horizon. A mild, gray day, which, while demanding fires, yet permitted the master of the house to bring his book to the front piazza. His feet were on the banisters, his chair was tilted back, and a soft hat was drawn a little over his eyes. Some pipes and a box of tobacco were on another chair beside him, and at a little distance a red setter lay, with his head on his front paws, watching his master wistfully, with now and then a nervous start and a tremulous long breath that was almost a whimper. Out on the bluff, under the trees, a negro woman sat sewing, and a little child, with long fair curls creeping out from under the deep frill of her white sunbonnet, played beside her.

It was very still, so still that as far away as she was the words of the child would now and then reach her father where he sat, and hearing, he would lift his head and look towards the little group. It was a dull-looking book that he held, bound in brown leather, and heavy; for when wheels were heard driving up to the side door, and he dropped it on the floor, it jarred loudly, so that the sound reached the child under the trees. She focused her long bonnet on her father as he moved quickly down the piazza and cut across the corner to the side steps, where an open vehicle had stopped; then catching sight of the traveler who had arrived, she ran towards him as fast as her little legs could move, crying, "Tad! Tad!"

The two men shook hands; a servant, coming round from the back, took a valise from the wagon; and Tad going to meet the child, the master turned to the coachman.

"Did your mistress give you any orders last night?" he asked.

"Yes, suh," the negro answered. "Miss Lise say fuh me to come to de P'int fuh her dis mawnin' des es soon es I bring Mass Tad from de station."

"Then go at once," and Mr. Beverley pulled out his watch. "Yes, and be in a hurry." When once more he had reached his chair, Beverley pushed the heavy book aside with his foot, then, as if on second thought, he turned it up so that the title would show.

Before he took his seat, he drew another big chair forward, then filling his pipe he lighted it slowly while he watched his friend, who, having returned the child to her nurse, was coming towards the house, stooping and patting the dog as he came. "Poor old doggie," he said, "who's been trampling on you? What ails him, George?" he went on, when he reached the piazza. "He's trembling as if he had a chill, and winces as if he were sore."

"I had to thrash him this morning," Beverley answered, and a gleam came into his eyes that seemed to stop the poor dog in his tracks, and he lay down as before, tremulous and watchful.

Tad's own eyes took on a watchful look. "Where's Lise?" he asked.

"Over at Aunt Bowman's."

Then, as sitting down Tad's foot struck the big book, he said, "Reading law, and beating old Dash, and writing me that extraordinary letter yesterday, something must be very wrong, George, by Jove, infernally wrong."

Beverley handed him the tobacco box and pipes. "Light up," he said.

Tad obeyed, and for a little while they smoked in silence; then Tad, still with the watchful look in his eyes, went on, "Your letter bothered me, bothered me because I could not come out yesterday."

"Yes," Beverley answered, "I meant you to come yesterday."

"I've wanted to come all winter," Tad went on, "but I've been away attending court, you know."

"Yes, I wish you had come," and Beverley blew out clouds of smoke. "That letter should have been written long ago. Well, I sent for you as my lawyer, Tad, and as you did not come yesterday, I reduced everything to writing."

"Reduced what to writing?"

"My instructions," then Beverley turned his head away, and added, "I've decided to sell."

Tad's chair came down on its front legs with a bang; his pipe, jarred from its stem, fell on the floor, and the dog sprang up with a nervous yelp.

Beverley nodded as if he had expected this outbreak, and taking his pipe from his lips he began to stir the tobacco in the bowl with his knife blade, watching his own motions attentively. "I know all that you want to say," he went on, "but there's no use in saying it. I know that no creature has ever owned this land but Beverleys; I know that I belong to the soil as that tree does; I know that it would have broken my mother's heart, and my father's," his voice shook a little. "Well, never mind; if he knew, he would commend what I have done."

Tad was still leaning forward, with the pipestem forgotten between his fingers, gazing at the pipe bowl forgotten on the floor. Beverley was looking out across the marsh.

"That club has offered me a fancy price," he continued, his voice growing more and more monotonous, as if he had rehearsed his speech, "and I mean to take it. They want this house just as it stands, the high lands, and the fields down to the barn; in short, all of the original Beverley tract, which will give them the best shooting and fishing. I want you to begin at once to look up the deeds, and to get everything in readiness; but I do not want the bargain concluded, nor the transfer made, until next autumn, and I shall put everything into your hands, as I do not wish to enter into any of the details. I shall keep all the up-river tract and continue to plant it, living in the overseer's house . . ."

"And Lise and the child?" Tad interrupted; and now he raised his eyes from the fallen pipe and fixed them on his friend's averted face.

"They will go to Europe and live there." There was a moment's pause, then Beverley went on," The money I get for this place, together with what I make planting, will enable me to keep them there, the child always under the supervision of a careful English governess, to whom I myself will give instructions, for I shall take them over. In case of my death, there is yourself, and my life insurance made out to the child."

Tad grasped his arm. "George!" And he shook him as if to waken him, "George, for God's sake, tell me all!"

"I am telling you all."

"But Lise has learned to love the place!"

"Yes, she has learned to love the place."

"And your aunt Bowman, and Jack, and Sandy are like your own brothers! George, you'll pull up the growth of generations."

There was no answer, and the look across the marsh became more set.

"George!" Again shaking his arm, "George, for God's sake, tell me all!"

"I am telling you all. Aunt Bowman? Yes, it will hurt her; this was her father's house . . ."

"And Sandy!" Tad struck in, leaning a little more forward, trying to get a better view of his friend's face.

Beverley glanced round at the dog. "Get away from here!" he cried, springing to his feet, his eyes flashing. The dog fled down the steps, and the men's eyes met.

"I am telling you all!" Beverley repeated, harshly. "And it will be better for the child." He sat down again, while a deathly, spent look came over his face, and the dog once more crept up the steps.

"Better—best," he went on, as if to himself. "Best, yes. And as I have no son, thank God, no son, what does it matter? Traditions? Memories? All marred and blotted, stained. And the place must not be called Beverley any more; the name must vanish. You hear, Tad?" lifting his head quickly. "You must stipulate about the name."

Tad put down the pipestem at last, put it into the tobacco box with an exaggerated carefulness as if it were spun glass, and began to walk up and down the piazza. After a turn or two he saw Beverley bend his head to one side as if listening.

"You think you hear the carriage," he said. "I wish Lise would come; I don't think she should stay away when you are so worried."

"It was my arrangement," Beverley answered, coldly, "and I do not need a keeper, Tad."

There was silence while Tad walked the length of the piazza and back, then he paused behind Beverley's chair. "George," he said, "I love you as I love myself, but as surely as my name is Thaddeus Marvin, I'll throw up your business, and even your friendship, before I'll help you to do this thing."

Beverley shook his head slowly. "No," he said, "no you won't," and again silence fell between them.

Somewhere within the house a clock ticked; a bird fluttered down to a rosebush in front, and the laughter of the little child came clear and sweet from the riverbank. Presently the dog lifted its head sidewise and grew rigid, and Beverley, putting his pipe slowly into the tobacco box, laid his two hands on the arms of his chair. Tad looked quickly from one to the other. The dog heard something that the master expected to hear. Then coming nearer on the still air was the thud of a horse's hoofs, and a mad rattle of wheels. The dog rushed out, barking wildly; the negro woman gathered the child up into her arms; Tad ran to the side steps, and Beverley rose slowly to his feet.

On the horse came, but now Tad could see that the driver was urging him, and that the lady on the back seat was leaning forward urging the driver. What was she fleeing from? It was scarcely a moment before they reached the steps, and Tad sprang forward.

"What is it, Lise?" he cried, and almost lifted her from the wagon.

Her forget-me-not-blue eyes looked as if they had seen some dreadful vision, which they would forever see; her fair hair, blown out here and there by the wind, crisped and curled about a pallid face; her colorless lips were drawn back squarely, as in a mask of tragedy, and her breath seemed hard to get.

"What is it?" Tad repeated.

She clutched his shoulder. "Sandy," she whispered, "brought home dead!" She drew a long, sobbing breath, "Shot!"

In Tad's honest eyes that looked into hers there dawned a growing horror of knowledge, and slowly, as if directed by some stronger power, he loosened her hand from off his shoulder and laid it on the railing of the steps.

"Call the carriage back," Beverley said, looking down on them from above, "I must be needed at the Point."

A rigidity crept over the trembling woman; she drew her lips together, catching the lower one with her teeth, and began to mount the steps as a blind person might. At the top, her husband stood aside, out of her way; their eyes met, it was not long, then she passed on slowly into the house.

It was very still at the Point when they arrived. Mrs. Bowman sent at once for her nephew to come to her where she had shut herself into her room, while Tad took his seat on the front piazza with others who were waiting about, and watching, and talking in hushed voices.

"It is so dreadful," said the distant cousin, who took her seat next to Tad. "Sandy was so handsome, and his mother's darling—me! me! It is always the dearest who is taken," wiping her eyes. "And last night he was the gayest of the gay, he and Lise Beverley. George went home early, just as soon as they began to dance. He is so quiet, you know, so deadly still. I always feel a little bit sorry for Lise, poor, pretty, gay Lise. But George left her here last night, and she was in a gale of spirits, she and Sandy, dancing like mad, and keeping us in roars of laughter. Cousin Bowman was so pleased to see the young ones so gay, and to think, oh me, to think!" and again she wiped away her tears. "Have you heard the particulars?" she went on, turning squarely on her silent companion.

Tad shook his head. "Only the bare fact," he answered.

"How strange!" Then she began eagerly, "Sandy went out very early this morning to shoot, he often does, you know, and told the boatmen to meet him at nine o'clock at the long bend below the far swamp. You know it?"

"Yes," Tad answered.

"And they found him lying there dead! Accident, of course, for both barrels of his gun were empty, and just by the trunk of a fallen tree; he must have tripped in stepping over it, don't you think so?"

"Yes," Tad answered again.

"They brought him home; we were all late at breakfast, laughing and talking, and those stupid negroes brought him to the front landing! Lise saw the boat coming. 'There's Sandy!' she said, and ran out. Oh, it was awful! Cousin Bowman and Jack were nearly frantic!" This time she sobbed a little, and others near wiped their eyes.

"Jack has gone out to walk by himself, poor fellow," she went on, recovering herself, "and I'm so glad George has come over; he'll be a comfort to Cousin Bowman. He and Sandy have always been so devoted; he's like another son to Cousin Bowman; she depends on him greatly, as the head of her family. Poor George! He adored Sandy."

"Yes," Tad answered, "he did. He did most of Sandy's work at school, and took many of Sandy's whippings."

"Poor George!" she repeated, "it will break his heart. And Lise, Lise stood there like a dead woman while they brought him, lying on an old door, straight up to her, past her! Oh, it was awful!"

Tad rose hurriedly, "Take this chair," he said, and gave his place to a newcomer. After this he kept himself as far from his late companion and as near to the hall door as was possible, and waited patiently through all the long, lagging hours, while people came to make inquiries and to offer help; and food was served in the dining room and eaten between whispered sentences that told the story of the unfortunate accident over and over again, and so sent it away through all the countryside, and into the town newspapers.

At last, as evening fell, Jack Bowman came in at the back door, and down the hall. Beverley came out quickly from his aunt's room, and Tad stepped in from the piazza. The three men paused a moment, then Bowman led the way into the parlor where, on a couch in the middle of the room, the dead man lay. He shut the door and turned to Beverley. "It was buckshot," he said.

Beverley nodded. "For our good names' sake there could be no scandal," he answered.

Bowman bent his head.

"He agreed in this," Beverley went on, "and arranged it all himself so that no living soul, and especially his mother, need ever know."

Again Bowman bent his head.

"And at the last," Beverley's voice broke a little, "at the last he fired both barrels into the air."

Bowman laid his hand on the folded hands of his brother, and Beverley turned towards the door with shudders as of mortal agony going over him.

Tad took the reins himself, leaving the coachman to walk, and he and his friend drove through the lonely night together. Through all the distance Beverley sat silent, bent over like an old, decrepit man, but as they turned in at the big gate, he laid his hand on Tad's arm.

"You must take the old dog with you," he said, "out of my sight! This morning I had to beat him to make him come away, and at the last he ran back and licked his face."

This story of a typically restrained proper Episcopalian being swept up in the fervor of a Baptist revival originally appeared in the August 1896 issue of *Harper's Magazine*. It was published in the short story collection *An Incident and Other Happenings* by Harper & Brothers in 1899.

MISS MARIA'S REVIVAL

Religion sat easily in Kingshaven, but was by no means neglected. The old church had been added to more than once, until at last it partially covered the grave of the first John Tremelstoun, who might have been called the founder of the town. But it could scarcely be said that religious enthusiasm had caused the building to be enlarged; it had to grow a little in order to accommodate the population, which, though it increased only naturally, yet did increase, and there being no rival house of worship in the place, the old church had to be added to.

In the thirties, however, there was a revival; it could be called nothing else, even though extremely quiet, for the people waked up spiritually, and in a way that went against all the teachings of the past, against all the training and customs, and that amounted almost to a scandal. Indeed, the extremely conservative people said, in so many words, that it "was scandalous to let a stranger and a Baptist turn the town topsy-turvy." Nevertheless it was done, and many who went to scoff remained to pray. The meetings were held in the Sunday school room day after day for a week, and at the end of that time Kingshaven was a new place, and a Baptist church was projected.

This awakening was epoch-making, and superseded, once for all, the war of 1812 as the thing to date from. Indeed, the war of 1812 was scarcely ever mentioned again, and the effects of the revival were not only numerous, but apparently everlasting. Among other things, the marriage of one of the youngest and loveliest of Kingshaven's daughters to a missionary was thought to be due entirely to the arousing visit of the Baptist preacher. Not that this marriage followed immediately on the stranger's visit, far from it; the young woman had scarcely finished teething when the revival took place, but in a town as conservative as Kingshaven even so ephemeral a thing as a revival remained new for a long time. So this marriage was looked on as one of the most decided results of the revival because, unless the environment of everybody had been spiritually changed, no one could possibly have married a missionary and have gone to live in China.

When all was done and said, and the girl gone, it was found that a great revival had been given to the cause of foreign missions, and the religious papers were read far more diligently than ever before; and when letters began to appear in their columns signed by Margaret St. Clair, the papers became fashionable, and those persons who had believed in the revival and in Margaret St. Clair's marriage became more important, and assumed an "I-told-you-so" air that was to some people extremely irritating. It was thus it affected Miss Maria Cathcart, one of the aunts of the town. She remembered the days when the diocesan convention, which was the spiritual event of the year, and the races, which were the secular event of the year, were always arranged to fall together, and were most harmoniously mingled, and she had never been brought to say that it was even incongruous, much less wrong. She had disapproved entirely of the revival, and had declared that those who had announced themselves as "converted" had cast a slur on their forefathers. She, for one, required no change in her religion; those who were gone had been good people, and nobody could ever have changed them.

Meanwhile Miss Maria prayed very earnestly for her niece Margaret, and wrote to her regularly and lovingly, but she did not give to China for she could not divert her charity fund from the channels in which it had always flowed, and she was not able to give more, for long division makes short provision, and if the division of the family property for generations had not in her case made short provision, it had at least made limited provision. She was not poor, for she had her comfortable house and servants, and a regular, if small, income from the family estate, she had her little carriage and her fat little horse, she could not have less for in Kingshaven the ladies lived in almost Eastern seclusion, and never walked, except to afternoon service on Sundays, when the overfed horses and servants were supposed to need rest.

It was a pretty sight to see the whole town walking across the wide greens and down the shady streets to the old church in the middle of the churchyard, where all their dead lay under the great live oaks and swaying moss. It was not a very tidy graveyard, but it was solemn and beautiful, and it gave one a reverential feeling. Time, and the genuine faith and love of those buried there, and of those who had buried them, transformed the place, maybe, and hallowed it. People lowered their voices when they came inside the high walls, and ceased talking altogether by the time they reached the church door, and the young men who waited for the young women after service—for even in Kingshaven this thing was done—waited for them outside the big gates.

It was a pleasant day in May when Miss Maria ordered her little carriage, and told her maid Kizzy to put her cap into a covered basket and her knitting into her reticule, and had herself driven to see her cousin, old Mrs. George Bullen. To "spend the morning" was one of the habits of Kingshaven, and this was what Miss Maria purposed doing. She was very fond of her cousin Bullen; and then, Miss Sophia having a large correspondence with the outside world, and Miss Phoebe being thoroughly practical and interested in everything, Miss Maria found a morning spent there a very pleasant thing, and always came away feeling herself fully abreast of the times.

Old Mrs. Bullen sat in her armchair, Miss Sophia, in her low sewing chair, was reading aloud, and Miss Phoebe, in a higher, straighter chair, near a window, was making a cap for her mother.

"I see Cousin Maria's carriage coming across the green," she said, interrupting her sister. "She must have a letter from Margaret."

"Possibly she has heard of this Mr. Bowers who has come," Miss Sophia answered.

"I doubt that," and Miss Phoebe rose. "I'll go down and meet her." So she did, giving orders on the way for cake and wine to be brought up to Mrs. Bullen's room; then she waited in the wide shaded doorway until Miss Maria arrived. "So glad to see you, Cousin Maria," she said. "Mamma is quite well today."

"I have come to hear all the news," Miss Maria answered, as she slowly mounted the stairs. "Living alone as I do, one hears nothing. Ah, Polly, how well you are looking," she went on, as she entered Mrs. Bullen's room. "Your daughters take such good care of you!"

"You are looking well yourself, Maria," Mrs. Bullen answered. "Take off your bonnet, my dear, and sit near me here out of the wind. What is the news?"

"Asking me for news! Indeed, I have come here for that very thing. Sophia has more letters than anybody in the town, and Phoebe is such a grand manager. Why, even at the sewing school her negroes do better than any others. Heard from Cicely yet?"

"Yes, she is to send Dick and the two little girls to us very soon. And what do you hear from Margaret?"

"Nothing since I was here last; she might be dead and buried for weeks before we could hear. I never thought that I should live to see one of my family a missionary. You need not remonstrate, Sophia," shaking her head. "I shall never approve of it, never."

"Have you heard of Mr. Bowers?" Miss Sophia asked.

"Bowers?" putting down her knitting and looking over the top of her spectacles, "who is Bowers?"

"He is staying at Eliza Tremelstoun's; he has just come over from China, and is begging through the country for money; he is going to preach tomorrow morning. He came yesterday evening on the boat. No one expected him, and Cousin James happened to be on the Bay, and, seeing that he was a clergyman, he spoke to him. He had brought letters from Cousin Richard Denny, so Cousin James took him to his house."

"Of course if he had letters from Richard Denny he must be a person of some distinction," Mrs. Bullen said. "Richard is very careful in such matters."

"But a clergyman, mamma," Miss Sophia remonstrated, "would have a right to hospitality."

"Not without proper letters," and Miss Maria reared her head back with much dignity. "You got that from that Baptist man, Sophia. You have never been the same since that disagreeable time when everything was upset. I have never given in to those teachings, and I never shall. But for that revival, and until that time I had never heard of revivals except among negroes, my niece Margaret would never have gone gallivanting off to China on any such wild goose chase, and I don't intend to encourage this man, for the first thing we know we shall have another revival on our hands, and I do not approve of such things."

"But you will surely go to church, Maria," Mrs. Bullen said. "If it were in the week you might stay away, but to stay away on Sunday would cause a great many remarks. It would be very disagreeable."

"I am anxious to meet him," Miss Sophia put in, looking out of the window with something like longing in her eyes. "I think it must be glorious to go out and work, to spend one's life in elevating one's fellow creatures, as Margaret is doing. I . . ."

"Sophia!" and Miss Maria turned on her sharply. "Don't you, a sensible woman, get any such nonsense into your head. There are plenty of ordinary people to go out and save Chinese souls; ladies and gentlemen are not meant for such work."

"There is no caste in souls, Cousin Maria," Miss Sophia answered, laughing, "and there is no danger of my ever accomplishing anything. Even if I could leave mamma and Phoebe, I have no strength."

"The 'Lord's mercies are ever sure,'" Miss Maria said, decidedly, "and even your delicate constitution, Sophia, is a mercy. Polly," turning to Mrs. Bullen, "you should let this make you resigned to Sophia's delicacy. Think if she were strong what might happen."

"I hope I have never rebelled, Maria," Mrs. Bullen answered, "and I hope that I should not rebel even if Sophia should go away as a missionary, but I think it would kill me."

"Of course it would kill you," Miss Maria assented, promptly. "If I, a maiden aunt, was almost killed when Margaret went, you, a mother, would die immediately, immediately. But I am sorry this man has come, and he would never have thought of coming to Kingshaven but for that revival, and Margaret's going out as a missionary. I wish we could have been left in peace, and perhaps the Chinese wish so, too. I am quite sure we should not like any one to come here and worry us about a new religion. I am sure we should not."

Miss Sophia laughed. "Cousin Maria, we have the truth," she said.

"That Baptist minister did not think so," Miss Maria retorted. "It is twenty years ago now, but I remember it as if it had been yesterday how he roared out, 'Ye are dead in your sins!' And I got up immediately and left the room, that a person no one knew anything about should speak to me in that way was insolent. But the Chinese, what worse can Margaret say to the Chinese than that? Only I hope she has been too well brought up to roar as that man roared."

"That may all be so, Maria," Mrs. Bullen answered, gently, "but that revival did great good in the town. Think of three of our gayest young men being turned to the ministry, think of it! That was a great blessing."

"You can't be sure of that, Polly," Miss Maria returned, "even though they are now middle-aged men, you can't be sure it was a blessing until they are dead; and, blessing or not, I did not think it was dignified to be converted by a man outside of the Church."

"But you will go to church tomorrow, Cousin Maria," Miss Sophia urged. "There can be nothing against Mr. Bowers. He is a regularly ordained clergyman."

"Well, if I go to church, it will be because it is Sunday, and I always go to church on Sunday, and not because I am the least interested in this man or his mission; I have suffered enough in that way. I never was more shocked in my life than when Margaret told me what she intended to do, but in these days people do not seem to realize what is due to their birth and position."

"Won't you have a glass of wine, Cousin Maria," Miss Phoebe asked, "and a bit of cake?"

"Yes, my dear, thank you. And, Sophia, you may right my knitting; I always drop stitches when I am excited, and I always become excited when I speak of missionaries and revivals. There, my dear, take it."

Sunday morning saw Miss Maria in her usual place in church. But there was no humility in her bearing, rather a lofty toleration and a resigned pity, presumably for those who had departed, or who might now depart, from the ways of their forefathers. She went through the service with an air of aloofness, and did not sing the hymns, and when the tall, thin stranger, with a worn, lined face, got up to preach, she turned her head aside to look out of the window, to the graves of those who had lived and died conservatively.

"Wist ye not that I must be about my Father's business?" was the text, and presently Miss Maria's eyes came in from the conservative dead and fastened themselves on a tablet to a former rector; a little later they moved on as far as the chancel railing, then gradually up the steps to the figure in the high old pulpit. Nobody saw her, for nobody's eyes seemed able to wander that day. She had brought her usual Sunday offering, which she deposited in the plate, and she spoke very little on her way from the church to the carriage, and Miss Sophia smiled to herself as she saw Miss Maria's preoccupied manner.

It was a very fine sermon, Miss Maria thought, as she ate her dinner, a really fine sermon, and a preacher like that should not be wasted on Chinese, certainly not, but of course Richard Denny would not have given him letters unless he had been a worthy person, of course not. She spoke to Kizzy, the girl who waited on table, and told her how thankful she should be that she was a Christian in a Christian land, and not still a poor deluded heathen, as her people were in Africa. And after dinner she went into her cool chamber and walked about with her hands behind her, thinking still of the sermon and of the blessings of Christianity. It might be very disagreeable to the Chinese to be disturbed, as she had said to Sophia Bullen the day before, but still it was good for them; it was a necessary thing, yes, quite a necessary thing; that man had shown it to be so. And that had been an uncommon sermon; the more she thought of it, the more impressed she was. How blessed to be able to preach in such a way, and how blessed to hear such preaching, how blessed she had been in all her life, how comfortable she was, and how good God had been to her, and how sure a Christian's hope was. Poor heathen. Poor Chinese. How sorry she felt for them.

She extended her walk to the front piazza, which was on the shady side of the house. How quiet and peaceful it all was, and a nice breeze from the water. Her lot had fallen in a fair place, and all who had gone before had lived in this same delightful town, and had died in this same sure faith. Up and down she walked, with her hands clasped behind her and her face filled with peace; then, in a quavering voice that was not at all true, she began to sing, "How firm a foundation." She sang it all through, rendering the last verse with much vigor, her voice quivering with excitement; then she walked hastily into her room and went down on her knees.

Fervently she prayed, then rose up. Alms and prayers went together, of course they did, so, taking a key from a drawer, she opened her wardrobe, and inside of that unlocked a moneybox. There was her supply in two neat piles, and she took out five dollars. Yes, she could give that much; she would take it to Sophia Bullen at afternoon service, and ask her to put it with the fund she was collecting for foreign missions. Perhaps she had been wrong in her views of missions, but of course the revival was another affair entirely, and she could never change her views of that. But the poor heathen. And again she began walking up and down the piazza in the pleasant summer weather. Poor Chinese, they had a bad climate, and Margaret had always been so good—not very sprightly, though. Perhaps she would help the deluded things. Poor child, she must be lonely sometimes, but God would reward her. Yes, "His mercy was ever sure." Once more she lifted up her thin, old voice, this time beginning, "When streaming from the eastern skies."

There were no passersby to hear and be amused and astonished, and if there had been, they would have said, "Only Miss Maria." So on she sang, wiping her eyes over the last verse, for, in spite of all her comforts and friends and relatives, she was very lonely sometimes. But she finished the hymn triumphantly—"To see Thy face and sing Thy praise," and at the last word she retired to her room and knelt down once more. This time her prayers were almost audible, and longer than before, then the moneybox was opened and another five dollars was laid aside to be sent to Miss Sophia Bullen. Of course she could give ten dollars—a small tithe from all that God had given her.

"Praise God, praise God !" she said, aloud, and broke forth into the doxology before she reached the piazza. This time she sang quite loud and long, beginning with, "There is a fountain filled with blood." How good God was—how His blessings surrounded her on every side. And she sang another hymn. How joyful she felt. She must pray again. She prayed aloud for all her friends and relatives, for all God's children, then laid ten dollars more on the pile for Miss Sophia Bullen. What better could any one do than push forward the glorious work of converting the world, of bringing all men to her state of happiness? Think if every one were as happy as she was this beautiful afternoon?

"Forth in Thy name, O Lord, I go," she sang at the top of her voice, that rang through the still evening air. That was what the missionaries did, aye, all good people could do it. She was old, past sixty, but she could praise and pray and give, yes, give of her substance. Pray once more, yes, and again she went down on her knees, and afterwards laid another bill aside for missions.

"Fain would I still for Thee employ

Whate'er Thy bounteous grace has given . . . "

She stopped abruptly, and looked at the pile of bills. "Good gracious!" she cried, "if I don't stop singing and praying, I shall give *all* my money," and she pulled the bell rope violently, then, locking up the moneybox and the enclosing drawer hastily, she stood still in the middle of the room, holding the key in her hand.

Presently her maid, Kizzy, appeared. "Is you ring de bell, Miss 'Ria?" she asked.

"Yes, Kizzy, I rang. Here, I want you to take this key and keep it until tomorrow; never mind if I ask for it, you keep it. Now put out my bonnet and mantilla; it must be almost time for church."

"Ki! Is you gwine chu'ch, Miss 'Ria?" the negro asked, as she opened the wardrobe doors, which Miss Maria had closed a few moments before. "I been yeddy you sing summuch, I t'ink say you is hab chu'ch up yer—'e soun' same liker "vival."

Miss Maria started. "A 'revival'!" she cried. "You are foolish, Kizzy, an extremely foolish girl. A 'revival'." She walked up and down nervously for a moment, then stopped, while the maid took off her cap and put it away and brought her bonnet. She put it on quickly, then her mantilla and gloves. Then Kizzy caught sight of the money. She looked at it a moment.

"Is you gwine leff dat money dey, Miss 'Ria?" she asked.

"No, *no*" Miss Maria answered, decidedly, "give it to me, that is to go to the heathen, Kizzy," and Miss Maria folded the bills together and slipped them into her prayerbook, that went into her silk reticule. "The poor heathen. I am going to take it to Miss Sophia to send off; it is to pay the preachers to preach to them, Kizzy."

"Yes, m'am, is dat what you been singin' 'bout, Miss 'Ria, gittin' yo' sperret up to gie dat money? Dat's de way, Miss 'Ria, singin' 'll sho git de sperret up; w'en we niggers gits to singin' en shoutin', 'e ent know what we do, but I ent t'ink say white people do dat."

Miss Maria hurried away, Kizzy's words ringing in her ears. A revival! What nonsense. Miss Sophia Bullen was trying on her spotted lace veil that fell full over her face, when Miss Maria appeared.

"I stopped to give you this money, Sophia," she said, "for missions."

"Oh, cousin!" Miss Sophia cried, "*can* you give as much as this?" holding the bills a little away from her. "Is it not too much?"

"I don't know, Sophia," Miss Maria answered, almost indignantly, while a little color crept up her face, "but I *do* know this, that I sang and prayed until I had to lock my moneybox and give Kizzy the key to keep for me. It was a most ridiculous proceeding, but that is the money, the result, and I hope it will help your cause."

Miss Sophia smiled. "A little private revival, cousin?" she said, and kissed the old lady gently.

This story of a mistress and her slave
becoming war refugees originally appeared
in the October 1896 issue of *Harper's
Magazine*. It was published in the short
story collection *An Incident and Other
Happenings* by Harper & Brothers in 1899.

FAITH AND FAITHFULNESS

"God's in His heaven, All's right with the world!"

EARLY IN THE SIXTIES THE TOWN OF KINGSHAVEN WAS SURRENDERED and abandoned, and, on entering, the Federal army found the place deserted save for the negroes. The people had only a few hours' notice, for they had felt quite secure behind the one small battery of light artillery at the mouth of the river. They knew nothing whatever of the warships that were approaching; but they did know that the battery was manned by the gentlemen of the town, and commanded by George Bullen, and what more could be needed?

George Bullen had warned them, and had warned the government, that the little battery would scarcely be heard by the warships; was, indeed, little more than a joke; but the government either agreed with the ladies, or was careless whether Kingshaven fell or not. So the battery retreated, and the war vessels only waited for the tide to steam up to the town.

It was during this short delay that the hegira took place, the inhabitants moving in a body, driving away in their wagons and carriages, taking with them what they could, and accompanied by many of their negroes. By night and by torchlight they marched up to the ferry, across which they were taken in flatboats to the mainland, then, some following one road and some following another, these people, who had lived and loved and disputed, who had wept and prayed and rejoiced together for generations, bade each other farewell, and went away into a well nigh unknown world.

Miss Maria Cathcart cast in her lot with her nephew, Charles St. Clair, as being her nearest of kin; and her little carriage and a wagon drawn by one mule brought away for her and her servants all that they could transport. In the front of the carriage, under the feet of Jack the coachman, was a basket of silver; on the seat beside him, a box of Miss Maria's caps, and another basket of ancestral candlesticks. Inside, piled all about Miss Maria, were her clothes and house linen, and in either hand she carried a cut-glass decanter. The wagon behind was driven by Kizzy, Miss Maria's maid, who was the wife of the coachman, and in it were Kizzy's little children and the children of other servants, and all that could be saved of household stuff. Behind came other carriages and wagons, and many negroes walking with their bundles on their backs—a patriarchal procession; but Jack and Miss Maria were in the lead, because, Mr. St. Clair having to go with his company to join the army, Jack, as the oldest and most responsible negro, had the care of the party as they journeyed to the nearest town within the Southern lines, from whence they were transported by rail to the interior.

Miss Maria and the St. Clairs took a house together, and Jack hired out the negroes and collected the wages, and took care of the place they had rented, and things were more comfortable than could have been expected.

"Indeed, we get along famously," Miss Maria asserted, "we have everything quite decent, and Jack is a very good servant—butler, coachman, overseer, and several other things rolled into one; and Kizzy is doing admirably; yes, we are surprisingly comfortable, and I am most thankful."

One day the news came of her nephew's death—killed in Virginia. It was a dreadful blow, and the results which followed were most disastrous to Miss Maria, for her nephew's widow took her many children and went to her own parents. Jack and Kizzy declared that it was "berry ha'd fuh Miss 'Ria to be leff wid nuttin' but niggers," but Miss Maria, who had no idea of being under obligations or of being a burden, bore it very quietly.

So the niece and the children went away, the children very reluctantly and with many tears, and Miss Maria moved into two rooms on the sunniest corner of the ramshackle old house, the owner agreeing to let her have them for a nominal rent, seeing that in the town, houses were going begging.

The neighbors seemed to feel with old Jack and Kizzy that Miss Maria had been hardly treated, and became more friendly.

But worse times came: old Jack died. Kizzy and Miss Maria did everything possible, and also the doctor and the neighbors, but nothing could save him. After this Miss Maria began to feel the want of money. She sold the mule and wagon, and later her little horse and carriage; but she did it quite pleasantly, not alluding to her needs. She and Kizzy consulted as to ways and means, and Kizzy took in washing, and her little daughter Milly became Miss Maria's maid.

The surrender came, and with it came absolute demoralization. This was a black period, a blackness that involved the whole country, and Kizzy spent much of it leaning over the back gate abusing the refugee negroes she knew, as one after another they came to ask if she were going home.

"Goin' back home!" she repeated, scornfully. "What you got down dey to go to? Who is gwine gie you bittle en close? You foolish; you t'ink say 'kase you free dese t'ings is gwine grow on de tree. No, I ain't goin'; I gwine stay right yer wid Miss 'Ria. Enty I done promise Jack say I would stay? Enty I got house yer fuh me en my chillun; enty I got fire, en close, en bittle? No, I ain't goin'. En I ain't t'ink say you would leff missis like dis; 'fo' Gawd, I ain't t'ink it!"

"Sis Kizzy, I 'bleeged to go," was the usual answer; "I cahn stay in dis po' red clay country no longer. I des wants to smell de ma'sh one mo' time, en tas'e dem fish, en crab, en 'yster, des one mo' time; en I wants to feel dat good lightwood fire 'gen. I 'clay, Sis Kizzy, I des 'bleeged to go; but I cahn tell missis goodbye; dat I cahn do."

And they did not, but disappeared one by one during the week, until Kizzy alone was left. She did not tell Miss Maria all at once, but when the last one was gone she opened up the subject gradually, when, one morning, she was putting Miss Maria's breakfast on the table.

"I des wish I had a good fish fuh you, Miss 'Ria," she began—Miss Maria's breakfast was bacon and hominy. "I done yeddy Mingo say turrer day dat 'e was hongry en trusty fuh dem crab en fish, en I ain't shum f'om dat day to dis, en I spec' say 'e gone home. Mingo ain't no 'count nohow, 'ceppen somebody stan' by um awl de time en meck um wuck."

Miss Maria looked up. "You think that he has really gone home?" she asked.

"Yes, missis, I spec' 'e is, 'kase I ain't shum fuh dese t'ree day."

"Perhaps they will all go, Kizzy," the old lady said, making no motion to touch her breakfast.

"I spec' so, missis," Kizzy answered, pushing the little dish of hominy nearer to her mistress, "'kase sence Jack daid, en Mass' Cha'lie is kill, de nigger ain't feel like dey's got no mawsa; en now when people tell urn dey is free, den dey awl t'ink say if dey kin git back home t'ings is gwine be des like dey is always be."

Miss Maria was silent for a moment, then the light kindled in her bright old eyes, and she drew herself up. "They are very ungrateful, Kizzy," she said, "and forget that I have cared for them all their lives, and that now they ought to care for me. I hope that you, Kizzy, will be better behaved, for you must remember that you have lived in the house since you were two years old, indeed, your mother died before you were two years old, and that for more than thirty years I have had you cared for and have provided for you. But perhaps," she went on, her voice softening," perhaps the poor things were homesick, perhaps they were; I am homesick myself sometimes; and, oh, my country, my poor country!"

And Miss Maria put her handkerchief, a piece of old linen, to her eyes and wept; and Kizzy, throwing her apron over her head, knelt down by her mistress's chair and sobbed too, begging pardon all the time for crying in Miss Maria's presence. But it was not long that Miss Maria wept, the tears of old age are hard, but they are few, and presently she wiped her eyes and blew her nose, which seemed to recall Kizzy's self-control, and rising, she took the dishes of bacon and hominy off the table.

"Dis is done git cole, Miss 'Ria," she said, "dis will do fuh me en de chillun; I'll git you some hot."

So the old lady ate her breakfast, and when she had finished, Kizzy beat up the cushions in the chair by the fire and brought Miss Maria her books for daily reading, then went away to her washing.

After this it seemed to Miss Maria that the whole country had dissolved, and her cheerfulness wavered a little. If she could have written to any one to ask for news, or have known where her kinsmen were, whether in prison, or killed in the last battles, or gone with the despairing to Mexico, if any one had sent her a line or a word, it would have been a great help; but there was such confusion that no one seemed to know anything certainly, and she knew nothing at all. For a few days she was depressed, then she took herself in hand and gave herself a good scolding. Where was the faith of her youth? Why should it fail now when the bread she had cast on the water in Kizzy's direction was returning to her in such substantial fashion? This thought made her laugh a little, and she began to walk up and down her two bare rooms and to sing her hymns as bravely and as badly as in her old Kingshaven home; and Kizzy, hearing the quavering voice, paused over her washtub to wipe her eyes.

Money became more scarce, so Kizzy began to work for barter, milking for a share of milk, cooking for food, and washing for a return in wood. Meanwhile Miss Maria got one or two notes, which told of nothing but death and disaster, of privation to the extent of need, and of great mortality among the uncared for negroes. Again Kizzy came in and knelt by her mistress's chair to weep.

"We's better off wey we is, Miss 'Ria," she comforted, "en I tell dem nigger dey is foolish. Mingo is des been gone 'bout free munts, en now 'e daid, po' Mingo!"

"And just think," Miss Maria said, "Mass George Bullen has just got home; he has been so ill; and Miss Phoebe has been cooking. Yes, Kizzy, God has been very good to us, for at least we have enough to eat and are in good health. And, Kizzy, think of your Mass Tom St. Clair ploughing in his field barefooted! Think of it—educated in Europe, and owning three plantations! Poor fellow! Poor fellow! And his wife cooking and washing. Kizzy, it is awful!"

"Yes, missis, it's berry bad, m'am," Kizzy answered, "en we's better off right wey we is; en ef dem triflin' niggers had stay wid we, dey is been better off too; 'kaze who know wey dey is gone now dey is daid? Nobody kin say, 'kaze dey ain't do right in leffin' we up yer by we seff. No, dat ain't been right, en I tell 'em so 'fo' dey gone; en Gawd ain't want 'em ef dey ain't do right—no, m'am, 'e ain't. Please Gawd, somebody will come en git we bime-by, please Gawd."

So Miss Maria and Kizzy set themselves to wait patiently for this "bime-by" but again for several days Miss Maria could not sing.

Cold weather came. Cracks were everywhere in the old house, and curtains and carpets nowhere. The big chimneys took a vast quantity of wood even to heat them so that they would draw, and Kizzy was dismayed. At length she and Miss Maria came to the conclusion that all the furniture had better be moved into the warmest room; then, by having a fire always, Miss Maria might keep comfortable.

"If you ketch a cole, missis, it 'll be berry bad, m'am," Kizzy agreed, "en now ebbrybody is so po' dat nobody ain't gwine t'ink nuttin' 'bout yo' baid bein' in de pahlor."

It was dreadful to live in one room, Miss Maria thought; but how much better than Tom St. Clair ploughing barefooted! And when the move was made she declared that the parlor looked much nicer for having everything in it, and it was much more sociable to have things closer to her, even poor sticks of furniture.

But Kizzy found less and less work, and she did not know what to do unless she hired out by the month. A place was offered to her by a new family who had just come to town—a clergyman and his wife. Kizzy had been scouring for them, and from her present standpoint they seemed to her to be very rich. They offered her good wages if she would come and do all the work, and she might spend the nights at her own home. She had a week in which to decide; but how could she do it—how could she leave Miss Maria and her own little children all day? She could take the youngest with her, but that would leave two besides Milly at home, and how would they keep warm?

The day before Kizzy's answer was due was cold, and Kizzy had no work at all. She thought a long time while she mended various articles, sitting on the floor by the fire in Miss Maria's room. At last she said, "Is you glad fuh simme settin' yer en sewin', missis?"

"Yes," Miss Maria answered, looking up from her book; "it seems quite proper, Kizzy; but how is it you are not working today?"

Kizzy waited a moment, then said, slowly, "I 'ain't got no wuck, Miss 'Ria, en I cahn git none."

"No work!" Miss Maria repeated; then, after a pause, she sat up straighter in her chair and looked down on Kizzy. "Why, girl," she said, "what does this mean?"

"Miss 'Ria, I 'clay, Miss 'Ria, dat is de trute," Kizzy asserted, so mournfully that she showed all the whites of her eyes. "De trute is de light, Miss 'Ria, en dat is de trute; I try en I try, en I cahn fine nuttin' to do; no, m'am, 'ceppen . . ." But here Kizzy broke down, and threw her apron over her head, crying.

"Well," Miss Maria said, "excepting where?"

"Scuge me, missis, I know 'tain't no manners to cry, but I cahn he'p it, Miss 'Ria."

"Of course I'll excuse you," Miss Maria answered, rather sternly, for she did not know what to expect, "but what does it all mean?"

Kizzy wiped her eyes. Miss Maria's sternness quieted her.

"I mean, Miss 'Ria, dat I kin git wuck, but I hafter go 'way from home to do it, m'am. I kin come yer to sleep at night, but I muss go by daylight in de mawnin', en come home after da'k, yes, m'am."

"Well?" said Miss Maria.

"Well, m'am, dey won't be nobody yer but Milly, Miss 'Ria, en de two nex' chilluns—I'll teck de younges' one wid me."

"Well?" Miss Maria said again.

"En who's gwine teck care o' you, Miss 'Ria, en git yo' dinner hot, m'am?"

"Milly," Miss Maria answered.

"En who's gwine teck care o' de chillun, m'am?"

"Milly."

"En how is dey gwine keep wa'm?"

Kizzy's voice was low, and her eyes were fixed on her mistress's face like the eyes of a dumb creature, and Miss Maria looked at Kizzy. This was the critical point. To have a fire out in Kizzy's room for these two children would be dangerous as well as expensive; to send them to the house of another negro would be expensive also, and not altogether safe; yet to expect that they should sit on the floor in Miss Maria's room was to Kizzy far more presumptuous than to expect that they should sit on the floor of heaven. A dozen little negroes might come into her mistress's room to be taught if Miss Maria pleased, or to serve Miss Maria, but for her to ask Miss Maria to let her children stay there all day while she was gone seemed to her to be preposterous, to be reversing things and asking Miss Maria to serve her. It had somewhat this look to Miss Maria too for a moment; then she saw an escape from the dilemma. In Kingshaven she had taught all the little negroes who lived in her yard, every day, hymns and such things; so to teach these children would be only to keep up old customs. It might entertain her, would surely do them good, and at the same time save appearances and embarrassment both for her and for Kizzy. Still looking in Kizzy's eyes, she said, "They may stay in here, Kizzy, and I will teach them; Milly shall give them their dinner in the kitchen. It can be easily managed, I think."

And so it was. Kizzy cooked food for the day, and left that for the children in the kitchen, and that for Miss Maria in the cupboard; and the children, spotlessly clean, waited in the back room until Miss Maria had dressed and breakfasted; then Milly, with stern disciplinary whispers, brought them into Miss Maria's room, and put them into a warm corner, from which point of vantage they, sitting crosslegged like little black idols, stared at their mistress, who was a part of their faith; or, with eyes that turned so far round in their sockets as to seem all white, they watched Milly as she pattered about putting things to rights. And Milly developed so wonderfully under their admiring gaze, and skipped about so nimbly and assuredly on her battercake feet and slim little legs, that Miss Maria, looking at her over the top of her spectacles, told her she would equal her mother some day. Whereupon Milly fizzed into mirth, like a siphon of Vichy, and the little black idols in the corner rolled their eyes from Milly round again to their mistress, and fastened them there.

The weather grew colder; the big chimney in Miss Maria's room "eat wood," and Kizzy's wages made very scant provision. One thing after another Miss Maria said that she could do without. Butter was not at all necessary, nor coffee, nor sugar; milk was quite enough for her to drink. Then lights were not necessary; Miss Maria could do her reading in the day, so that for the evening the firelight would do. Fuel, too, must not be burned with any view to a special blaze for the sake of light. Sitting alone in the dusk seemed to double the desolation, and putting on two shawls and her rubbers for warmth seemed to deepen the poverty; but it could not be helped; and every evening, as Kizzy came in to make Miss Maria comfortable for the night, to bank up the precious fire and to take the children away, she seemed to bring a little freshness in, a little cheer; and as she rubbed her mistress, in an old-fashioned way, it is true, but soothingly, Miss Maria would say, "We are one day nearer to going home, Kizzy; for somebody will surely come to fetch us."

"Yes, missis," Kizzy would answer, "somebody will come en git we bime-by."

Then with a sigh and a smile Miss Maria would go to sleep as quietly as a child, and Kizzy would steal away.

One day, in going his rounds, the new clergyman heard of Miss Maria—of her age, her loneliness, her poverty, and her cheerfulness. It made a moving story, and impressed the good man; but in the faithful, humble servant "Kizzy" he did not for one moment recognize his wife's dignified treasure, who had introduced herself as Mrs. Kezia Adams. He was full of the story, and at supper he retailed it to his wife, who was also deeply moved. They did not observe that Kizzy left the room hastily, nor that they had to ring twice before she returned, nor that when she did come her eyes were flashing, and her head was held unusually high. Indeed, they were so busy planning relief for Miss Maria that they did not observe Kizzy at all; but very little escaped Kizzy of the plans they made to send the stores they would buy to Miss Maria before they called, so that she would not trace the gift to them. The things should be sent in the morning, and they would call in the evening.

"Think of her having so little wood, and no lights at all, not even one candle!" Mrs. Jarvis said. "How pitiful to sit alone in the dark! I wonder if she would use a stove; but these Southern people are so devoted to their open fireplaces that I doubt if she would; yet these big chimneys are dreadfully wasteful."

Mr. Jarvis shook his head. "To send a stove," he said, "would be to tell her who sent the things, and she might not accept them. Feeling runs high, you know; I meet it at every turn, poor people!"

Kizzy almost dropped a dish at this juncture. Her white people poor! No deeper insult could be offered to ex-slaves than the suggestion that their former owners had not been born in the purple and with the wealth of Croesus, and Mr. Jarvis unwittingly had offered this insult. Kizzy was in a fury.

That night she took an armful of wood. "If he t'inks I is po' buckra nigger," she muttered, vindictively," I'll do like po' buckra nigger; en if he is so rich, Gawd knows I ain't gwine let my missis look po' 'fo' him, not me. Any nigger'll hab better manners en dat." But Kizzy kept the secret of the coming stores to herself, for she had caught the idea that Miss Maria might refuse them.

The next morning there was the most marked change in Miss Maria's room; there were extra touches everywhere, a much larger fire than usual, and the two little black idols had disappeared. Gone to help their mother, Milly said.

Just as Miss Maria finished her reading, the front door was heard to open and steps sounded in the hall. Miss Maria waited, thinking some friend had come in; then hearing the door close again, she sent Milly to investigate; then following herself, found a large basket and an uncovered box filled with all sorts of bags and bundles, addressed to Miss Maria Cathcart.

Miss Maria and Milly stared; then Miss Maria said, "It is a present. How kind!" Her face lighted up like a child's. "You can't move the basket or the box, Milly," she went on, "but you can bring in the packages." And forthwith Milly began work; and sometimes running and sometimes staggering, and at all times puffing with excitement and delight, she transported bundle after bundle to the table in the back room, Miss Maria walking back and forth with her, touching and pinching each thing to guess what it might be.

"A very handsome present indeed," Miss Maria said, when everything was at last on the table, "a very handsome present. Crackers, very good. Here, Milly. Coffee, butter, grits, rice, gingersnaps. Here, Milly. Tea, flour, candles, pickles, nuts. Here, Milly. Sugar, lump sugar. Here, Milly. Cheese. Here, Milly. Bacon, lard, raisins. Here, Milly." By this time Milly was holding her apron. "And wine," Miss Maria finished. "A very handsome present. I shall put some in the decanters at once. Two bottles of wine. Suppose I had not saved the decanters! A glass of wine and a cracker will be very comfortable at twelve o'clock, very comfortable indeed; quite like old times. Get the scissors, Milly."

So the cork was poked out of one bottle, and the contents divided between the two decanters, which had stood on the high mantelpiece for safety. Miss Maria placed them on the table, with a plate of raisins, a plate of nuts, a plate of crackers, and a plate of gingersnaps, and her only wine glasses, three in number and three in shape; then she stood off and surveyed it; and Milly, standing on one foot in her excitement, surveyed it too, and smiled an ear-to-ear smile.

"Very comfortable," Miss Maria repeated, nodding her head at the table. "Put on more wood, Milly."

"Missis!" Milly cried, returning with a log in her arms, "dey is a big new pile o' wood in de back ya'd, yes, m'am."

Miss Maria stepped briskly to the window. There it was, a very large pile, the biggest pile she had seen since leaving home. The old lady's face beamed as she folded her hands together.

"God is good," she said, softly, "very good. Now Kizzy can return to her proper duties. Yes, with all that has been provided, we can live decently once more. Praise the Lord!" She felt like sending Milly off immediately to call her mother home, but her eyes falling on the boxes of candles, she thought of something she wished to do at once. The candles must be put into the candlesticks—for what else had she saved them? So from the mantelpiece and the closet all the candlesticks were taken; and Milly, seated on the floor, rubbed them with a woolen rag, munching the while from her store of confections piled away in the corner; and Miss Maria, hunting up a piece of white paper from around one of the packages, cut little frills with which to make the candles stand firm in the sticks.

It was a very busy day indeed, Miss Maria scarcely wishing to stop for dinner; but by the afternoon the candles were all put into the sticks, with the jaunty little frills about the base of each, and were arranged—and every few moments rearranged—about the room.

The big branches were on the table, where the wine and other refreshments still stood; the smaller branches were on the mantelpiece, flanked by two straight candlesticks; the others were put about in various places, for Miss Maria had decided that she would have a plenty of light. The candles had been sent to give her light and comfort and pleasure, and as soon as it was dark she would gain all this by lighting them. Things had been very bad, but they had taken a turn for the better, and she was weary of darkness and loneliness. In the back room she had stuck the candles into bottles, and Milly had made a fire in there too, so that her mistress could go in and out without fear of taking cold. Miss Maria felt as if she had been keeping house once more; and all being arranged to her satisfaction, she waited anxiously for the evening and the illumination.

By five o'clock she and Milly were in a glow of light. Fine fires were blazing on both hearths, and Miss Maria was walking up and down singing, when a knock came at the outer door. Not a remarkably loud knock, but one that made Milly spring to her feet and Miss Maria stop in her walk. The neighbors usually came to the inner door, and this knock, being on the outer door, was a stranger's, and being loud, was a man's.

"Put another log on the fire, Milly," Miss Maria said, as she stepped over to the glass to see if her cap and kerchief were straight. "It must be the new clergyman. And sweep up the hearth, quickly, before you go to the door." Then Miss Maria took from a box filled with dead rose-leaves one of the squares of old linen which she had hemmed for pocket handkerchiefs, and holding it by the middle, resumed her seat, while Milly put away in the corner the bunch of feathers that served as a hearth broom.

To Milly and to Miss Maria the room looked very fine and cheerful, while to the strangers entering it seemed inexpressibly incongruous and pathetic.

Miss Maria rose and stepped forward to meet them, bowing graciously, and extending her delicate hand as they introduced themselves as Mr. and Mrs. Jarvis. There was wonder in their eyes, and putting it down to the brightness of her apartment, Miss Maria was pleased that they should be surprised.

"It has been such a cloudy day," she said, cheerfully, when they were seated, "that I lighted the candles early, and lighted them all. I enjoy light and warmth, and am so thankful to have it; of late it has not been plentiful," and she smiled a little to herself at the mild way in which she had stated her case.

"It looks very cheerful indeed," Mr. Jarvis answered, slowly, while Mrs. Jarvis, suffering "pain and grief" for the wild waste she saw, looked on the solidity of the candlesticks and not on the candles, and on the sparkle of the old decanters rather than on the wine.

"A kind friend has sent me quite a batch of nice things," Miss Maria went on. "Won't you try a glass of wine and a cake?" She rose and filled the glasses; but Mrs. Jarvis declining, the ceremony was between Mr. Jarvis and herself.

"Your very good health, sir," she said, with a bow.

"Your very good health, madam," Mr. Jarvis returned, and felt as if he had suddenly reverted into his own grandfather.

"Things have been very bad for everybody," Miss Maria continued, as she sipped her wine, "but I knew that they would get better, and they have. I have always been of a very hopeful and cheerful disposition. I had begun to think too much so," nodding gaily, "and that I was being chastened for it; but now you see how little good the chastening has done," making a gesture that took in all the flaring candles, "for at the first opportunity I have an illumination, and change my mind."

After this the conversation ran on smoothly, but chiefly between Mr. Jarvis and his hostess. To Milly, standing at attention between the strangers and her victuals in the corner, Miss Maria seemed a new being—so quick and ready of speech, laughing so gaily, and gesticulating so vivaciously, but with no mention whatever of woes or wants, save as they were the woes and wants of the country.

And Mrs. Jarvis felt defrauded. As they closed the gate she said, "Those candles should have lasted her all winter."

And her husband answered, "I feel like spending my whole salary on candles."

Kizzy was enchanted, especially at the illogical command to come home. Her eyes and teeth reflected all the lights; she looked over the stores, felt the height and length of the woodpile, deposited the three little black idols in safety, then ran back to Mrs. Jarvis.

"I cahn come yer no mo'," she said, breathlessly, to that astounded lady; "I got to stay home. Miss 'Ria Cat'cart, wey you sen' de t'ings, is my missis."

"Is she sick?"

"No, ma'am; but we hab plenty now, en I can stay yer no mo'."

"Miss Cathcart ought not to take you."

"Ki! I b'longs to urn."

"But you said you'd stay . . ."

"I say dat when we 'ain't hab nuttin'."

"You promised."

"'Kaze we 'ain't hab nuttin'."

"You must keep a promise."

"Who gwine meck me? Nigger do what 'e wants to do, en what 'e meck to do. Who gwine meck me?"

"I won't pay you."

"You 'bleeged to pay me fuh what I done do, 'kaze it is done do."

"Not if you go without warning."

"I muss go."

"Why?"

"'Kaze I wants to, en 'kaze my missis wants me, en I tired. If you doan pay me, well, you doan pay me; I cahn he'p dat; but I gwine. I'll sen' somebody fuh cook you breakfuss."

All the way home Kizzy chuckled.

"Dey call me po' buckra nigger; I'll do like po' buckra nigger!" and she clapped her hands and laughed aloud as she ran through the darkness, and remembered the stores only as a further revenge on Mrs. Jarvis for the imagined insult.

Of course Mrs. Jarvis sent Kizzy's money, but she prophesied dire want for Miss Maria and her manage; poetical justice must take account of such childish improvidence.

But no harm came to Miss Maria; Mrs. Jarvis herself would not have permitted it; still, it did not even threaten, for before the stores were exhausted, Mr. George Bullen came to bring Miss Maria and her retinue home to her own people.

So the remaining supplies were given away with much generosity, and, to Kizzy's proud delight, she was sent with a pair of the silver candlesticks as a parting present to Mrs. Jarvis. For, as Miss Maria said to a neighbor, she had not been able to pay anything towards Mr. Jarvis's salary, which had mortified her very much.

This story of sacrificed principles in the reconstruction South set in Alabama originally appeared in the May 1890 issue of *Harper's Magazine*. It was published in the short story collection *An Incident and Other Happenings* by Harper & Brothers in 1899.

AN EX-BRIGADIER

"KNOW GENERAL STAMPER?" and the speaker looked at me with an expression of wonder in his eyes that amused me; then he smiled. "Know General Stamper—'old General Billy'? Of co'se I do. Where were you raised?"

"Not in Alabama," I answered.

"I thought as much," came with a ring of pity in the voice. "There's nobody in *this* State has to ask who is General Stamper."

We were standing outside the door of the only thing in Booker City that could be called a building; Booker City, that might have been described as a "wide place in the road."

Over the door of this building was the sign, "*G. W. S. Booker, General Merchant;*" a little lower down came a smaller sign, "*Post Office.*" On either side the shop, and out behind it, stretched the unbroken pine barren; in front the trees had been cut away, and the wheel tracks between the ragged stumps showed dimly the street of the future. Beyond the stumps came a ditch that cut through the sandy soil and deep into the red clay, and across this ditch two old "cross-ties" made a bridge to the railway.

Across the railway there was a blacksmith's shed, and one or two shanties where some bloodless looking people, with straight, clay-colored hair and vacant eyes, made shift to live. And this was Booker City.

The train had left me there ten minutes before this true story opens; my valise stood just inside the door of the shop; my overcoat was buttoned against the chill February wind. I had come straight through from New York, sent out by a great railway syndicate as a sort of private detective to look into the merits of Booker City. By profession I am a civil engineer.

"We send you because you are a Southern man," my chief had said, "and will therefore understand the people and win their confidence. I want you to go down to this 'Booker City,' and see this 'General William Stamper.' Look the whole thing up incog; be anything you like, and draw for anything you may want. Here is a map of the city."

So I packed my valise and started for Booker City. Arriving, I asked the only man I saw as to General Stamper, with the results given above.

"Where does General Stamper live?" I went on.

"Cross the railroad 'bout a mile. He owns moster this county; I own some, though. I own this store and down the railroad 'bout a mile; but our fam'lies were always friends, and me and General Stamper persuaded the railroad to have a station here. I've got Stamper in my name." This last was said proudly.

"And you got the station in order to make your land more valuable, I suppose?" in a mild tone.

My companion turned on me slowly.

"Not exactly," he answered; "for it couldn't be made much more valuable. We've got coal and iron right back here in the hills, and a big syndicate behind us; we'll have five thousand people here by next month."

"Roosting on stumps," I asked, "and feeding on pine knots?"

"Maybe, and maybe not," he answered, quietly, "and maybe by that time you'll have money enough to come back and see."

"If not, will you have money enough to lend me a dollar or two?"

"I'll have it, you bet; but whether I'll lend it to you or not, that's another question; and yonder comes General Billy."

I looked in the direction indicated, and coming through the pines I saw a muddy old buggy, very much bent down on one side, and drawn by a gray mule; of course the harness was helped out with pieces of rope, and the slim, rascally looking negro boy who drove was ragged; so natural were these things to that kind of vehicle that I scarcely observed them; but the man pointed out as "General Billy" caught my attention instantly and firmly. When the buggy stopped I saw that his left arm and right leg were missing, but, in spite of that, he leaped out quite nimbly. He was a large, ruddy man, dressed in a baggy suit of gray jeans, with a soft black hat drawn well down on his head, and from under it some fine gray hair curled over his coat collar. His eyes were bright and deep set, and twinkled as merrily as if a third of him were not in the grave. He swung himself along with great agility, and had a cheery voice.

"And how is the father of my country today?" he cried, as he hopped into the shop. Then, balancing himself skillfully, he hit my friend Booker a pretty solid blow with his crutch. "George Washington Stamper Booker! By gad, man, if your name had done its duty it would have destroyed you long ago; every day I am expecting to hear that it has struck in and killed you. And your name?" leaning on his crutches and eying me keenly. "You look very familiar somehow."

"Willoughby is my name," I answered.

"Willoughby? The devil! Kemper Willoughby?"

"John Kemper Willoughby," I amended, in some surprise.

"Oh, blast the John! Here, shake!" extending his one hand, that seemed to me to be marvelously small. "What kin are you to old Kemper Willoughby of Chilhowie?"

"Grandson."

"Bless my eyes, my *dear* boy!" and he wrung my hand painfully almost. "I wouldn't take a thousand dollars for this meeting; no, sir, not five thousand; no, not Booker City itself," throwing back his head with a ringing laugh.

It was a sweet laugh, and his voice had a tone in it that made me think of my father; his face was clean shaven, too, like my father's, and his mouth and teeth and laugh reminded me of Joseph Jefferson.

"There was something in the cut of you," he went on, "and in the setting of your eyes, that took me back to some fig trees in your grandfather's back yard. You looked as your father Kemper used to look when we were stealing figs. It was not really stealing, you know; only Mrs. Willoughby was saving the figs for something. God knows what women save things for, but they are always doing it. But you looked just like him, surprised and amused, and a little disgusted with yourself. All the Willoughbys look alike, all cut out of the same piece of cloth. See here, General Washington Booker, look alive, and hand out the mail. I want to take the boy home," rattling on without drawing a breath. "Fifty years ago we were in those fig trees. And your father?"

"I am the only one of the name left," I answered, briefly.

"Good heavens!" taking up the one letter that Booker laid on the counter, "only one, and there used to be such lots of them—Willoughbys world without end; only one left, only one!" and, leaning on his crutch, he looked at me sadly. "The war, I suppose?" he said.

"Yes."

"And at the last we went under, all for nothing; and now we must be patient, and say we were wrong, or, at the least, unwise, and forget those who lie under the sod! Never! And, by gad, sir, I'll make something out of them, something! Forget, sir? No, sir. There's too much of me under the sod—me, myself. I'll not forget. But come, my boy, we'll have some supper and a talk, and maybe some' condensed corn, ha ha! Will you have sugar in yourn? And I'll tell you about those figs your dear grandmother did not save. Ah, we had ladies and gentlemen in those days, ladies from afar. I have a little girl at home, God bless her! She keeps house for me. Come on; where are your traps? Here, look alive, you young imp!" to the negro. "Get out, sir, and put this gentleman's bag in, and you hang on behind; and don't you dare to drop off, or to get hurt. Get in, my boy" to me. Then, calling back, "Don't answer any telegrams without consulting me, Booker; not about your own land even. Do you hear?"

"All right, General."

"Now we are off," as with wonderful ease he got into the buggy. "You can drive, of course, and will not be afraid of a runaway," laughing. "Booker City has not made my fortune yet, so I drive a mule; but just wait a little bit, just wait. I will sell every stump and tree before long, and come out on top. Have you anything to invest?"

"No," I answered, leaning forward to thrash the old mule, and for the first time realizing my position, almost a spy! Well, I need not be; but how to get out of it? Write that I preferred not to report? That would kill Booker City as dead as Hector. Write what had come to me from the general's talk? Die the thought and the thinker! Besides, *what* had come to my knowledge? Nothing really; but one thing was certain. I *could not* be his guest, and at the same time hold my present position. I thrashed the mule again, but a wave of the ears was the only answer; then the general turned to the back of the buggy.

"Get down, there, you miserable rascal!" he cried. "How dare you ride at ease, and let a gentleman exhaust himself on this beast! Get down, sir; yes, and be in a hurry." The riding at ease meant that Jupiter was hanging on to the back of the seat with his hands, while his feet were clinging to the springs of the vehicle.

He dropped off now as nimbly as a monkey, and picking up a stick as he ran, came abreast of the jogging mule very easily.

"Hi! hi! Git up, you w'ite debbil; git up!" he cried, prodding the mule as he ran. "Hi! hi! I'll make you know; I'll make you go; I'll poke you troo an' troo—hi! hi!"

"That's you, Jupiter," cried the general, "poke him lively! You'll be President of these United States yet, ha ha! Get up now, quick, you lazy dog," as, with a grin that seemed to meet at the back of his head, Jupiter made a dash at the buggy, and swung himself into place once more. It was a wild race we were having then. The mule was cantering, with his ears backed, and his tail going round and round like a windmill.

"Negroes and mules were made for each other," the general said, as he pulled his hat on more firmly. "They understand each other in a way that can be explained only by affinity; and to see a negro on a mule is like hearing a mockingbird sing on a moonlight night in summer, the 'eternal fitness' is satisfied."

While he talked we had come at a rattling pace through the pine woods, and now were moving more slowly along a red clay road, that, fringed with blackberry briers, ran narrow and deep between rail fences. Presently we began a long ascent, still between rail fences, and the mule settled down into a walk once more.

"We are nearing home now," the general went on, "and soon we'll see the ancestral rooftree, which will be turned into a foundry shortly, I hope. I used to have some sentiment, sir, but poverty unscrews the spinal column of sentiment. I'll be hanged if I can stand living from hand to mouth here, where once I lived on the fat of the land. No, sir. I'll sell every stick of timber, and every foot of land, and throw in the malaria for nothing. I've starved long enough on 'befo'-de-wah' memories. I'm sick of it, and it is not wholesome. I want to take my child away from this African atmosphere. Her blood and breeding will show anywhere, sir; and with a few shekels to put a halo around her head, why, she can do and be what she likes, God bless her. And I'll make those shekels; I have a few already. But just after the war, I'll give you my word, sir, I was an absolute beggar. I borrowed money, and went to Mexico; well, that is a story."

We had reached the brow of the hill by this, and halfway down the other side I saw an oasis in the red fields and a glimpse of a white house. A square white house it proved to be, with deep piazzas, and a long wing running back, and an old garden in front, with cedar trees and flags, and woodbine on trellises; there were some oak trees and locust trees, all bare of leaves; and the fence and gate were on their last legs. I had seen innumerable places like it in the inland South, felt familiar with the gullied gravel walk and the "corn shucks" doormat, even with the red clay footmarks that extended into the hall, and felt that I knew quite well the slim, fair haired girl who greeted us with "How are you, Pappy darling?" Then she stopped, looking at me frankly from a pair of handsome brown eyes.

"A friend of my youth, Agnes, my dear; a Willoughby of Chilhowie, where my happiest holidays were spent. Kemper Willoughby, his father, was my boyhood friend, and this afternoon I found him stranded in Booker City. I knew him by his eyes, good eyes. Shake hands; both hands, if you like. If he is true to his blood, you'll never find an honester gentleman."

So we shook hands, smiling the while, and I was glad of my blood when I looked in her eyes, and hated, without reason, my good chief in faraway New York.

A Willoughby of Chilhowie—poor old Chilhowie, lost in the war, and now a great phosphate works. The old name had a goodly sound to it, and the brown eyes took a reverent expression almost. Evidently she had heard stories of the old place and people. The rooms were carpetless, desolate expanses rather, but the fires were grand, and the few homely chairs were most comfortable. After a while we had a good country supper, then Agnes brought some tumblers and sugar, and Jupiter appeared with a kettle, that soon was singing on the fire, and the general hopped over to a cupboard in the wall and brought out a black bottle. My case was full of cigars, but the general preferred his pipe.

"I got that pipe in Mexico," he said, "a long story."

"A disgraceful story, Pappy," his daughter added, bringing her workbasket from a far table, "a story that will shock Mr. Willoughby." She was seated now, with the firelight playing on her delicate features and fair hair, and as her little hands filled the battered old pipe, she looked up lovingly at the old man. "You must give Mr. Willoughby your pedigree before you tell that story."

"Oh, confound the pedigree! Willoughby *is* a gentleman, therefore he knows one under any disguise. Will you have sugar in yourn, my dear boy, and the story of the pipe, or rather of the time when I got the pipe? It is the joy of my life, that time; it was life! And that old pipe was the beginning of the first comfort I had after the war. I had fought for four years in the cavalry, part of the time with Forrest. We were not what you would call a godly set, Agnes, but good fellows, who would die, or worse, would come near to lying, for a friend, brave fellows: God bless every man of them. We were a reckless set, and death meant nothing to us, but we lived, ye gods! Life since has seemed a faded rag. Well, I lost my leg first. I had a hand-to-hand scuffle for it, and I will not say how many I sent to their long homes, it hurts Agnes, but well, my leg went, and not a year after, my arm. I killed the rascal who shot me in the arm. Then came the surrender," his voice losing its cheery ring, "and I was fit to murder right and left. I could not stand it, or I thought I could not, and trundled off to Mexico. Beautiful country, my dear fellow, lovely, but the lowest down nation on the face of the earth to call themselves Christians, not morals enough in the whole nation to satisfy one respectable old-time darky. I could not stand it, and determined to come home, no matter what was the state of the country.

"But how to get here. I had the whole kingdom of Texas to cross, and no money and no railways, and only half rations in the way of legs. I worked my way to the Rio Grande on a broken down old mustang. About ten miles from the river I came to a Mexican jacal, and hesitated about going in, they are such treacherous villains. But I was hungry, and pausing outside the door I heard a groan. Somebody in distress, I thought, and, cocking my pistol, I pushed my way in. An Englishman lay there. He had passed me two days before, travelling across country with a party of Mexicans, but I had caught him up again, and at the last gasp. The place was empty, save for him, and a pot of tamales steaming near the fire.

"I looked at the Englishman first, but he was dead. I had heard his last groan probably, and his murderers had been run off by my approach. His pockets were rifled of everything save this pipe, a good pipe in its day. A meerschaum, you see, and had a fancy stem, but I prefer a joint or two of cane. I was glad of the tamales, but I did not think it safe to linger, as I did not know the number of the Mexicans.

My clothes and shoe were too ragged, however, to leave a dead man as well clothed as that Englishman was, so I helped myself to a part of his wardrobe. I had not been so well dressed in years, and I laughed a little at myself. 'You look as nice as a preacher,' I said. Then folding up my old clothes, I left them near the dead man, and taking some extra tamales, I left the house.

"'As nice as a preacher,' the words came to me again. It had been a phrase in the army when a fellow was specially well dressed. 'As nice as a preacher?' Why not? Who had a better time than preachers? Why not be a preacher? I could not help chuckling a little at the thought. Why not be a preacher for the time? And visions of fried chicken and hot biscuit came over my mind, and fiery steeds furnished by adoring flocks . . . why not? I laughed out loud as I jogged on in the darkness. A preacher? What kind? What kind? Out on the border that did not matter. As far as my experience in that country went, all one had to do was to swear one had had a call, then preach and eat. That was more than twenty years ago, you see. So I did not come to any decision, but left it all to chance.

"I was so much entertained by my thoughts that I was surprised when I found myself at the river. It was day dawn, and, as luck would have it, I found some Mexicans with a boat just where I reached the bank. I seemed to strike terror into most of the party, and I shrewdly suspected that it was the Englishman's clothes that did it as most probably they had been among his murderers. Some ran away, but two remained, and agreed to put me across. Of course they thought I had money, but I kept my pistol lined on them, and when we reached the other bank, my pay was to jump ashore, and tell them in their own language that I was to meet a party of Americans there, and that they had better skip with my blessing and the old mustang. They did.

"I shall never forget my first day as a preacher. I thought of the character so much that at last I began to imagine myself one. I arranged sermons with the utmost facility, and all that I had ever learned of catechism and hymns and prayers came back to me. The day passed swiftly enough, although hopping along on crutches was such weary work that I began to think longingly of even my old mustang.

"About sundown I reached a settlement, a cattle ranch, but evidently not of the highest character. Yes, they would take me in. The woman of the house had a pathetic face, and looked at me searchingly, almost suspiciously.

"'I am a man of peace,' I said, in answer to her look, 'and I have lost my way.'

"'You look like a preacher,' one of the men said.

"I bowed my head.

"'I thought as much,' he went on, turning to the woman, whose face had brightened up.

"'I ain't seen a preacher in five years,' she said. 'Ain't you hungry?'

"'I am, indeed, my sister,' I said, 'as hungry as your spirit must be.'

"'Now you're shoutin'!' the man cried, slapping his leg. 'That's the way to talk it. I've heard 'em a hund'ed times, an' mammy would always come to me an' say, sof'ly, 'Go kill fo' chickens, Billy.' I'd know that talk anywhere.

"'Golly, go kill something, 'Liza, a horse, the baby, anythin', an call in all the fellers; bound to have somethin' to eat. Gosh, your stomach thinks your throat's cut, don't it, mister?'

"I was wild to laugh, by gad, sir, the rascal hit the nail so squarely on the head, but I answered quietly enough, 'I *would* like a little food,' adding, meekly, 'if you have anything to spare.'

"The man went out roaring with laughter, and the woman came close to me.

"'Did you ever marry anybody?' she asked.

"It gave me a sort of chill for a minute.

"'No,' I answered, 'I am not married.'

"'That ain't what I mean,' she said. 'Me an' Billy have changed rings, an' promised befo' the boys, an' mean it, too, but we ain't had no minister nor no magistrate, an' somehow I'd ruther have some words said. It's been three years gone now sence we changed rings.'

"'And you wish me to say a few words?' I asked, my compunctions fading as the woman's story went on.

"'Yes, if Billy's willin', but he don't like preachers much. He don't believe in 'em, but I do. I'll ask him,' and she went out.

"This was a position I had not counted on, for the official acts of the clergy had not occurred to me, and for a few moments I wished myself well out of the dilemma, but I must go on now, for to show these men that I was deceiving them might mean death. So while I waited I trumped up, or tried to trump up, the Episcopal marriage service, but something else would come instead, and looking into the matter afterwards, I discovered it to be the catechism, but then I knew only that it would not serve my purposes, and I was still at sea when the woman returned.

"This time she was followed by several men, among them 'Billy.'

"'Come in, boys,' he cried, 'we're goin' to have a weddin', me an' 'Liza, an' that means a supper, don't it, Liza? An' tomorrer we'll have to loan Brother—What's your name, mister?'

"'Stiggins,' I answered, with a back glance at Mr. Weller.

"'Stiggins,' Billy repeated. 'We'll have to loan Brother Stiggins a horse. I tell you, boys, it's a good thing we've got somethin' to drink tonight, an' me an' 'Liza 'll change rings again.'

"It was a trying moment. To save my life I could not remember anything to begin with, and as the couple took their places in front of me I felt puzzled to death, but I *could* not fail, and I made a mad dash.

"'What is your name?' I asked, solemnly.

"'Billy Sprowle,' was answered, promptly.

"'What is your name?' to the woman.

"'Liza Dobbs.'

"'Who gave you that name?' was the thing that seemed to come next, somehow, but I realized at once that it would not do, so determined on a commonsense question, and asked, 'Are you both of one mind in this matter? Answer as you shall answer at the last great day!' and I let my voice fall into profound depths.

"'Yes,' came from the couple, and from the subdued expression of the company I saw that my voice had impressed them. This encouraged me, and I made another grab among my memories.

"'William, will you have this woman to be thy wedded wife, to have and to hold until death us do part?' And the words tumbled out so glibly, once I got started, that I left the 'us' unchanged, and recklessly plighted my troth along with them. But they did not notice this, and Billy's 'Yes, sir,' came like a shot. 'Eliza, will you have this man to be thy wedded husband, to have and to hold until death us do part?' I said once more.

"'Yes.'

"'Change rings,' I went on, 'and both of you say, 'With this ring I thee wed, from this day forth for evermore.' They obeyed, Billy looking meeker and meeker as the service went on; then joining their hands, I looked at the company sternly, saying, 'I pronounce William and Eliza Sprowle to be man and wife.'

"By this time lots more of the service had come to me, but somehow I could not bring myself to say it. It seemed to stick in my throat. But what I had said *had* made an immense impression. Every man there looked at me with something of awe in his eyes, and I heard one whisper, 'A rale sho-'nuff preacher,' and the answer, 'You bet. He crawls me.'

"'The ceremony over, I sat down by the fire to wait for further developments, and the men stood about awkwardly. By this time, however, I felt quite in character, and said, in a mild tone, 'Have you much of a settlement here?'

"'Not much,' the oldest man of the group answered, 'an' the nighest neighbors is ten miles off. It's a right lonesome country.'

"'Yes,' I answered, 'but good grass.'

"'That's so, an' free. Billy Sprowle has made a right good thing of comin' out here, him an' these boys. I 'ain't been here long.'

"'Do the Mexicans trouble you much?' I went on.

"'Not as much as they'd like to.' Then with an effort, 'Do you think killin' a Mexican is any harm?'

"'No,' I answered, promptly, then clearing my throat slowly, 'no, not if they molest your property.'

"The man passed his hand over his face, looking at me curiously, while I gazed sadly into the fire. After a moment's reflective scanning of me he drew nearer, and, putting his hands in his pockets, stood looking down on me.

"'You've got commonsense, mister,' he said, 'if you *are* a preacher, an' you answered mighty lively at first 'bout killin' Mexicans; you *know* they oughter be wiped off the face of the earth?'

"I gave him look for look. 'My brother,' I said, 'I fought for four years in the war, and, as you see, half of me is in the grave. I don't stand back on killing or on being killed when it is necessary. And I like hunting too,' I went on, 'but I don't like to hunt buzzards.'

"'Shake!' he cried, holding out his hand, 'that's good 'bout buzzards. Mexicans an' buzzards is one. Sakes-er-mussy!' turning to the rest, 'that's sense, boys, preacher or no preacher.'

"They all drew up after this, and sat down near the fire. They had fought, too, and war stories were plenty, and before supper was over we were the firmest friends.

"Next morning, however, after the night's reflection, Billy came to me, confidentially.

"'Are you a sho-'nuff preacher?' he said, 'or did you jest put it up on the old girl? It won't make no diffrunce to us boys, you know, an' 'Liza's done eased off 'bout bein' married, an' we won't make her onressless by tellin' her no better, but are you a preacher?'

"'Why not?' I asked, drawing myself up. 'What have I done that a preacher should not do?'

"'Oh, nothin', nothin',' rather hurriedly, 'only you've got so much horsesense, an' preachers, you know . . .'

"'My brother,' I said, gravely, and I laid my hand on his shoulder in a way that would have done credit to an archbishop, 'you don't understand. I got my sense before I was called to be a preacher. I was a man first, and then a preacher. Do you see?'

"'You bet, an' you'll *always* be a man?'

"'Always.'

"'Thet's good,' heartily. 'I'd like to hear you preach.'

"Well, those fellows could not do enough for me. They lent me a horse that was to be left at the next town. They rode a long way with me, and Billy gave me a Mexican dollar as a marriage fee. But poor 'Liza, her gratitude was pathetic, and she brought her little child for me to bless. That got me, rather, but I gave him the best I had. It was the last blessing my dear old mother gave me, 'The Lord bless and keep you, my boy, and bring you home at last,' she had said. I gave it to the little fellow, and the mother cried. And I did not feel mean a bit for deceiving them, for I had done *good*. I had made that woman happy, and had raised the clergy in the estimation of these men. To tell you the truth, I felt myself a missionary.

"About sundown I reached a little town, a very small affair, and stopped at the largest house I could find, and the hardest looking case I had ever seen came to the door. I asked if I could stop there. He said he would see, and went back into the house. Then a woman came, harder looking than the man, if that were possible. I told her I was a man of peace, and wanted to spend the night; that I made a point of going to the houses of the best people in a town, because they would have the most influence, and could help me in my work. That woman's face was like a flint when I began, but before the end of my speech the whole expression had changed.

"'I ain't no 'Piscopal,' she said, the defiance that had left her face still lingering in her voice.

"'Of course not,' I answered, glibly. 'I take you to be a Wash-foot Baptist.'

"'How'd you know that?' she cried.

"'There's a look in your face,' I said.

"'My soul an' body! Come in,' and she flung the door wide. She put me in a very decent room, and presently I heard wild shouting and a cannonade of sticks and stones. As I had distrusted both the man and the woman, I was startled for a second, but the screech of a chicken restored my equilibrium. 'Fried chicken for the preacher,' I said to myself, and determined that I must become accustomed to that side of the ministerial life, and a very good side too. In a marvelously short time I was called to supper.

"'I s'pose you don't mind havin' a bate,' the woman said, 'so I jest killed a chicken, and knocked up a few biscuit.'

"I did have a little feeling that the chicken was scarcely dead, and that the biscuit had rather a jaundiced look, but I had been intimate with starvation too long to be fastidious, and I ate with a will, and as I remember it now, the coffee was not bad.

"'Is you goin' to have a meetin'?' was the woman's first question as I took my seat at table. 'I 'member you said somethin' 'bout your work, an' we 'ain't had nothin' but 'Piscopal religion here for a long time.'

"'And you don't like it?' I parried.

"'No, I don't. There ain't no grit to it. I want my religion to have some sperrit. I'd ruther have a revival now than money, and the 'Piscopals jest keep right along quiet an' easy, an' I 'ain't got no mo' patience with 'em. I'm tired.'

"'Is there a clergyman here?'

"'No, he's dead. He come for his health, an' worked an' died 'bout a month ago. We 'ain't had nothin' sence, but if you're a Baptist preacher, there's nothin' henders why you can't have a meetin'.'

"'If you think so . . .'

"'Yes, I *do* think so. You look like you kin preach.'

"'Yes, I think I can.'

"'Then I'll send John out. John! I say, John!' The man who had opened the door for me came in.

"'I want you to go round this town, John,' she began, 'an' tell the folks that Brother— What's your name?'

"'Stiggins.'

"'That Brother Stiggins will have a meetin' tomorrer, startin' right early.'

"'John looked at me slowly, then said the one word, 'Piscopal?'

"'No!' and the woman looked as amiable as a sitting hen. 'Ain't you got *no* sense, John Blye? Did you *ever* see a 'Piscopal look like him? He looks like he's got grit. Go 'long an' tell Brother Williams to come over an' help 'range 'bout it. Go 'long.'

"I must confess I felt rather queer as the combat thickened round me. After all, suppose I could not preach? And I said, mildly, 'Is Brother Williams a good preacher?'

"'No, he ain't, frankly, but he's a mighty good prayer. I've heard him pray right along for a hour, an' it never seemed like he drawed a breath. Yes, he's a mighty upliftin' prayer; he'll help you, don't you fret. Jest you preach, an' hit hard too, an' Brother Williams he'll raise all the hymns an' do the prayin', an' he does line out hymns beautiful.'

"This made me more comfortable, and it was easy enough to arrange matters with Brother Williams, a small, red-headed man, a druggist, with a long red nose that he used as a speaking trumpet. Very soon he and Sister Blye had arranged all the details; even the hymns were chosen, and nine o'clock the hour fixed on. I was awfully tired, but I chose my text, and dreamed out my sermon, for by morning the whole thing was in my mind—a grand thing, with enough fire and brimstone in it to destroy the universe. 'Where the worm dieth not, and the fire is not quenched,' that was my text. I tell you, Willoughby, I have often thought that I missed my vocation in not being a preacher. If you could hear me once, I believe you would be converted yourself. By Jove, sir, all the town was there the next morning, in a big place like a barn, which all creeds used in common. Brother Williams was there, and his nose looked longer and redder than before.

"We started them off with a hymn, then Brother Williams prayed: such a prayer! It was ridiculous, sir. I was dying to laugh. If you could have heard his instructions to the Almighty, and his fault-finding too, it was awful. But Sister Blye, the way in which she groaned and grunted over Brother Williams's presentation of the shortcomings of the Lord was edifying in the extreme. Then we had another hymn, a regular dynamite fuse, but nobody showed any signs of religion except Sister Blye. Then I began. I began quietly, but in the deepest voice I could muster. First, I gave a picture of heaven, quoting Milton copiously, but my audience was quiet under that, and I realized that they were in a coolly critical frame of mind. Further, I realized that *I* had no idea of heaven, or eternal bliss, or *anything* eternal for that matter. I could not conceive of heavenly bliss, for the happiest moments of my life had been passed in battle. I tell you there's nothing like the rush and madness of a charge, and you know that is no vision of heaven.

"I think I failed in my description of heaven, so, according to my plan, I came down to this life. I knew that through and through, and I flayed humanity alive and rubbed salt in. Then they began to prick up their ears, and Sister Blye looked uneasy. I liked to see it, and a determination came over me to do a little good, if possible. And I believe I did. I gave them the devil for a good half hour, straight from the shoulder. Then I dropped down to hell, and *then* I made the fur fly! I knew sin and remorse," and the general's face grew grave, and he laid his hand on his daughter's shoulder. "Yes, I knew hell better than heaven; it came easy, and I drew it strong. In twenty minutes that place was like Bedlam.

"I have never heard or seen anything like it, and never want to again. Such howls and screams and shouting! I did not know what to do exactly, for nobody could hear me, so I stopped and sat down. Well, sir, little Williams, who had been lying flat on the floor, howling, hopped up as spry as a cricket, and lined out a hymn. It was the best thing he could have done. It served as a vent for the excitement, and they sang with a will. Then he prayed, and exhorted people to come up and be prayed for, in fact, he got up a first-class revival on top of my sermon; then he took up a collection, to pay my expenses, he said. I don't know how much was given him, but I think he and Sister Blye got a very good return for their labors. They gave me five dollars.

"I refused to preach any more that day, and told them I must go on. Well, sir, people followed me to the next town, followed to hear me preach again, they said. There was a real Baptist preacher there, a very good fellow, who kept a shoe shop. He was delighted with the thought of a revival, and he and Sister Blye and little Williams arranged the programme. I had caught on to their methods by this time, and determined to take up my own collections. I did the work, and was determined to get my pay. We were in that town three days, and every one of them field days. You never saw the like. Such a raging, tearing time I have never conceived of. But the funny part was that when the collecting time came, and I started out on my own hook, Sister Blye and Williams and the other preacher all dashed after me full tilt, and it was simply a race, but many refused to give to any one but me, which made me have fewer compunctions about taking the money, for it showed me that they understood each other.

"By Jove, sir, at the end of three days everybody wanted to be baptized, and I nearly exploded when their own preacher told them that there was not enough water anywhere short of the Gulf to wash away their sins, but that he would do the best he could for them in the waterhole outside the town.

"I did not take any hand in that. The official acts I did not touch, nor did I ever pray in public, but I did not see any harm in telling them their sins, and in making them wish they had never been born because of the fright I put them in. It was pitiful. But I did *good*. I know I did good, and I made money. By this time I had learned all the tricks of the trade, and my brother preacher proposed that we should agree to work Texas for three months, I doing the preaching, and he doing everything else; that we should dismiss Sister Blye and Williams immediately, and divide the proceeds into two parts instead of four. That fellow, Stallings was his name, was something of a wag, and he told Williams and Sister Blye that we had entered into a partnership, and did not want them any more; that we had concluded to stop the circus business and teach religion.

"It was astonishing how much money we made after that, and how wonderfully successful we were. The papers took us up: 'Stallings and Stiggins,' and their grand revivals; their preaching and praying and singing, and the rest of it. We went from town to town in style, lived on the fat of the land, and had as many horses as we wanted. And I added a postscript to my sermons that any people who changed their creeds under stress of excitement were renegades and fools. I wish you could have seen Stallings's face the first time I tacked that on, but it took like wildfire.

"All the preachers in that town came to hear me, and thanked me for my sermons, and after that, Stallings and I gave something always to every Protestant church in every town, with always the proviso that it was to go to the preacher's salary, that much extra. Well, that got out, and the effect was miraculous: money flowed in. Don't you see that I did good? Then the scoldings I gave! By gad, sir, they should have taken the skin off. Bless your heart, how I went for the people for not doing their duty by the ministry. Why, Dante's lowest round was nothing to what I promised them if they did not do better.

"But the end of it all was wonderful. We were at a little town not far from the Louisiana line, and I was preaching fire and brimstone for dear life, when a face in the congregation caught my eye. It was the saddest face I had ever seen: past middle age, with sunken cheeks and silver hair. But it was the eyes that took hold of me—big, pitiful brown eyes that looked hunted and starved.

"After I had seen that face I could not preach anything but comfort and hope: I could not say anything hard to that woman. When I came out she was waiting at the door.

"'I want to speak to you,' she said, and took hold of my arm. 'You come from my part of the country, I know it by your voice, and you are a gentleman, if you are . . .' And she paused.

"'If I am an itinerant preacher,' I put in.

"'Yes, it does seem strange to me,' she answered, frankly, 'but you *are* a gentleman, and you come from the South Atlantic coast.'

"'Yes,' I admitted, beginning to feel thoroughly ashamed of my position, 'and is there anything I can do for you?'

"'I have come to you for help,' she answered, tremulously, 'because I seemed to recognize you in some way, and yet your name is not a coast name—Stiggins—I have never heard it.'

"'Outside of *Pickwick*,' I amended. 'But where do you live? Can I go home with you and talk to you?'

"'Just around the corner: we have one room. Yes, you can come, my daughter is there.'

"In five minutes we reached the room, a poor, miserable little place, but absolutely clean, and sitting there sewing, a young girl, not more than eighteen. She looked up in surprise.

"'Mamma!' she said, and I seemed to hear my own little sister speaking, so familiar were the accents.

"'This is Mr. Stiggins, dear, the preacher; he comes from home, and will help us.' Then motioning me to a seat, she went on, 'My name is Vernon, one of the South Carolina Vernons, you know.'

"'And your maiden name?' I asked, rising in astonishment.

"'Asheburton?'

"'Marion Asheburton?'

"'Yes,' her eyes dilating with wonder.

"'And a long time ago, when I was a little boy, you were engaged to Jack Stamper, and he died?'

"'Yes, oh yes! Who *are* you?'

"'Willie,' I said, 'Willie Stamper, the little brother. Don't you remember?'

"'How, then, is your name Stiggins?' said the daughter, severely. But the mother asked no questions, needed no proofs. She simply fell on my neck, and cried as if her heart would break.

"You see she had gone back to her first love, and her first sorrow, had gone back to days when prosperity and luxury were the rule. Poor thing, poor thing! Then our stories came out: hers pitiful beyond compare; mine, that seemed to grow more vulgar and disgraceful as I told it. The telling of that story was an awful grind until the girl laughed, the sweetest laugh I had ever heard. God bless her!

"They were destitute, these Vernons, had moved to Texas, and the father had died, leaving the mother and child to struggle alone, poor things. When I met them they had not tasted food for twenty-four hours. I took charge of them at once, and sent them over to New Orleans to wait for me. I had a good deal of money by that time, but could not break my engagement with Stallings, and it lacked a month of being out. But I preached for all I was worth that last month, and tears and dollars came like rain, and at the last I had literally to run away from Stallings. He said we would make our fortunes if we stayed together, but I explained to him that I was not so anxious about making money as I was about looking up some heathen I knew across the Mississippi.

"So we parted, and I left Texas with two hundred dollars in my pocket, besides what I had sent Mrs. Vernon.

"Well, we were married, the girl and I, and came home here to Alabama, where I have managed to live ever since. But I have never been as rich as I was when I was a preacher, for all my expenses were paid, I had horses to ride, I lived on the fat of the land, and had more clothes made for me by adoring sisters than ever since. It was a wonderful time. Agnes here thinks it was disgraceful, but she laughs sometimes when I tell the old story, just as her mother did. They are forgotten now, those happy-go-lucky old days, and my little wife lived only a year, only a year."

The fire seemed to burn low as the old gentleman paused, and the girl laid her head on his shoulder.

"But I *have* lived," and he drew a long sigh. "Yea, verily, life was worth living when I first set out, and the war," shaking his head, "I would not take anything for those years of excitement. By gad, sir, that was life, sure enough! And just after the war it was not so very bad. There was some novelty in being poor, just at first, before we learned to strive and grind, but now the grind is awful, perfectly awful. For everybody is grinding now, rich and poor, old and young. Rich people do not stop to enjoy, because they want more, and poor people cannot stop to enjoy, because they have nothing. We have lost the art of being satisfied—an art the South used to possess to a ruinous extent. We are losing the art of having fun, the art of enjoying simple things. We are learning to be avaricious, for now in the South position is coming to depend on money. So all grind along together, and I hate it."

"But when you sell Booker City, papa," suggested the daughter, with an earnest faith in word and look, "then you will have enough?"

The twinkle came back to the general's eye, and he tossed off the last of his toddy with a wave of the hand.

"That is true, little girl—when I sell Booker City."

But I did not want to talk of Booker City, and the keen old fellow noticed it, and cocking his head on one side, he said, "You don't believe in Booker City?"

"I don't know anything about it," I answered, "but I believe in *you.*"

"And so you *may,* my boy," heartily, "and I tell you Booker City has a grand future."

I lifted my hand. "Don't tell me," I said, "until I tell you." Then I blurted out my story. "Of course I will resign," I finished, "and they may send another man."

The general rubbed his chin. "Don't be rash," he said. "Write your chief the whole story. Let him recall you. Let him come out himself if he likes. To resign because I happen to be a friend of your father is a 'befo'-de-wah' sensitiveness which we cannot afford now. That fine old sensitiveness! It was silly sometimes, but exquisite. We cannot afford it now, however, and by the time we can afford it we will have been made so tough in the grind for money that we will have lost the cuticle necessary to it. That is the reason it takes three generations to make a gentleman. For myself, I don't think he can be made under five or six. However, accepting the proposition, the first generation cannot afford to be a gentleman; the second generation might be able to afford it, but don't know how; the third generation can afford it, and maybe has learned the outward semblance, and so the saying has come. But to have all the 'ear-marks,' to have the thing come naturally, to have it so bred in the bone that a man can't help being a gentleman, and has hands and feet and ears all to match, that kind of thing takes five or six generations. And even after six generations I have seen the 'old Adam' crop out in broad thumbs or big ears.

"Now you have all the points, Willoughby, but you cannot afford that 'befo'-de-wah sensitiveness. Don't resign, but tell your story, and give your honest impressions. For the first generation cannot afford even a comfortable lie. It requires 'a hundred earls' to let a man lie with impunity. Humanity is still too crude, all except the French and Africans, to put up with a lie, except under very extraordinary circumstances of success or position.

"So after you have seen Booker City, and have heard all my plans, then write, but don't resign because you happen to find a friend in

me, and so may be suspected of collusion. If you have no idea of collusion, don't be afraid of suspicion. Tell him that I am your friend, then,
if he suspects you, he will send another fellow down, but if he has any
sense he will not send to *supersede* you. If he does, why you come over
to my party, me and George Washington Stamper Booker," laughing,
"and by gad, sir, we'll work those fellows for all they are worth. We'll
never let them rest until our fortunes are made, and Booker City is the
London and Paris and New York and Chicago and Rome and Athens
and everything else of the South all rolled into one, not to leave out
Pittsburgh and Boston, yes, sir, and we'll invite your chief down, and
we'll take him to drive with Jupiter and the mule, and tell him about
those palmy days in Texas over a good hot toddy, and by Jove, sir,
he'll be one of us in twenty-four hours.

"We'll make him build a memorial for Sister Blye, and save a
corner lot for Stallings. Just let him dare to supersede you, and so help
me over the fence if I am not such a friend to him as will make him
wish he'd never been born. I have not forgotten how to preach, and
I'll make that old Dives think he's reached an infinite prairie on an
infinite August day and not a waterhole in sight, but don't you resign."

I took the general's advice, but it was a hard letter to write, and I
am afraid it was a little stiff. Nevertheless, the general was right. I was
not superseded, and in time my chief did take a drive with Jupiter and
the mule, and heard the story of the Texas days told as no pen on
earth can write it.

THE DURKET SPERRET

Elliott's novella, *The Durket Sperret* was published by Henry Holt & Company in 1898. The story reveals the clash of cultures which took place on the Cumberland Plateau as the "Covites," who lived a hardscrabble existence close to the land, began to interact with the faculty and students of The University of the South. The location and people were beloved by Sarah Barnwell Elliott who moved to Sewanee with her mother in 1870.

In this story, the main character, Hannah Warren, was raised with the burden of her grandmother's desire that the girl live up to her own proud family name of "Durket" and the proud spirit (or "sperret" as Mrs. Warren says it) of that line. Hannah charts her own path to self reliance, defying her grandmother's will even as she shows she inherited that same strength of spirit.

"But when I saw that woman's face,
Its calm simplicity of grace—"

~The Italian In England
Robert Browning

I

It had been a wild morning up among the Cumberlands—a March morning full of rain, of clouds that veiled the mountains, and of wind that tore the clouds to shreds. But at the turn of the day the wind had fallen, and the great masses of trees that purpled the mountainside from base to apex had ceased their tossing, and stood in dark monotony, save when a gray cliff thrust itself out, or a wild, snow-swollen stream dashed its spray toward the sky as it flung itself down into the valley.

The shadows are gathering early over a little valley known as "Lost Cove." On all sides the mountains rise about it in soft, sweeping curves, until they stand out against the sky a level, unbroken line. There is little of rugged wildness in these old mountains, for no stormy outburst marked their birth. They stand the perfect work of the ages. Their gray old faces looked out across the slow Silurian sea, whose wandering waves began the patient work of denudation.

No rugged wildness, but a silent grandeur of repose smoothes every curve of every spur that stretches out across the plain, and a great unspoken dignity lives in the straight sky line that marks the summit.

On three sides the mountains guard Lost Cove, on the fourth the barrier that shuts this basin from the world is lowered. But though lowered, the little stream that through all the years had hollowed out Lost Cove, found here an obstacle that its patient zeal could not remove. It could not rise above it, it could not wear it through, and so it sank, and, burrowing deep among the "hidden bases of the hills," found victory and freedom. From out the black-browed cave it flashed again into the glad sunlight, with a mocking laugh for the barring cliffs that rose two hundred feet above it, to face the eastern sun.

Near the upper end of the Cove, which is nearly a mile long, there stands a house built of squared logs, carefully mortised at the corners, and neatly chinked with plaster. Seventy years ago it was built by the first Warren as a defense as well as a shelter. Three rooms, a lobby, a loft, and two piazzas make the extent of it. A room on either side the lobby that connects the front and back piazzas, and from which a rough stairway leads up to the loft. The third room is made by boarding in the end of the back piazza, and through its single window a modern cooking stove pushes its pipe. The floors look worn with scrubbing, the small, deep-set windows shine like eyes, and the great stone chimneys that grace either end of the house, look as if built for eternity.

Around the house there is a rough picket fence; within this enclosure there are some cedar trees, some common rose bushes, some chickens, and some much-scratched grass. Beyond, and rising and falling with the swells of the mountains, is a rail fence which shuts in from the public road the lot where the hogs, and cows, and horses are kept, and where stand the few outbuildings. From the lower end of this outer lot the fields stretch down the Cove to where the stream sinks, and a stately beech grove crowns the rising ground. The public road from across the mountains turns at Mr. Warren's gate, and zigzags along these fields to the beech wood, then it marches over the divide to the far off valley.

A young woman leaned over the outer gate. The rain had ceased, and the wind came softly with a touch of spring. It would be clear on the morrow, the girl thought as she looked up from the shadows of the Cove to where the cloud-broken sunlight flashed and faded on the mountaintops. A clear spring day, and, as the warm wind swept by, her fair cheeks flushed with gladness for the coming spring.

The winter had been hard, and for the first time the Warrens had felt themselves poor. This girl's father had been killed a few months before, and she and her grandparents had had to fight through the cold weather alone. And now, as she waited for the cows, the touch of warmth in the wind brought to her mind a new problem—the planting. Some help would have to be hired, and where was the money? They had bacon, and apples, and potatoes that could be sold if she could take them to the town on top the mountain. The color flamed into her face; she had never peddled in her life. Her grandfather was held fast by rheumatism, and her grandmother would far rather starve than go on such an errand.

Presently a cowbell clanked, and down the mountainside, in dignified procession, came the rough, long-legged, patient-eyed cows. The girl roused herself with a sigh, and, holding the big gate open, remembered one more article that could be sold—butter.

She fetched two wooden piggins, white with scouring, and some fodder, then brought the cows in, one at a time, to the inner lot. She moved with the deliberation of age, and milked with patient sedateness. This quietness was a class habit, but increased in this girl's case through her having lived always with old people, and now the heavy responsibilities that crowded upon her seemed to have banished all youthfulness.

The Warrens had always been well to do, making at home almost everything they needed. After his sons left him the old man had been quite able to carry on the place, and before his strength failed his eldest son had returned with his motherless baby, Hannah. So there had been little need for money until now, when, her father dead and her grandfather disabled, Hannah needed to hire help. She might have paid in kind, but everybody that she knew made all they needed. The only people she had ever heard of who bought everything and saved nothing, were these new people on the mountain, who were held throughout the country to be strangely "lackin'." Old Mrs. Warren pronouncing them "darn fools, a-settin' round with books in their hands."

The milking done, Hannah took the pails into the kitchen. With the same lack of haste she stirred the fire under the kettle, opened the oven to look at the corn bread, strained the milk, then taking up an axe went into the back yard. Her face grew graver as she looked at the woodpile; she would have to go for more tomorrow, and she sighed as she pulled a log into position for cutting.

There was an outlet from all this. She could marry her cousin Si

Durket. She would rather cut wood all day! And the axe swung into the air with an ease and swiftness scarcely to be looked for from a woman.

No good would ever come to Si. She rested on the axe as she turned the log with her foot. Peddling would be better than Si; hiring out, starving, *anything* would be better. Yet, if something were not done very soon, she would have to marry him, or let the old people want. Mrs. Wilson, from the far side of the Cove, went up to the mountain to peddle—she could go with her. Mrs. Wilson was a creature much scorned by Mrs. Warren, still she knew the ways at the University, and could direct a beginner. It was worth thinking of. Gathering up the wood, she went into the house to her grandmother's room.

It was low, and the walls, finished up to the rafters with wood, were painted gray, spattered with white. A pine bedstead, with tall posts, and piled into a dumpling with feather beds, filled one corner. In another corner there stood a high chest of drawers, above which hung a spotted looking glass and some peacock feathers. A spinning wheel, a small table full of dusty odds and ends, a large rocking chair, covered with a patchwork quilt, and a few splint-bottomed chairs, finished the furnishing of the room.

In the rocking chair, close to the great fireplace, sat an old man, and an old woman stood near a window catching the last light on her work. She had been a handsome woman once, and, like Hannah, was tall, but here the likeness ended. Mrs. Warren's face was sharp and hard, the girl's face was grave and strong; Mrs. Warren's eyes were keen, while Hannah's eyes were thoughtful, almost sad. Further, Mrs. Warren's temper and tongue were famous, while Hannah seemed still and gentle.

Perhaps time was needed to reveal Hannah; perhaps the temper of her grandmother had made her esteem peace as the greatest good. Each son had had to take his wife away, and Hannah's father had only come back after his wife's death, when, seeing that his father needed him, he stayed. A gentle, patient man, he could put up with the temper his mother, whose maiden name had been Durket, was proud to call the "Durket sperret."[1] With regard to his child, he knew that no real harm would come to any creature absolutely dependent on his mother. "Her own" meant a great deal to Mrs. Warren. Her sons' wives she had looked on as aliens. The kitchen stove, introduced by one of

---

[1] The Durket Sperret refers to the "Spirit" of the Durket Family.

these unworthies, had caused the final breaking up of the family. The young woman had declared the open fireplace to be old fashioned, and her husband bought the stove. The "Durket sperret" could not stand this, and the young people had to go, but not the stove; Mrs. Warren kept that, and for the future vented much of her superfluous wrath on it.

As Hannah entered, Mrs. Warren turned sharply, "I wonder you don't git tired a-playin' nigger, Hannah Warren," was her greeting.

The girl put down and arranged the wood before she answered, "Thar is wuss things," then stood looking down into the fire. Straight as a young poplar, with the grace and roundness of perfect strength and youth in every curve, Hannah, in her scant black frock, was dowered with a beauty rare in any class. A grave, clear cut face, waving brown hair taken straight back and twisted in a knot, a full throat that showed exquisitely white where the little faded shawl fell away from it, and hands that, if hard and brown, were very shapely.

Her grandmother looked at her intently as she stood there, and grumbled a little under her breath.

"Ain't you none better, Gramper?" Hannah asked pityingly of the old man, bent nearly double in his chair.

"I'm some easier," he answered patiently, "but I'm tore up a-steddyin' 'bout the crap."[2]

"The crap wouldn't count if Hannah had a shavin' o' sense," the old woman struck in sharply.

"Supper's ready, Granny," Hannah said, and left the room.

"You pesters Hannah moren human, Mertildy," the old man suggested mildly, "an' she's a good gal."

"I reckon I knows my own flesh a' blood, John Warren," his wife retorted, "an' but for you, I'd larn her some sense, or know why. Si Durket's my own brether's son, an' as good as Hannah Warren will ever git. He's got a plenty, an' is free-handed an' hearty, an' he'll do to look at too. He's a Durket through an' through."

"All the same, Mertildy, Hannah don't favor Si."

"Don't favor Si! You makes me weak, John Warren! Do a steer favor a yoke? But thet's all a steer or a yoke is made fur. Gals is the same; an' all yokes is jest alike as fur as I kin see."

Mr. Warren shook his head, "You've missed the furrer, Mertildy," he said, " 'tain't the yoke, hit's the t'other steer thet's the trouble. The

---

[2] "Crap" is how "crop" was pronounced in dialect.

yoke is fur all, one way or anether, an' we gits our necks sorely galded, thet's true, but hit's the t'other steer thet mostly gits us, an' Hannah shan't be yoked ginst her will. You worn't, Mertildy."

"I reckon the difference would abeen wore out by now, anyhow," Mrs. Warren answered ungraciously, "an' I'd abeen jest as well pleased," and she left the room.

For more than a year Si Durket had been courting his cousin Hannah. Hannah's father and grandfather had supported her in saying no, agreeing that a man who could strike his mother and curse his old father, was not to be desired, but Mrs. Warren championed Si vigorously. That a woman lived who could refuse a Durket, she would not believe. A Durket who would be rich when his father died, for there was much land and only two brothers to divide it; further, a Durket who had been to school. Mrs. Warren had a great contempt for education, nevertheless she urged Si's "larnin" as a point in his favor.

Another potent cause for Mrs. Warren's earnestness was that the wife of Si's brother Dave, a young woman from a town, had openly laughed at Si's choice of Hannah, a country girl who had never been out of Lost Cove a half dozen times in her life, and who was poor compared with some girls Si might have won.

These considerations did not sway Si, but he was keen enough to repeat this speech to his Aunt Warren, who in her rage declared that Hannah should marry Si, if only "to down thet sassy hussy, Minervy!" And Si, seeing how work and poverty were pressing the girl, felt his hopes rise.

Mr. Warren was troubled for Hannah in the present crisis, still he felt that *any* work was better than marrying a man she despised. Hard work made rest sweet, he thought, as he sat by the fire weary and disabled; made any food seem good, and left a peaceful satisfaction when the day was done, when one could smoke one's pipe and think of the long dark furrows, and the well-stacked woodpile, and the cattle penned from harm, and think that, when the winter came, there would be a plenty and to spare. Ay, work was a good friend. But now his son was gone, and he could do nothing. It was hard on the girl.

"He knocked hisn's mammy—he's hard." The musing ended aloud, and Hannah, coming in with his supper, heard him.

"I'll never tuck[3] him," she said, in her soft slow voice, as she put

---

[3] "Tuck" is how "take" was pronounced in dialect.

the cup and plate on a chair near the old man. "Si kin cuss, an' Granny kin blate, I'll tuck hit, but I'll never tuck Si." She kneeled on the hearth with her hands fallen together in front of her. "An' 'bout the crap, Gramper, I 'llows I kin git thet Dock Wilson what's come to the Cove to he'p me do the plowin', an, Granny kin drap, an' I kin kivver."

"Don't say nothin' to Granny 'bout drappin', chile," the old man said, with patient experience in his voice, "hit 'll jest gie her anether handle to grind on."

"Jest so," Hannah responded, "but, Gramper, if Dock's like hisn's stepmammy he'll strike fur high wages."

"Thet's true as true, an' thar ain't no money."

"Thar's things to sell," Hannah suggested, "I could tuck ole Bess, an' pack truck to the 'versity."

"Peddle?" the old man said, in a lowered tone, "a Warren woman peddle?"

"Hit ain't no sin."

"No, but no Warren woman ain't never peddled yit—never yit!"

"You said onest that I could go," the girl persisted, "an' hits peddlin', or hirin' out, or marryin' Si, Gramper."

"That's true, gal, but I hates hit"

"No moren I do, Gramper." Then hearing a chair pushed back in the kitchen, she rose. "I'll hev to git wood tomorrow," she added, "but I'll go on Friday. Don't say nothin' to Granny."

Mr. Warren nodded, and Hannah, taking the cup and plate, reached the door just as her grandmother entered.

"The cawfee's 'bout out," she said, "an' the sugar's right low too."

"I knows hit, Granny."

"An' I can't git on 'thout cawfee an' sugar."

"I knows thet, too, Granny," and Hannah closed the door.

"An' whar hit's to come from *I* dunno," Mrs. Warren continued as she filled her pipe.

"I reckon Jack Dunner'll trade her some fur meat," Mr. Warren answered. "Jack knows we's pushed, an' he's mighty 'commydatin'.'"

"Pushed! Thet *is* true, John Warren, if you did say hit, but if you hed any grit we'd not *be* pushed. You keeps on a-stirrin', an' a-stirrin 'bout Hannah tell nuther one o' you is stiffern hog slops."

"An' if Hannah *did* tuck Si," Mr. Warren said patiently, "hit'd leave us 'thout *no* help, Mertildy, fur thet gal is all we hes."

Mrs. Warren laughed. "Thet's easy fixed," she answered, "goin' to Si's is jest a-goin' home to me an' you kin bet youuns hide I'd go."

"Then you'd leave me, Mertildy," and the old man straightened himself. "I couldn't rest under no shed but John Warren's, an' I won't, kase thar ain't no shed big enough for two famblies, nummine if thar's only one apiece in them famblies. Moren thet, thar ain't never been a Warren beholden to nobody fur a shelter yit, an' John Warren ain't gwine to start hit. If you goes, Mertildy, you'll leave ole John to his lone."

Mrs. Warren smoked furiously, and, "You're sappy yit," was all the answer she vouchsafed.

Pondering his wife's words, the old man began to see the wisdom of Hannah's plan, while Hannah, at her work, was busy devising ways for the carrying out of this same plan. The coffee and sugar made a good excuse for her journey to this new mountain town that was a market for all the country. She could arrange her load in an out house, and leave before the old people were up. When she went for the wood she would stop at the Wilsons' and find out about the people and prices at Sewanee. She had been there as a sightseer, but *never* to peddle. There were worse things than peddling, however, *and Si Durket was one.*

"Ofttimes like children we are led to meet
Our life—or driven like slaves by circumstance.
And suddenly it crowds us down to earth!
And in the thick we have no time to cry,
Only to fight! Then all is still. And through
The deadly calm of peace we moan—'Oh, fool!
Oh, fool! now all thy life is done—is done!'
Yet, still, like children we were led to it;
Or driven like slaves by lashing circumstance,
And knew not of the ambush waiting there."

~Unknown

II

At the time this story opens, the railway station, known as Sewanee, consisted of a few shops, the post office, and one or two small houses, built about a barren square. From this a broad road led to the "University," and the other end of Sewanee. Up this road the butcher and shoemaker had planted some locust trees in front of their shops, and beyond them the confectioner had laid a stone pavement for the length of his lot, and planted some maple trees, that, in the autumn, burned like flames of fire. Beyond the confectioner's the road was in the woods for a short space, then more houses. About a half mile from the station this road ended in another road that crossed it at right angles, and up and down this the University town was built.

Between the houses, between the public buildings, wherever any space was left free from carpenters and stone masons, the forest marched up and claimed its own, while the houses looked as if they had been convinced of their obtrusiveness, and had crept as far back as possible, leaving their fences as protection to the forest, and not as the sign of a clearing.

Very still and bare the little place looked on the gray March morning, when, under Mrs. Wilson's guidance, Hannah made her entrance as a peddler. Down the road, beaten hard by the rain, and dotted here and there with clear little pools of water, Hannah led old Bess, bearing the long bags, in the ends of which were bestowed the apples and potatoes, the bucket of butter being fastened to the saddle.

They had not stopped at the station, for Mrs. Wilson said the people in the town paid better prices.

"They don't know no better than to tuck frostbit 'taters," she explained, "an' they'll give most anything fur butter jest now. All the 'versity boys is come back, an' butter's awful sca'ce. To tell the truth," pushing her long bonnet back, "thar ain't much *anything* to eat right now. What with layin' an' scratchin' through the winter fur a livin', the hens is wore out, an' chickens ain't in yit, an' these 'versity women is jest pestered to git sumpen fur the boys."

Hannah listened in silence. She had her own ideas about trading, and besides had very scant respect for Mrs. Wilson, either mentally or morally. She knew that her things were good, but she was determined to ask only a fair price for them. It was bad to cheat people because they were simple or "in a push." She was in a push herself, and felt sorry for them.

"An' ax a leetle moren you 'llows to git," Mrs. Wilson went on, "kase they'll allers tuck some off. Thar *air* a few that jest pays what you says, or don't tuck none, an' I axes them a fa'r price." They stopped at a gate as she finished, and she directed Hannah to "hitch the nag an' stiffen up."

"I ain't feared," Hannah answered, while she made old Bess fast, "but I ain't usen to peddlin', an' I don't like hit, nuther."

Mrs. Wilson laughed. "Youuns Granny keeps on a-settin' you up till nothin' ain't good enough," she said. "Lots o' folks as good as ary Warren hes been a peddlin' a many a year."

"Thet don't make hit no better fur me, Lizer Wilson, an' nothin' ain't agoin' to make hit better any moren a dog ever likes a hog-waller," and she took down the bucket of butter with a swing that brought her face to face with her companion. One glance at Hannah's eyes, that now looked like her grandmother's, and Mrs. Wilson changed the subject.

"Leave the sacks," she said roughly, "hit'll be time to pack 'em in when they're sold." She led the way in along a graveled walk, Hannah looking about her curiously, and trying to conquer her rather unreasonable anger against Mrs. Wilson, before she should meet the people about whom she had heard such varying reports.

At the front piazza Hannah paused, and Mrs. Wilson laughed exasperatingly, "Lor, gal!" she said, "these fine folks don't ax folks like weuns in the front do'; weuns ain't nothin' but 'Covites come to peddle; come to the kitchen."

That people lived who thought themselves better than the War-rens or Durkets was a new sensation to Hannah, and she wondered if her grandmother knew it. Her astonishment stilled her wrath until the thought overwhelmed her that perhaps these people would look on her and Lizer Wilson as the same! She had followed mechanically, and before she had reached any conclusion they were at the back door.

A negro woman stood wiping a pan, while a lady, holding an open bucket of butter, was talking scoldingly to a woman who, as Hannah saw instantly, looked very different from the lady, and very much like Lizer and herself. There was a moment's silence as the new-comers appeared; then the negress spoke.

"Mornin', Mrs. Wilson," she said familiarly.

"Mornin', Mary," Mrs. Wilson answered, in an oily tone; then to the lady she said, "Mornin', Mrs. Skinner."

"Good morning, Mrs. Wilson," the lady answered, while the woman she had been scolding turned, and Hannah recognized a per-son who lived near the Durkets, and who was looked down on by them just as Lizer Wilson was by the Warrens. They did not greet each other, but Hannah felt the woman's stare of wonder, that "John Warren's gal" should peddle with Lizer Wilson! She seemed to hear the story being told to the Durkets, and repeated to her grandmother by Si.

Things seemed misty for a moment, then, through the confu-sion, she heard Lizer's voice. "No, I ain't got nothin' left but a few aigs, but this gal has a few things she'd like to get shed of 'fore we starts home."

Hannah listened, wondering, and remembered a saying of her grandmother's, that Lizer could "lie the kick outern a mule."

"What has she?" questioned Mrs. Skinner.

"Taters, an' apples, an' butter," Lizer answered, "nothin' much to pack back if the price ain't a-comin'."

"What is the price of the butter?"

"Thirty cents; I've done sold mine at thet; the taters is a dollar an' a heff a bushel, an' the apples a dollar."

"I have just paid twenty cents for butter; why are your things so high?" was questioned sharply.

"Ourn is extry good," Lizer answered. The negro woman smiled. Hannah's indignation was gathering, but she did not speak. Mrs. Wilson must know the ways of the place—she would wait.

"I'll take the apples," the lady began compromisingly, "but I will *not* take the butter nor the potatoes. How many apples have you?" to Hannah.

"A bushel," Hannah answered quickly, afraid that Lizer would say a cartload.

Mrs. Skinner looked at her keenly. "I have never seen you before," she said.

"She ain't never peddled befo', an' ain't got no need to come now," Lizer struck in, looking straight at the woman from the other valley. "She jest come along fur comp'ny, an' brung a few things fur balance— she ain't pertickler 'bout sellin'."

The first part of this speech soothed Hannah's feelings somewhat, but the final clause, representing her as coming for the love of Lizer Wilson, was worse than the peddling.

She began to wonder if this woman *could* tell the truth.

"Run git youuns apples, Honey," were the next astonishing words; Lizer calling *her* "Honey!" She felt a sudden hatred for the woman. What had happened to her? Was she really no better than Lizer? She drew a bitter sigh. Never mind, she would get a dollar for the apples instead of the "six-bits" she had thought to demand, and shouldering the apples she went back. They were carefully examined by the mistress, and generously measured by the servant.

"Hit's a good bushel," Hannah said, astonished that her bushel should be re-measured.

"Three water buckets with a rise," the lady put in quietly, and the negress piled each bucket carefully. Mrs. Wilson laughed, then stooped to help her, and Hannah watched them with her share of the "Durket sperret" rising within her. A Warren cheat!

"With all youuns risin', Mary, some's left," and Lizer laughed again. Hannah looked down the cavernous bag, where about a dozen apples were huddled into one corner. The color burned in her face, and with a quick movement she emptied them on the floor.

"They wuz in my bushel," she said, "they misewell go in yourn."

The negress laughed. "I'll tek dese, Miss Josie," she said to the lady.

There were two spots of color on Mrs. Skinner's face as she paid Hannah. "I should like some more apples if you can spare them," she said.

Hannah paused, her anger fading before the hope of more money. If she could bring them the next day? But by Sunday the storm about peddling would reach her from the Durkets, and she had no security that she would be allowed to return.

"Hit's a fur way to come an' only a dollar at the end," Lizer struck in, mistaking Hannah's hesitation, and Mrs. Skinner answered, " She can bring me two bushels for two dollars and a quarter."

"I can't bring 'em atter tomorrer," Hannah said slowly.

"Very well, bring them tomorrow."

When they turned the corner of the house, Mrs. Wilson said, "Thet wuz a good trade; you'd asold fur nothin'. Miss Harner thar, she hed put her butter at two bits, an' only got twenty cents. These folks beats a pusson down to nothin'."

"She riz on the apples," Hannah answered coldly.

"Riz on the apples," Lizer repeated derisively, while Hannah untied the horse, "she done thet kase you acted so biggity. My soul, but thet'll tickle Si Durket when Jane Harner tells hit."

"'Pears to me like she done hit kase she lit on a honest pusson," Hannah retorted.

It was Mrs. Wilson's turn to be angry now, but as the Warrens were her rich neighbors, she only comforted herself with a promise to remember, and walked on without giving a hint as to their destination. At the next house she did not wait while Hannah tied the horse, but walked in rapidly, leaving her to come alone. Hannah was glad, for if there was danger of meeting acquaintances, she preferred not to be seen with Lizer. She walked in quite confidently, but when she reached the back door, Lizer had vanished.

She paused a moment before several closed doors, some belonging to an out house and two to the main house. She knocked at one of the latter. She might be mistaken, but there was no harm in trying. Her knock was answered by a little boy, who asked her business, then called to someone within, "It's a woman with butter." There was an indistinguishable answer, then the child led the way to a small room where Hannah saw so much china and glass that she wondered if they kept it for sale. She would have liked a longer look at it, and if she had known more she would have waited here, but the child had gone through another door, and she followed.

Once or twice she had heard descriptions of how the people lived in this town, that to the surrounding country was as yet an enigma. Stories of how they had no object in life but "book larnin'," and were little better than "Naytrals." Once her grandfather had said, "God made all the critters, book-larnin' critters, too, an' all hes a right to live." This was the only excuse she had ever heard made for them. But she forgot all she had ever heard when she passed through the second door. It was as strange as a dream. The various kinds of furniture she had never seen before, the covered floors that made no noise, the books, the curtains, the pictures, all were new to her, at least, in this reckless profusion.

"Come near the fire," a voice said, and Hannah caught a glimpse of a fire, but it seemed a long way off, and a young man in the middle distance was an almost impassable barrier. She saw no signs of Lizer, but only the young man, and near the fire a young woman who had spoken. She moved forward slowly. The room seemed so full, and she felt herself so unusually large, that she was afraid of knocking things over. A new and disagreeable sensation, at which she could only wonder as she took her seat carefully, doubtful if the chair the young woman had placed for her would hold her.

"How much butter have you?" the young lady asked.

"Six pounds," Hannah answered, then waited to hear again the voice that was so different from any voice she had ever heard; different even from Mrs. Skinner's, that itself had been strange to her.

"And what do you ask for it?" the voice went on.

"Two bits, a' hit's good."

"That will be one dollar and a half," then to the child, "call Susan for me."

"I've got some taters," Hannah suggested hesitatingly, pushing her bonnet back a little, "taters, a bushel, good measure an' sound, for a dollar."

"I will take them also."

Hannah rose.

"If your things are at the front gate, this is your shortest way out," and the young lady opened a door that led into a hall, then opened also what Hannah recognized as the front door, which Lizer had declared was sealed to traders.

"Did you observe how very handsome that girl was?" the young lady asked of her companion when she returned from the hall.

"I did not," he answered, looking contentedly into the face before him.

"Very handsome, and I am sure she will bring the potatoes in here—she seems quite bewildered."

"I thought she seemed quite at home."

"Not at all. Her voice was very soft, too."

"Yes, and her English had about it that sweet simplicity that dispenses with all extra syllables. The way in which she said 'taters' was lovely."

"I am in earnest; her voice is sweet. I have never seen her before; I wonder what Cove she comes from."

"Ask her, and ask her to call again."

"I shall." Here the door opened, and Hannah, with the long bag over her shoulder, entered and stood looking from one to the other. Her bonnet had fallen back, letting the light touch the delicately flushed face, and the dark eyes grown wistful in their uncertainty. She was unquestionably handsome. She put the bag down carefully.

"Did I ax you too much?"

"Oh, no!" the young woman exclaimed. "Here, Susan," to a negress who had entered from the back, "empty these things." Susan raised the bag with some difficulty.

"Dat Wilson woman's in de kitchen, Miss Agnes," she said, "she's got aigs."

"You know I never buy from her," the young lady answered.

Hannah listened, and Susan went away chuckling.

Agnes turned to Hannah. "Sit down and take off your bonnet," she said, herself taking a seat. "What Cove do you come from?"

"Lost Cove."

"Where the stream sinks?"

"Thet's hit; hev you seen hit?"

"No, but I wish very much to see it."

"Hit's a smart piece," Hannah went on, looking into the fire as if making calculations, "but you could go it on a nag."

"Where do you live in Lost Cove?" Agnes went on.

"Hit most all b'longs to Gramper. Mrs. Wilson owns a leetle piece . . ." then her face burned as she remembered what had just been said about Lizer.

Agnes remembered too, and asked, "Is Mrs. Wilson a friend of yours?"

"She is a neighbor," Hannah said, then, after a moment's pause, "she come alonger me this mornin', kase I didn't know the ways ner the folks, but we couldn't 'gree, an' she leff me at youuns gate."

"I am glad of that. If you had come with her I should not have bought your things; she asks two prices."

"She do thet! But she's mighty poor."

A smile flitted across the young man's face as the words reached him, and he wondered what Hannah's idea of wealth was. "Quantity," would have been her answer, for, to her, this was the only difference. In her world the rich demanded no better quality, only a greater quantity, and, after a certain stage of plentifulness was reached, life was taken with folded hands.

"You have never been here before?" Agnes asked.

"Not to peddle, I ain't."

"Will you come again soon?" as the servant put the bag and bucket down by Hannah.

"I hes to bring some apples to a woman tomorrer."

"Then you can bring me some—a bushel?"

"I reckon," and Hannah rose, feeling as glad about coming again as about the much-coveted money she was putting into the old deer-skin purse; then Agnes shook hands with the girl over whom she had cast a spell.

"So you sold out at Agnes Welling's front do'," Mrs. Wilson said mockingly, when she met Hannah at the gate.

"I did, an' I'll wait fur you at the sto," then Hannah mounted old Bess and rode away. She did not want to talk to Mrs. Wilson just yet.

"And you did not ask her name?" the young man said when Hannah was gone.

"I forgot it; but was she not handsome? I shall go to Lost Cove this summer."

"We will make up a party," the young man suggested.

"No, I will go alone."

"Honest, at least."

Agnes laughed softly. "Still, I mean what I say, Mr. Cartright."

"It is too far for you to go alone, your brother will not permit it."

"We will see." Then Cartright went away, slamming the gate sharply, while Agnes laughed.

"Turn, Fortune, turn thy wheel with smile or frown;
With that wild wheel we go not up or down.
Our hoard is little, but our heart is great."

~Unknown

III

It had been a successful day, and as Hannah rode through the falling
shadows, with Mrs. Wilson mounted behind her, her heart felt light.
She had the coffee and the sugar, besides two dollars toward the plowing, and three bushels of apples engaged, making five dollars—to her
a fortune. And this success *would* mitigate the displeasure of her grandmother, unless talk from the Durkets reached her; that would stop
everything.

But above all, she had looked into a new world, and her life
seemed to have changed. All the fear of Sewanee was gone. The people
up there were strange, that is, different from any people she had known,
but she liked them. She was anxious to see that "Miss Agnes" again.
She would take more potatoes tomorrow, and some meat; there was
no telling how much she might make.

She began to hum a tune as they jogged along; for, although Mrs.
Wilson's feelings permitted her to ride behind Hannah, they still pre-
vented conversation. It was only at the Warrens' gate that Mrs. Wilson

vouchsafed a dignified "Far'well, Hannah Warren," and trudged away across the fields.

Hannah was preoccupied and excited. She had been dead, and now, in some strange way, vigorous and uncontrollable life had come to her. Her impulse was to defy her grandmother, but habit bade her avoid any meeting until she had found out from her grandfather the state of things.

She hung the bag containing her purchases across the fence, and unsaddled the horse. In the kitchen she went through the evening's routine with forced quietness, and ran upstairs for the fodder with a lightness and haste hitherto unknown, laughing softly as, opening the end window farthest from her grandmother's room she tossed the binds out. This would let her carry the milk pails out when she went down, and lessen, by one journey into the house, the danger of meeting Mrs. Warren.

She leaned on the gate as on the afternoon when she decided to peddle, but how different was everything. She felt that she controlled her own fate now; that she could resist her grandmother and defy Si Durket. In short, she was free, and with the rare joy of having realized her bondage and freedom in the same moment. She might have gone on forever in the old dull path, but for the necessity that drove her to peddling. The fruits of the earth and the beasts of the field had become her protectors against Si Durket. She would never tire of work again.

A shadow fell on the joy, and she leaned her head on the gate. "Poor Daddy! If he hed downfaced Granny, an' peddled stiddy, an' not jest traded what happed over, Granny couldn't hev jawed him the way she did, kase he'd hev hed as much as the Durkets. Poor Daddy." And she recalled the silent, sad-eyed man who had thought himself a failure. The tears rose to her eyes, but did not quench the anger that burned in her heart against her grandmother. "An' I'd abeen jest like him but fur peddlin'."

The clank of the cowbells broke on her musings, and at the sound happiness brimmed up again. "Does you feel well, cows?" she said. "Si Durket kin say farwell now," and, holding open the gate, she patted the animals as they came in.

This elation lasted until she had to carry wood into her grandmother's room, then unexpectedly her heart failed her.

All she kin do is to kill me, she thought, with an incredulous smile, an' thet's heap better marryin' Si.

"Hardy, Gramper!" she said as she opened the door, and there was such a cheery ring to her voice that Mrs. Warren put her great silver-rimmed spectacles in place to look at her. "How'd you git on 'thout me?" she went on, smiling reassuringly into the old man's eyes as she put down the wood.

"Hit's been some lonesome," he answered, "hit's never been afore thet I've set all day an' never hearn a holler, ner a whistle, ner a step 'bout the ole house thet kin 'member so many a stomp. My Par, an' my brethers, an' my boys, all gone, all gone. But I kin 'member how ever one sot hisn heel to the flo'. I don't see how I'll ever spar' you to go clean away, Hannah,"

"You'll never need to see hit," Hannah answered. "Supper's ready, Granny," she went on, and turned to the door.

Mrs. Warren rose slowly. "You gits meallyer ever day, John Warren," she said, pushing the odd needle through her knitting.

"Thet's right, Mertildy, a good, ripe apple is allers meally."

"An' gits rotten-meally—mebbe you knows thet."

"An' you speaks thet to me thet hes been youuns man fur moren fifty yeer, Mertildy?"

"Yes, I do say hit 'bout Hannah," she answered. "Did I think I'd live to see a Warren gal a-tradin' taters like any trash? She'll be a-peddlin' next, an' mebbe you'll marry her to Dock Wilson, jest to hev her a-nigh you."

"Hit mout all come true, Mertildy," and the old man's gentle eyes flashed, "fur peddlin' ain't no sin, an' Dock Wilson ain't never knocked a woman yit."

A dull color came into Mrs. Warren's face. "Si were wrong," she admitted, "but thar's one thing a Durket can't stand, an' thet's bein' jawed by a fool, and Si's Mar were a p'in-blank fool." At the door she met Hannah. It looked almost as if she had been waiting there, in spite of the cold wind that was sweeping through the lobby.

And now the happiness that had left her at the woodpile came back, as, kneeling in front of the fire, Hannah drew the two silver dollars from her pocket.

"Didn't you git no cawfee an' sugar?" Mrs. Warren asked.

"I did thet, an' brung home this fur the plowin'," and she shook the money triumphantly. Then she told her story, impressing on the old man that she had gone to the shop with money. But she lowered her voice as she told of her meeting Mrs. Harner, and of her engagement for the next day. Mr. Warren, eating slowly, made no comment until she came to the description of her being received in the Wellings' parlor, while a servant emptied her things, and Lizer waited in the kitchen.

"Thet'll tickle Mertildy," he said with a chuckle, "but if you 'lows to go ag'in tomorrer, you must git off 'fore youuns Granny hes time to hender you."

"She can't hold me all day, Gramper, an' she can't tie me."

Mr. Warren regarded his granddaughter curiously. "Granny's ole now, chile," he said, "an' don't you go to makin' her wuss mad 'an is needful. You ain't never seen her rayly mad. I ain't never seen hit but onest, but thet's enough," rubbing one hand slowly round on his bald head. "'Fair-an'-easy' is a good horse, Hannah, but 'Don't keer' is a galding nag. Thar's no use a-flyin' in Granny's face 'thout thar's a needcessity."

Hannah felt her independence slipping away, and she asked, "What hev you told Granny?"

"Thet you hed gone to trade fur cawfee an' sugar, an' I ain't a-goin' to tell her nothing mo' tell I'm obleeged to. She's been worrited an' onsettled all day, mad 'bout Lizer a-goin'. Lizer ain't to say a clean-tongued woman."

"Mrs. Wilson's feared o' me," Hannah said contemptuously. Then told again of emptying the apples, and the snubbing she had given Lizer at the gate.

"Thet's what Granny 'll call the 'Durket sperret,'" and the old man smiled as if at the vagaries of a child. "But she sets a heap o' store by you, Hannah."

"She's too hard, Gramper," the girl said coldly. "She stomps youuns feelin's dead, an' *then* she ain't sati'fy, kase then you've got to feel her way," and the girl's eyes filled with tears. "If I coulder lied or stole, or if I coulder left you an' Daddy, she'd hev druv me to hit long ago. Poor Daddy!" But she dashed the tears away, for, without warning, Mrs. Warren entered. She looked at them sharply, then seated herself near the fire with her knitting. Hannah did not move; she would do nothing that looked like retreat.

"An' what's you been a-cryin' 'bout, Hannah; is you sick?"

"We's been a-talkin', Mertildy," Mr. Warren answered, "'bout you, and me, an' Joshaway, an' Hannah."

Mrs. Warren was silent, for, unknown to anyone, her heart was sore about her son Joshua. Her last words to him haunted her. She had abused him in the presence of his child. When she ceased, he had shouldered his axe and had gone into the woods, and in the evening had been brought home dead, his life crushed out by a falling tree. Her grief for his death had been unfeigned, and she had spent all she could lay her hands on for his funeral; but she had never said that she was sorry for any of the hard things she had dealt to him throughout his life, and Hannah's young heart had grown hard toward her. But Mrs. Warren remembered, and any mention of his name was a keen pain.

"Youuns daddy were a good son, boy and man," Mr. Warren went on. "He never tole a lie as I kin 'member, an' he never done nothin' he were tole not to do, nur he never hurt nothin' if he knowed hit; an' when youuns Granny were ailin', thar worn't no woman more soffly than Joshaway. An' from the time he were born he hed them kind o' askin' eyes like the critters thet can't say what they wants. An' hit allers hurt me, Joshaway's eyes did, an' when he were leetle I were allers a-givin' him ever'thing he looked at, but all the same hisn's eyes kept on askin' an' askin' to the last."

There was a dead silence in the room save for the click of Mrs. Warren's needles, and the whispering of the fire. Presently Mr. Warren spoke again. "I reckon hisn eyes is satisfy now. I reckon so. An' weuns never hed no words, me an' Joshaway, but I've been right sharp on Pete, an' Dave, an' John, but Joshaway never hurt nobody, an' nobody never hed no 'casion to hurt Joshaway. An' now he's gone afore me. But I reckon hisn eyes is satisfy—I reckon so."

Hannah rose, she could not listen any longer; she would cry out against the hard old woman sitting there with that immovable face. Her taste of freedom that day had unfitted her for the stolid submission of the past. She could not bear it, and she left the room. It scarcely seemed fair that her father should be brought back from his grave to blunt her grandmother's temper. She might be mistaken, and the words have been only loving recollections.

"Ole folks don't hev nothin' to do but 'member things," she whispered, wiping her eyes with the corner of her little shawl, as she stole away to the loft where the apples were stored. She put down the sacks and the measure carefully, and, hanging the lantern on a nail in the low rafters, kneeled down cautiously. "An' Daddy would a-been willin' to be spoke 'bout to save me," the whisper went on, as she carefully picked out the apples and laid them in the measure. The fall of one might call her grandmother up to investigate, and prohibit. When the sacks were filled she lowered them from the window with a rope. It took a long time, and she was shivering uncontrollably when she took the lantern from the nail and crept downstairs.

The meat and the potatoes were easily arranged, for they were in an out house. In the piazza she piled wood for the morning, and laid the kitchen fire ready for lighting. Her grandmother should have no extra work to complain of.

She took the milk pails and the kettle into her own room, for all must be done before day. And in after years it seemed to her that her life dated from that cold, dark March morning. She milked, with the lantern casting weird shadows about her, refusing to listen to the strange noises of the wind, and trembled like a thief when she took off her shoes and stole into the kitchen with the milk. She was glad now that the wind was wild and high; she could hear the branch of a tree her father had planted close to the house, scraping against her grandmother's window, and drowning any little noise that she might make.

She drank a bowl of milk, and put a piece of cold cornbread into her pocket, to serve until she came back, and, as the first light broke in the east, and flashed a crimson flame from point to point of the low flying clouds, Hannah closed the gate softly and rode away.

The shadows were still black in the woods, and the wind that came tearing down the mountain seemed to wrap round her, and to bend the trees down as if to bar her from this journey. Never before had the sunrise affected her as it did now, and realizing dimly a change in herself, she wondered a little, stopping to look down over the wild, mist-draped scene.

"Everything seems purtier now," she murmured.

A thread of blue smoke rose from among the trees below, she started, gathering up the reins; she knew where that came from.

An' now poor Gramper's a-steddyin' what to say!" and she urged old Bess forward as if her grandmother might yet sally forth and stop her.

"But my being is confused with new experience,
And changed to something other than it was."

~*Astarte*, Robert Bulwer Lytton

IV

"Where are you off to, Max?" The young man addressed was adjusting a shabby gown with much precision.

"To Miss Welling's," Max answered, as with the same care he put on his square cap.

"If *I* had such a fossil gown," his companion went on from the bed where, though the day was young, he was lounging with a cigarette between his lips, "and such a crummy mortarboard, I'd not put them on with such solemnity and jurisdiction."

"If you could show such a cap and gown, Melville, you'd not be a 'Squab,'" and taking up some books, Max left the room.

It was early, but formal visiting hours were ignored in the village of Sewanee, and people kept open house, and dropped in on each other when they liked. So Max dropped in and found Miss Welling sewing.

"I have brought the book I spoke of," he began, without further greeting. "This poet ought to capture you, to convert you to himself, for he makes one long to live bravely."

"Or die bravely," Agnes suggested.

"To live is harder. Death cannot be dodged, so there is no use in being afraid, but many things in life can be dodged. I often wonder if education makes any difference in the way one meets death. Is it easier for these country people to let life go than for us?"

"They live like moles," Agnes said, "in comparison we are squirrels; and I think they take a pride in dying. I think the ignorant die calmly because they do not know, and the educated because they do know."

"What?"

"What? Why, why, everything, which comprehensive everything is, after all, very limited. Still I believe in education. I *know* that educated people are happier and better."

"Whew," and Max pulled his mustache slowly. "If I were sure of that, I should this day begin a crusade with a 'blue-backed' spelling book as my banner. And you," leaning forward a little, "your duty is to begin at once to teach. If once we realize what is best to be done for our fellows, we *must* do it."

The door opened and Hannah stood before them with a sack of apples across one shoulder. "Hardy," she said, her face lighting up as she caught sight of Agnes, "har's youuns apples."

"I am glad to see you," and Agnes held out her hand. Max looked from one to the other curiously, then placed a chair near the fire for Hannah. "It is cold," he said. Hannah looked at him a moment, then taking off her long bonnet, sat down on the edge of the chair.

"Yes, and she has come a long way," Agnes answered for her, then turned away to call the servant. Max took up the bag and followed Agnes into the next room, and she going still further, he returned to his place. Hannah watched him until he came back, then looked at the fire, and Max watched her. It was a beautiful face as he saw it now with the firelight on it, and he spoke to her.

"What Cove do you come from?" he asked.

"Lost Cove."

"Then you must be connected with Mr. John Warren, and with his son?"

"He's my Gramper," she answered, in a surprised voice, "and hisn's son, Joshaway?"

"Yes, I met them out hunting last October."

"Joshaway were my Par," the voice faltered, and the eyes sought the fire. "He were killed in November."

"Yes, I heard that. What is your name?"

"Hannah," watching Agnes as she returned.

"And is your grandfather quite well?" Max went on in a quiet way that put Hannah at her ease and surprised Agnes.

"No, he ain't; he can't stir fur the rheumatiz, an' he ain't done a hand's turn sence hog killin', jest atter Daddy died, an' I'll hev to hire Dock Wilson to help me plow."

"You plow?"

"Yes, sir."

"Can you read?"

"Some. Mammy hed schoolin', an' she larned dad, an' he larned me. But I don't hev no time, what with the cows, an' the hogs, an' the wood, an' the cookin', an' washin', an' Granny says book-larnin' is foolishness."

"You must have too much to do, though work is a good friend."

"Thet's what Gramper says. He says work b'ars no gredges an' tells no lies; good work stan's up an' says 'good,' an' bad work stan's up an' says 'bad,' an' thar's no hushin' them, an' hit's true," then rising, she took up the bag the servant had brought, and held out her hand to Agnes.

"Farwell," she said, "weuns'd be rale proud to see you down home."

"Thank you," Agnes said, smiling as Hannah, instead of shaking her hand, turned it over and looked at it curiously.

Then she turned to Max. "You must come, too, an' what name shell I name to Gramper?"

"Max Dudley," shaking hands in his turn, "we camped together one night. I was lost and came on his camp. I will bring Miss Welling down," then he opened the door for Hannah.

"And answered with such craft as women use,
Guilty or guiltless, to stave off a chance —
That breaks upon them perilously."

~*Idyls of the King*, Alfred, Lord Tennyson

V

Successful as before, Hannah was happy, for, besides a little bag of flour, she had more money than she intended to show even to Mr. Warren. If he knew of this surplus he might reveal it in order to save her from hard words, and if Mrs. Warren knew, it would be stored away and she'd be left as helpless as before. She had made a long detour to reach the Wilsons and engage Dock to plow, as she had the money to pay him. She would say four dollars, the rest she must save for other purposes.

Once more on the main road, she urged old Bess on. There was much excitement in her position, and she was anxious yet afraid. How would it be possible to see Mr. Warren alone first? She stopped the horse. "If I keeps on bein' afeard o' Granny," she said aloud, "I'll do sumpen rale mean some day." Old Bess was urged on again. "I'll go right in an' face her, crooked chance or straight chance."

She dropped the reins on the horse's neck, and took the old deer-skin purse from her pocket. It was quite full with her two days' gains, and she drew a long sigh. She took out all the money save the four dollars intended for Dock's wages, and tying it up in her glove, hid it in her bosom, then put the purse back in her pocket.

"Hit looks right sneakin', but I must save hit 'ginst Si."

Reaching the gate, she unsaddled the horse with unusual celerity, and shouldering the saddle and the little bag of flour, went quickly into the house.

It had been a long and weary day to the old man. Hannah's errand was a bitter pill to Mrs. Warren. She had never done such a thing in her life, nor was it customary with women of her station. In those early days, "the man who would let his women-folks peddle was a poor sort of man." But the concealment of the expedition had wounded Mrs. Warren also.

Often she had complained that she did not understand Hannah, for though she usually held herself very much aloof, Hannah would yet do work and associate with people that shocked Mrs. Warren, and the irritation caused by what she deemed the girl's peculiarities was a very constant thing.

"A goat raised a pup once, Mertildy," her husband had often said to her, "but she never could larn thet pup to butt, an' you'll never larn Hannah youuns ways."

All this ground, and the grievance about Si, had been gone over many times during the day. Mrs. Warren felt herself outwitted, for she was sure the difficulty of plowing had been solved. Her sequence had been: no man to plow, no money to pay a man, no crop, then want, *or* Si Durket.

"An' why not?" she had asked, "he's well-lookin', he's well off, he's a *man*. He cusses some, he gits drunk some, and when he's mad, he *is* mad. But all the Durkets hes sperret, an' Si ain't none o' your soft-walkin', still-tongued folks like the Warrens, an' when he walks, he stomps!"

Mr. Warren had told her of Hannah's first venture, how she had sat in the parlor, leaving Lizer in the kitchen, how she showed the "Durket sperret" about the apples, and how, after her purchases, Hannah had two dollars left.

These things had mollified her, until she remembered that they had been concealed from her, and when Hannah entered she turned her face away.

"Is you done dinner?" Hannah asked, then looked at her grandmother's averted face.

"Yes, Honey," Mr. Warren answered, twitching her dress furtively, "an' was the woman glad to see you?"

"Yes, and I had a rale nice time. Thar wuz a young man to Miss Agnes Wellin's that knowed you an' Daddy. Says he stayed all night to youuns camp. He's coming to see you, an' Miss Agnes is a-comin' too."

"That's right," Mr. Warren answered heartily, "I 'members that feller, he's named Dudley, and he's rale well-spoken."

"That's hit," Hannah assented, "an' I said as you and Granny would be proud to see 'em if they'd come, an' they said they'd come sure. An' Miss Agnes said I must come again." Then, more slowly, "Them folks at Sewanee is good folks, Gramper, an' the lies Mrs. Wilson tells 'em, an' tells 'bout 'em, is scan'alous! But they knows Lizer."

"And was you all the time a-doin' that?" Mrs. Warren asked curtly.

"No, I stopped a piece at Mrs. Skinner's and at the sto'. Aigs is awful sca'ce; Mrs. Skinner says she'll gimme twenty cents a dozen."

"Thet's a good price, sure," Mr. Warren said. "Did you promise any?"

"You said not to say I'd go again," Hannah answered.

"When you is done rubbin' 'gainst the pot, thar ain't no use a-fearing smut," Mrs. Warren put in sharply. "Hannah Warren is done knowed fur a peddler alonger Lizer Wilson an' sich, an' she misewell sell the aigs."

"If you sesso, Granny, I'm surely willin'," and Hannah did not give a sign of the surprise she felt. "An' Dock Wilson says he'll come a-Monday, Gramper."

Mrs. Warren looked up quickly. She saw some of her suspicions being made facts, and realized that Hannah was escaping her. "An' who's to pay?"

"I've got the money," Hannah answered. Then she went her way to the kitchen, where she stood still and drew a long breath of relief.

Is she wronged? To the rescue of her honor, My heart!
Is she poor?—What costs it to become a donor?
Merely an earth to cleave—a sea to part.
But that fortune should have thrust all this upon her!

~Songs from Pippa Passes, Robert Browning

VI

"Dock Wilson!" Mrs. Wilson stood in the open door of her small log house. Dock turned and looked from where he sat on the wood-pile whittling, but did not answer, and she raised her voice, "Dinner's done, an' I wish you'd come!"

Dock went on with the whittling, whistling softly. He was tall and fair, with a grave, kind face and his eyes were true. His stepmother, Lizer Wilson, ruled him "to the last notch," people said, but Dock had his own code and went his quiet way, with few words or friends. He had not been in the Cove long. When old man Wilson was dying, he sent for this son, and since his father's death Dock had worked faithfully for his stepmother and her two boys.

In Mrs. Warren's eyes he was contemptible. "Any man that kin stan' Lizer Wilson must hev cotton insides,' she would say conclusively, and Hannah began to think of Dock with sympathy.

Just now he took his own time about obeying Mrs. Wilson's call. He was in deep thought that he seemed to work into the butter paddle he was fashioning, whistling softly. He regarded it with some satisfaction, as he shut his knife and dropped it into his cavernous pocket.

"A piece o' glass 'll make hit smooth." He put it away in the hollow of a tree near by, and went into the house.

"'Pears like you ain't much honggry," was Mrs. Wilson's greeting.

"I dunno," Dock answered, "I'll try an' see."

For a few moments there was silence; then, eying Dock closely, Mrs. Wilson asked, "What did Hannah Warren want?"

"She wanted to hire some plowin'."

Mrs. Wilson grunted. "Hiren plowin' an' been up twicest this week a-peddlin'. *She* to set up to run the place on hired han's; she'd better tuck Si Durket an' be done."

Dock shook his broad shoulders a little.

"Is you a-goin' to plow?"

"I am."

"An' I bet you ain't made no trade, jest said you'd do hit."

"Jest so."

"An' what kinder trade is you a-goin' to make?"

"If Hannah Warren hes to peddle to pay me, she kin pay what she hes a mind to pay, Hannah is a Sunday gal!"

"An' me an' the boys 'thout rags to ourn backs," rising, as if to keep up her voice; "an' you eatin' like a horse! I ain't a-goin' to stand hit, Dock Wilson, I tell you I ain't! An' thet dratted Hannah Warren thinkin' herself too good to go alonger me. You're a fool, a dead-gone fool! I ain't a-goin' to stand hit!"

Dock, rising, drew his shirtsleeve slowly across his bearded lips as he rose. Mrs. Wilson seized his arm. "Is you deef?" she cried shrilly. Dock looked down on her.

"No," he answered deliberately, "I ain't deef, an' I b'lieve you could raise the dead, Lizer, much less make the deef hear."

The woman swung away from him. "I sw'ar you'll wish yerseff dead if you don't make a good trade," she said, "I sw'ar you will."

"Thet won't be nothin' new." Then Dock went to a little shanty he had built for himself, where Lizer was denied entrance. He pushed up the fire, and, sitting down, lighted his pipe. Hannah Warren! Her worth had dawned on him gradually. He was first struck by the difference between her and the other women he knew. She reminded him of a pool of water deep under the rocks, where there was no sound of trickling stream, no ripple. In the evening, when the sun was setting and all was still, the purple light on the mountainside seemed like her.

He could not put it into words, but, when he saw these things he would whisper, "Hit 'minds me o' her." He did not dream of lifting his eyes to Hannah, he had scarcely ever spoken to her, but this far-off influence had changed his life. Now she had sought him.

She had called him, softly, "Dock," and when he stood beside her horse and looked up, the fair face seemed doubly fair, shining from the depths of her long bonnet. Drive a bargain with Hannah! He would see Lizer dead and buried first. It hurt him to think of her going about Sewanee peddling. It was very well for Lizer and the like, but Hannah was different. He had heard enough to make him sure she was peddling to save herself from Si Durket, and that she peddled against her grandmother's will. He had seen her cutting wood, and hauling it, too. Already he had carried wood there in the night, not enough to attract attention, but enough to help her. He must help her against Si, or he would have to kill Si. A quarrel was "easy picked."

Presently Mrs. Wilson's voice, ordering the boys to bring in wood, reminded him that the more wood he cut today, the more time he would have to help Hannah next week. He put down his pipe, and soon the quick, sharp strokes of the axe rang through the stillness, until Hannah could hear them between her own less powerful blows.

She listened, and wondered what wages he would demand. Speaking to him, she had become sure of his goodness, and felt that if he knew how hardly she was bestead, he would not push her. "But I can't tell him, if his heart *is* kind."

Si would come over the next day, it being Sunday, and she longed for snow or rain, even to the detriment of the plowing, to keep him at home. But before evening the clouds were swept away before a stinging northwest wind, and the morning dawned brilliantly clear.

"You'll hev a good week a-plowin'," Mr. Warren said, as he ate his breakfast.

"But we'll hev Si today," Hannah answered, "an' Granny will r'ar an' pitch if he riles her 'bout the peddlin'."

"Mebbe he won't say nothin', an' you kin keep him pleased."

Hannah looked up quickly. "If I makes b'lieve to favor him, I kin," she said, "but that's a big lie, Gramper, an' surely you don't mean hit, kase if you goes against me I'll go and hire out."

"Lord! Youuns Granny'll die!"

"Well, she'll hev to die 'fore I'll tuck Si." She felt strong now that she had a little money laid by; nevertheless her heart quailed a little when she saw Si dismount at the gate. She heard him come into her grandfather's room, and she longed to run away; instead, she emptied the water from the buckets, and, when the dishes were put away, sat with buckets on either side and her bonnet on.

Presently a chair was moved, and Hannah was gone. Si found the kitchen empty. But, lengthen it as she would, the work was done at last, and when Mrs. Warren called her she had to go. She took her seat close to her grandfather, who laid his hand on hers, that rested on the arm of his chair.

Si was giving a grand description of a visit he had made lately to Chattanooga. It was something to have traveled on the railway, but a visit to Chattanooga was a thing to date from. He had brought back some *"seegyars,"* one of which he now smoked with much ostentation.

Mrs. Warren looked and listened to her nephew with undisguised admiration, every now and then putting in an encouraging exclamation.

This great man was a Durket—the Warrens could not have produced him. She had tried her best to make her boys Durkets. She had showed them the "Durket sperret" faithfully, but each son, as he married, chose the quietest woman he could find. And now her granddaughter, who had this golden opportunity of mating with the flower of the Durkets, refused, and stood to her refusal with a strength in which Mrs. Warren might have seen a strain of "Durket sperret," if she had not been convinced that it was Warren obstinacy.

Presently Hannah was sent to see after dinner, then Si said, "We'll walk a piece after grub, Hannah."

"I dunno . . ."

"Yes, you do!" Mrs. Warren struck in, "I'll clean up, go 'long."

Hannah was tempted to hide, but the storm would then fall on her grandfather, who was bound to his chair, and always at the mercy of that merciless tongue. She must go with Si, and if there was a battle to be fought she must fight it.

"If there's a bad place in the road, pick up youuns foot an' cross it quick," she said to herself as she put the dinner on table, "thar' ain't no use in doubtin', git over." Then she helped her grandfather, and went back into the room as Mrs. Warren and Si left it.

She found that as yet nothing had been said about the peddling, and Si seemed in a good humor.

"But he hes hearn," Hannah thought, and took as long as she could to eat her own dinner.

At last the time came, and she passed quickly through the gate that Si held open, and turned into the public road going down the Cove. The bare trees along the mountaintops seemed to be cut in ebony against the brilliant blue. The buds were swelling, the moss and lichens on the gray boulders looked a brighter hue, the fields spread brown and ready for work, the birds were flying about busily, and through the stillness came the sound of falling water. The winter was done, and all nature was glad for the warm, soft wind that touched it into life again. The feeling swept over Hannah, too, a thrill of health and strength. The young year called to her youth that sprang forward to meet it. How happy she could have been! Si was still telling of the glories of Chattanooga, and Hannah had begun to hope that the walk would terminate peacefully, when he turned and said, "Would you like to live to Chattynoogy?"

Hannah started, and answered, more sharply than was wise, "No, I wouldn't."

"An' why not?"

"Kase I ain't heard you tell 'bout nothin' thar 'ceppen cussin' an' whisky, an' I hates both."

Si laughed and pulled a flat bottle out of his pocket. "Thet's the best friend in the country," he said, "an' you'd soon larn to like hit, hit's good. Why, gal, thet cost nigh onter *two* dollars a gallon! But Si Durket ain't feared o' spendin'."

Hannah was silent, hoping that Si would go on talking as he had done before, but he had other intentions.

"Would you like to live 'cross the mountain?" he asked, stooping to look under her bonnet.

Hannah drew back quickly. "No, I wouldn't," and the tone of disgust in her voice cut her cousin like a lash.

"Damn it, then, you needn't!" he answered viciously, kicking a stone into the fields that lay below them. "An' peddlin' is what you likes. Peddlin' alonger Lizer Wilson an' Jane Harner an' sich, sittin' round folks' back do's alonger the niggers till the fine ladies come to buy; you likes thet."

"Peddlin' is hones'," Hannah answered, and turned toward the house. She was afraid to go farther away with Si in this humor.

"Whar's you a-goin'?"

"To milk the cows!"

"Damn the cows!" but Hannah walked on, and he had to follow her or be left. He made a long step. "Hannah!" and he caught her sleeve. She stopped and looked at him quietly. "Is you a-goin' to marry me?"

Hannah turned her head away and moved forward as if deliberating, but Si held her sleeve.

"Is you?" drawing nearer. Hannah took off her bonnet and turned it about in her hands.

"Weuns don't suit, Si," dropping the bonnet, and Si, stooping for it, let go her sleeve.

"Hit suits me, an' hit suits Aunt Tildy; you is the only one that can't be satisfy."

"Well, I'm the main one," her voice growing firmer, as she caught sight of Dock Wilson in a field near by. But Si went on with a patience that surprised her.

"An' what about me don't please you?" he asked.

Hannah shook her head, "Fire don't suit water," she answered, "An' corn won't grow outer 'tater eyes, but I dunno why."

"An' you won't?"

"I can't."

"An' who's a-goin' to run this place an' feed the old folks?"

"I is."

"Peddlin'? Not if I knows hit. None o' my women folks ain't a-goin' to do thet, an' I'll show Aunt Tildy why. I knowed you were up to some trick when I hearn Jane Harner a-tellin', but you'll not go agin. If you do, thar'll be sicher talk raised as'll compel you to tuck anybody that axes you. An' everybody knows thet whoever comes nighst Hannah Warren is got Si Durket to fight."

Hannah walked on, silent.

"Does you onderstan'?" Si repeated, his head seeming to flatten in his anger like the head of a snake.

"I do, an' I tell you right now, Si, thet Hannah Warren 'll stay Hannah Warren furever," her eyes burning ominously into his. "You ner Granny can't skeer me, an' you kin tell all the lies you wants to 'bout me, kase if lies grows fast, truth grows strong."

Si uttered a great oath and raised his arm.

Hannah smiled. "You knocked youun's mammy, but . . ." then she paused, for at her words a livid hue overspread his face, and his arm dropped. For a moment she watched him, then walked away; and Dock, out in the fields, kept her well in sight.

The cows were gathered round the gate, and, letting them in, she went for the pails and food. Mrs. Warren met her.

"Whar's Si?" she asked. Hannah pointed to an elevated part of the road, where Si could be seen leaning against a tree, and Mrs. Warren let her go. She was trembling with excitement, and longed to warn her grandfather of the gathering storm. She led the cows to a position that her grandfather could see from the window, and Si coming in would not pass near. She heard a cheerful whistle, and saw Dock leaning on the fence, looking over the fields they would plough the next day. She took no notice, but was glad he was near.

Steadily she went on with the milking, wondering why Si did not come. It was possible that he was emptying the bottle he had shown her; if so, anything might happen. At last he came, and passing without a word, went into the house. She saw that he still had her bonnet in his hand; perhaps he was not very drunk, but she shivered a little. She was milking the last cow when voices reached her. Her grandmother's voice, rising higher and higher, and Mr. Warren's weaker tones calling out, "Mertildy! Mertildy!"

Dock's whistle rose with the voices, and she saw that he had climbed the fence and was sitting on the woodpile. He nodded as she looked, and she nodded in return.

"Hannah Warren!" She started. Her grandmother was standing in the open lobby. She took up the pails and went in. There was no fear or nervousness in her demeanor, except that her hands trembled a little as she strained the milk, but even that had ceased by the time she washed them, and, pulling down her sleeves, turned to face her grandmother.

Mrs. Warren did not understand the expression on the young face that looked so full in hers; an expression of cold hardness mixed with a little contempt; a look the old woman had never met before. For the moment she was disconcerted and turned toward her room, then, the spell of the look being broken, her voice rose sharp and clear. "This away," she called, "come right in. I'll hev the truth o' this dratted business or die, come in!"

But Hannah felt secure; her grandmother had flinched before her look, and instantly she felt a pity for what was weaker than herself. She would explain and keep the peace if possible, and she took her seat near her grandfather, just opposite Si.

"An' now, Hannah Warren, jes say what you mean by a-lyin' 'bout apples as were promised; jest tell the truth if you kin, fur I'll hev it outer you or die!" and Mrs. Warren's voice was rasping in its bitterness as she stood with arms akimbo, glaring at the two who sat so close together.

"Hit worn't no lie; I did tuck up apples I hed promised to Miss Agnes Wellin' and Mrs. Skinner."

"An' the meat an' the taters, whar'd you sell them?" stamping her foot as she came near.

A faint color came in Hannah's face, but she answered, quietly still, "I dunno what thet woman were named."

"No, thet you don't!" coming nearer still, and working herself up to a pitch of anger that would soon be beyond control, "but Si knows, he's 'cute as you, stealin' fust an' lyin' atterwards. How dar' you tuck them things, how dar' you go a-peddlin' 'thout axin' me, how dar' you, how dar' you do hit!"

"I never lied, an' I never stole, Granny," the girl answered, rising to her feet, "an' if you're a-goin' to keep Si Durket to crawl round an' spy on me, I'm a-goin'." She had risen because she expected now, what had always come with any burst of anger, quick, hard blows. And as she finished speaking the brown, sinewy old fist flashed up, but as quickly the girl caught it in her strong young hand, an action that was more to Mrs. Warren than a return blow would have been, for it meant not war, but victory.

"Granny," the low voice trembled, and the dark eyes flashed, "I've done tuck my last orders, an' I've done tuck my last blow. I'm a woman now, an' you must larn to 'member hit."

A silence fell that seemed the silence of death, as the anger on the old face changed to terror, and a gray hue spread from lips to brow, a deadly gray hue as the fierce old eyes grew dim, and a slight foam came on the parched lips. It was an awful change, scarcely realized by the girl until a low cry from her grandfather made her spring forward and catch the reeling figure.

"Help me, Si!" she called, and between them they laid Mrs. Warren on the bed. "Open the winders an' fetch some water," and while Si, half dazed with liquor, clumsily obeyed, Hannah loosened the old woman's clothes, and Mr. Warren, unable to move, wrung his hands.

"She's hed hit afore!" he wailed, "an' they said not to make her mad no mo', an' we never did, oh, Lord, hev mussy, hev mussy! I oughter hev tole Hannah, an' I never did. I never hed no 'casion, she were such a peaceable chile, an' now Lord, hev mussy, hev mussy!"

No, they had never told her. With the old man's words there came to Hannah the memory of the years through which all had bowed to the relentless will of this old woman. She had thought there *was* some truth in her grandmother's scorn for the weakness of the Warrens that yielded so quietly to the "Durket sperret," and she had determined to vindicate the Warrens. Alas, those strong men submitted because they were strong, and the old woman ruled because she was weak. And now in her pride she had made all those years of sacrifice of no avail.

There came a weak sigh. "Hesh, Gramper," she said, softly, to still the old man's wail, and motioned Si from the room. The sight of him would recall too much.

Dock watched him go, then walked away slowly.

"I'll help her agin Si to the tune of a bullet, if thar's a needcessity," he said to himself, "an' never feel myseff no sinner, nuther." And Hannah missed the friendly whistle that had helped her.

"Yet, ah, that Spring should vanish with the Rose!
That Youth's sweet-scented manuscript should close!
The nightingale that in the branches sang—
Ah, whence, and whither flown again, who knows!

"Would but some wingèd Angel ere too late
Arrest the yet unfolded Roll of Fate.
And make the stern Recorder otherwise
Enregister or quite obliterate!"

~*The Rubaiyat*, Omar Khayyam

VII

Monday was bright, and only cold enough to remind people that frost might still come to harass them. An exquisite morning, with that "sense of tears in mortal things" that seems ever to veil the glory of the spring.

Agnes Welling always declared that she liked Sewanee much better in winter than in the rush of summer gaiety. Question her, and it would be found that by "winter" she meant from the end of August to the first of July. From the crisply cool days of September, when the first touch of crimson is on the tall black gums, and the blue gentian bells bloom by the clear, brown streams; when the white shell flowers, like fallen stars, look up from among the shadowy ferns, it is as a dream—a dream where the air is sweeter than life; where the sky melts into illimitable depths of blue, and the purple haze, like the shadow of light, spreads over all the land.

Then, in the great, still forests, the leaves float down softly, tenderly to death; the nuts fall, the squirrels drop from limb to limb, the brilliant lizards bask in the last warm sun, and the partridges whir up and away from their hiding in the dry, brown leaves. Through the long white winter, when the trees bend with the weight of ice, and the snow hushes all to the silence of death, when the pulse of nature beats so slow, and only the cold winds cry and move. Through all the sweet waking of the flowers, and the fresh budding of the trees, through the glory of June to the glare of July, all this Agnes called "winter." And leaning on the gate this Monday morning, she thought, 'Only to live is enough.'

"A penny for your thoughts!" and Max Dudley joined her.

"I am mooning over the seasons, wondering which I like best."

"Which is the saddest? Tell me that, and I will tell you which you like best. Young people, ignorant of sorrow, have usually a leaning toward the melancholy."

"You being very old."

"Measuring by experience, yes. But about the seasons?"

"The saddest season in life must be when we have outlived our longings."

Max gave her a quick look. It was not often that she showed herself, yet now she had turned deliberately from the lighter side of the subject. Was it confidence in him? And he answered, "That we cannot do. In youth we long for the future; after that, we look back with longing."

"And when is 'that'?"

"I do not know. In the turmoil we do not seem to see the line; then we look up, and all is behind us, save our longings."

"And regrets? They seem immortal."

"'Oh, last regret, regret can die!'"

"Poetry scarcely counts for proof."

"True poets are prophets," Max answered. "They glorify common things, purify all things, and interpret the universe."

"Does 'common things' include people?" Agnes questioned. "And does the poet make *them* glorious, or only cast a glory about them?"

"Yes, to both questions," looking at her with a smile, "because I have that great liking and respect for the lower classes which you say you cannot understand. I like them, even if they be moles and our favored selves squirrels."

"That is a very good simile," Agnes maintained, "for their lives are passed in the blackness of intellectual darkness."

"And ours in the high tree tops of culture. Even so, but to what better purpose? The mole makes a living; what more does the squirrel? And what difference does it make to the mole so long as he does not know what it is to be a squirrel? Of course I am thankful that I am a squirrel; still, if I were a mole, I hope that I should be in this same state of mind, and burrow diligently into the best potato-patch I could find."

"And you do not think you would want to rise if, for instance, you were a Covite?"

Max shook his head. "If you should ask a Covite that question," he answered, "he would very soon show you that he did not consider your condition any better than his own. And if you changed his environment, he would not thank you any more than the mole would thank you if you should take him from his burrow and put him up a tree. Yet this is what you aim at in your educational crusade. I object to it. I like these people through this country, who have the habits and even the thoughts of eighty years ago, and with it a sturdy independence of opinion."

"And you do not think that Hannah Warren, for instance, would be better for an education and a little civilization? Think how charming she would be if well dressed and speaking good English."

"But not molded by a free school. From that she would return, probably, with frizzed bangs and a great love for chewing gum."

"Horrid! But here she comes now; see how pretty she is."

Max turned and saw Hannah leading her horse. She was walking very slowly, with her bare bead drooped, and in her hand her bonnet and a tin bucket.

"She is almost beautiful," Max answered, "but do you think that drapings and a fantastical hat would improve her?"

"I think a simple white frock and a big white hat would make her altogether beautiful, and the mole would not be 'up a tree,' but developed into an ideal squirrel, for it would have the cornbread training of the mole and the graces of the squirrel. She would be *your* ideal. Shall we civilize her?"

Max looked at her questioningly for a moment, then laughing, he answered, "By all means."

Hannah was about to fasten her horse, when she became aware of their presence, and a wave of color swept over her face, while her soft eyes looked from one to the other.

"How do you do, Hannah?" and Agnes stretched her hand over the fence in greeting. Hannah looked puzzled, then Max taking her

bonnet and bucket, she gave him a grateful glance and took Agnes'
outstretched hand.

"I'm well as common, Miss Agnes, but Granny's sick. She were
tuck bad yisterday; she's deep in the bed this mornin'."

"And you have brought some butter?" Agnes went on, holding
out her hand for the bucket.

"Let me bring it in for you." Max said, but Agnes shook her head
and walked away. Max watched her a moment, then turned to Hannah,
who looked so wearily dispirited. "What ails your grandmother?" he
asked.

"She got mad fust, an' then she hed a fit, tell I 'llowed she were
dead."

Here Agnes came back. "Your bucket will come in a moment,"
she said, "won't you come in and rest?"

"I'm obleeged to you, Miss Agnes, but I'm after the doctor; I'll
stop back for the bucket."

As she turned away she looked up at Max. "Gramper 'members
you, Mr. Dudley, and wants to see you an' Miss Agnes powerful; but
when you comes," looking pleadingly from one to the other, "for the
mussy sake don't say nothin' 'bout peddlin'."

"Of course not, and if there is anything I can do for you, Hannah,
you will promise to let me know?"

"Yes, sir." The low voice was tremulous, and the dark eyes full of
tears. "I'm in a dark trouble, Mr. Dudley; far'well."

"That was a picturesque expression," Agnes said, "some love affair, I suppose. They are usually the dark troubles of youth."

"It seems to be her grandmother, not a likely hero for a love affair, and she begged us not to mention peddling."

"Here comes Mrs. Wilson," Agnes said, "let us ask her."

"But not betray Hannah."

"Of course not," looking at him curiously for a moment.

"Good-mornin', Miss Agnes, is you hearty?"

"Yes, thank you, Mrs. Wilson, What is it this morning?"

"Jest a few aigs. I coulder sold 'em, but I allers brings 'em here
fust."

"I do not think I want them. Is Mrs. Warren very ill?"

"Nothin' but tantrums," grunting contemptuously. "She's sot on
Hannah a-marryin' her cousin Si Durket, and Hannah's sot agin hit.
An' Hannah slips off an' peddles for money to run the place, an' ole
Mrs. Warren 'llowed that Hannah couldn't run the place, an' would

jest hev to tuck Si, an' she's mad tell she's sick, an' thet's the jig they're dancin' to now."

Max looked indignant. "Poor girl." he said.

"Hannah 'll not git hurt," Mrs. Wilson sneered, and went her way.

"A 'mole romance' for you, Mr. Dudley," Agnes said. "I suppose there is a 'true love' somewhere to whom Hannah is faithful."

"And you laugh at true love? Give me time and I will prove it to you," a betraying earnestness creeping into his voice.

"As much as you like," and Agnes turned away.

"Alas! shall hope be nursed
On life's all-succoring breast in vain,
And made so perfect only to be slain?"

~Unknown

VIII

Mrs. Warren's attack seemed to have taken all hope out of Hannah's life, for opposition to the old woman's will might mean death. She longed to go away and work, and send the money back, but she could not. For years her father and grandfather had lived lives of purest self-abnegation, and as they had borne so she must wait and bear; and some words her father used to say seemed now to have been the keynote of his life, "Hit's easier to hurt than to heal," he would say, and leave the house to smoke his pipe outside. And now, as she rode through the glancing lights and shadows of the sweet spring day, she had a great longing to tell her father that she understood him now, and would follow in his footsteps. "I'll do jist what he done, kase if I kills Granny, all he done is gone fur nuthin', an' what he planted shell be gethered." She had been taught by example, and the lesson had gone very deep.

Mrs. Warren had refused to talk the night before, and this morning had spoken only to find fault and to order the doctor. This would diminish Hannah's savings sorely, and there was an unacknowledged suspicion in Hannah's mind that the physician had been called on purpose to absorb this money. In this, however, she was mistaken, and this demand for medical attention was a pledge of safety. Mrs. Warren was far more afraid of having another fit than Hannah was of causing it. The thought of death coming in this sudden way terrified her, and she was pitifully eager to avoid it. All her life she had been superstitious about the number three, and now saw death in the third fit.

She had dressed herself and put things to rights as usual; then, taking her knitting, sat down near the window, watching, with miserable but silent anxiety, for Hannah. She was feverishly anxious that things should seem as at other times, and the deprecating tenderness of her husband was dreadful to her. "For the Lord's sake, John Warren, quit a-whinin'!" she cried nervously, "you needn't be afeared that I'm agoin' to hev any mo' fits. But Hannah's got mo' sperret 'an any Warren I ever seen. Hit's better to git mud on you by prancin' 'an by crawlin', but she ain't a-goin' to prance on me."

Hannah found things so much as usual on her return that Sunday began to seem like a bad dream. "The doctor's a-comin'," she said, then, as Mrs. Warren neither looked up nor answered, she turned to leave the room.

"Ain't thar nothin' mo' to tell?" Mrs. Warren said sharply. She was anxious to be diverted, and angry because she knew that, in her absence, Hannah would have much to tell Mr. Warren.

Hannah came back and knelt in front of the fire. "Miss Agnes were leanin' on the gate, an' Mr. Dudley," she began, "an' I tole 'em I come fur the doctor kase you were sick, an' they were mighty sorry, an' Mr. Dudley says if thar were anything he could do, jest to let him know."

"I'd be rayly proud to see Mr. Dudley," Mr. Warren said, as Hannah paused, "when he talks I think I'm hearin' the paper read."

"An' the doctor axed a-many a question," she went on, "an' he prophesied thet you'd be up 'ginst I got home, an' you is." The old woman listened eagerly. If the doctor could tell that much from questions, perhaps he could cure her entirely. She felt much happier, and answered Hannah's next question amiably.

"Yes, you kin make a few biscuit, an' make some rale strong cawfee. I reckon the doctor 'll tuck a swaller."

Hannah went out to the fence after this, and as she waited for

Dock's slow plow, she wondered what had happened to sweeten her grandmother's mood.

"You hev done a heap," she said, as Dock paused and drew his shirt-sleeve across his forehead, "I'll bet you ain't rested."

"I ain't tired yit," Dock answered, then looking away, "the doctor don't tuk no pay from po' folks," he said, "but he'll tuck pay from you."

"I know hit," wondering how much Dock knew of her difficulties, "an' I've got hit, an' for you, too, Dock."

"Hit don't make no difference 'bout me," seizing his plow handles as if for instant departure, "I kin wait . . . or never," he added after a moment's pause.

Hannah looked at him curiously. She remembered his waiting until Si left, and how this morning he had come at the first streak of dawn and cut a great pile of wood, and as she watched him standing there with averted face, her eyes filled with tears of gratitude.

"I'm 'bleeged to you all the same, Dock," she said, "but I've got the money."

After dinner Hannah "geared up" old Bess and joined Dock in the fields, and when the evening fell she thought she had never seen such an honest day's work. And while her grandmother and Dock were eating their supper in the kitchen, Mrs. Warren talking so affably about the doctor's visit that she astonished Dock into a brisk conversation, Hannah told her grandfather all Dock's goodness and gave him the money to pay Dock. "I can't do hit, Gramper," she said, "kase thar's a heap that money can't pay fur, an' I 'llow he'd ruther git hit from you."

Tuesday rose clear, and Hannah hurried through her housework, for, in spite of all Dock's exertions, her absence the day before had made a difference. If her grandmother would only get dinner as usual, but she did not suggest it. While she plowed, her thoughts wandered off to Agnes Welling, so fair and delicate. The white clouds brought Agnes back to her, so did the soft, fresh wind as it swept by. A sense of coarseness came over her. She was like the clods her plow turned: she was clumsy, like her own heavy shoes that she had silently compared with Agnes' dainty slipper. What made the difference? Her thoughts glanced from Si Durket, as lowest in the scale, to Max Dudley, and to the other young man she had seen first with Agnes. That first day she had decided that he was Agnes' "sweetheart," but she was doubtful about it now, for Max Dudley was with her so much oftener. She tried to think of Agnes as mated with Si, and blushed at the thought. What was it made the difference?

Until she had gone to Sewanee, she had thought herself the best. Her grandmother had taught her this, but now she knew her grandmother had been mistaken. And the valley people who had laughed at the Sewanee people as "fools, 'llowin' they wuz extry fine kase o'book larnin'." They were mistaken, too. She saw at once that there was a difference in favor of the Sewanee people, and if books made this difference, they were right to care for books. Had anyone observed this before? She would ask her grandfather; he would know.

Suddenly the sound of the horn blown sharply, roused her, and seeing her shadow gathered close about her feet, she hoped that Mrs. Warren had prepared dinner. She was loosing her horse from the plow when another sharp blast made her drop everything and run. Reaching the yard, she saw Mrs. Warren hurrying about, and she felt relieved.

"Fur mussy sake hurry!" the old woman cried. "Youuns Uncle Durket's a-dyin', an' Si hes sent fur me. Git me sumpen to eat quick, while I gits my things," her voice was tremulous, "My po' brether, an' I ain't seen him so long. Po' Dave, po' Dave! Jest to think!"

And while she talked, walking back and forth, putting things together in a bundle, Hannah prepared dinner, and Mr. Warren watched his wife uneasily. She ought not to go, but, in her present state of nervousness, opposition might do more harm than the ride and the tumult she would find "over the mountain," so he said nothing except "Po' Dave, who would hev thought it?"

This monotonous little refrain seemed to please Mrs. Warren, for she paused sometimes to hear it, at last she said, "Sure enough, who would hev thought hit? But when the Durkets start to do anything, they don't mind what folks think." She became less nervous after this, for her own speech reminded her that she had the Durket name to sustain, and a little accident like death must not upset her. At last all was arranged, and Hannah went with her to the gate.

"I'll stop tell atter the buryin'," she said, "an' see how things is left; I most knows hit'll all come to Si, kase young Dave ain't got good sense, if he is oldern Si. An' if I sends fur you to come to the buryin', Hannah, leff Dock alonger youuns Gramper an' come."

"All right, Granny," and as the little procession moved away, she hurried to the kitchen, shutting her grandfather's door as she passed, and carrying with her the picture of him so helpless, so patient. The old man's mind was back in the days when he was courting Matilda Durket, the handsomest, richest, tartest girl in the county with one brother David, who managed afterward to get all the property.

"If I hed a-married Mertildy fur her money, I woulder made some fuss 'bout Dave gittin' everything, kase half were rightly Mertildy's. But I hed enough, an' mebbe I'm a-doin' Dave a onjustice, an' him a-dyin'. Mebbe hisn's par give hit to him far' an' squar, but he's got white eyes, an' thet ain't a good color fur a hones' man." Then he sat silent, gone back into days that had come to seem like dreams, and started with a cry when Hannah came with his dinner.

"An eye to everything—keen eyes like gimlets:
And a tongue—there are no words for that!
So bitter, sharp, so hard, so swift to probe
Into the heart of things; and for excuse—
For making black look white—no tongue like hers."

~Unknown

IX

From inertia solely, Mrs. Warren had fallen into the habit of staying at home, until at last she looked upon it as a virtue. From this she came to rail mercilessly on those whose habits were different, calling them "slip arounds" and "light heels," and other unpleasant names that made her own going impossible, except in cases of necessity. But this journey was such a necessity, and Mrs. Warren enjoyed it in spite of its occasion, or, rather, *because* of its occasion, for nothing makes people so important as affliction. The Warrens and the Durkets stood on the same social level, and as the two aristocratic lines met in Mrs. John Warren, she was regarded as a very important person, indeed, and, assisted by her temper and tongue, she kept people greater than Lizer Wilson in much awe.

Of course it would be noised abroad that Mrs. John Warren was coming, and this would insure a gathering of the "upper ten" from all the valleys. People would come even from the "Beech settlement." The Budds would be there: not as rich as the Durkets, but more traveled, for they had been not only to Nashville and Chattanooga, but one member of the family had penetrated as far as Atlanta on the one side and Memphis on the other. Thus, although without the blood of the Durkets, the Budds had achieved a position that in some respects rivaled theirs. Then Dave Durket, Jr., had married Minerva Budd.

Mrs. Warren knew that she was going where she would be treated with some distinction, and was pleasantly excited. She shuddered once or twice when she remembered that Jane Harner had probably spread the report of Hannah's peddling, and as the exploit could not be denied, she must tell them that Hannah had gone to visit a friend in the University. It was true that Mrs. Warren had a contempt for Sewanee, and so far had ignored it, but the Sewanee people could not be despised save for their thriftlessness, born of love of books, for no one could prove that they were not as well born as any family in the valley. They behaved as if they were above their neighbors, but this mistake, she felt, came of that same pride of knowledge.

Young Mrs. David Durket, Mrs. Warren's dearest foe, was a graduate of a country college, and thought herself learned, but she knew no Sewanee people, and if Mrs. Warren could emphasize the fact that Hannah had friends among these new people, who ate and drank books, it would be pain to Mrs. Dave. Further, she could say that one combining Durket and Warren blood could do what she pleased. She went so far as to acknowledge to herself that she had made a mistake in railing at the girl, and in not presenting this view of things to Si; for Mrs. Warren still clung to the thought of the Durket alliance. This visit could be turned to good account, if used properly, and enable her to rectify many things. She had never been able to *prove* that her brother had cheated her out of her share of the property, but she knew that it had happened only because of her absence. Her brother had taken the position that his father did not want the property divided, and that he, David Durket, would, in his turn, leave the land intact to one son. And Si thought, and the community thought, and Mrs. Warren was sure, that the heir would be Si, for the other son, David, was weak-minded.

But David had married a woman, Minerva Budd, who was far from weak-minded. She never resented the opinion that Si should be the heir, instead, she made much of Si, almost as much as she made of the old man, who never before had received such flattering attentions.

It was a long, rough ride across the mountains, and Mrs. Warren was tired before her horse began to bog along the red clay valley, and was thankful when at last she arrived.

Nothing seemed changed since her girlhood. The fences seemed the same, with about the same number of rotten and of missing rails. She seemed to see the same cows and horses, the same stumps. She could swear to the stumps, for who ever wasted time on a stump? The enclosures about the house were absolutely unchanged, only that the apple trees looked a little older. The branch was full, as always in the spring, and she could have declared that the geese had not changed even a feather.

Si came out and helped her down, looking supernaturally solemn. Mrs. Dave waited in the doorway. Her front hair painfully frizzed, long earrings in her ears, her stumpy fingers much beringed, and her jaws working patiently and doggedly on a piece of chewing gum, for, in spite of her travels and mental attainments, she had retained that barbarism.

"How sweet *too* welcome those we love, Aunt Warren!" she said. "And are you well?"

"Well as common," Mrs. Warren answered.

"An' had you an enjoyable ride *too*-day?"

"No, hit were dratted rough, Minervy Budd, an' you knows hit. How's my po' brether?"

"My dear papa is weakenin' sadly," leading the way upstairs. "You'll want *too* remove your ridin' skirt, dear Aunt," opening the door into a gaudily papered but fireless bedroom. "My dear papa's apart-*ment* is on the right side as you descend, an' I must return *too* my dooties," and, waiting for no reply, she left the room.

Mrs. Warren's ire was rising. "Hit's enough to make a hog sick," she muttered, "to hear that fool go on, an' she as ugly as a pot o' home-made soap. *Her* dear 'pup-par,' Lord, what is we a-comin' to? A Budd as much as callin' a Durket daddy, let alone 'pup-par!' An' her 'dooties,' an' 'too-day!' Work is good enough fur anybody, an' *ter*-day is too good fur a Budd. But when a man marries a parry-toed, whinin' fool like my po' brether done, they must speck to hev chilluns like young Dave, an' only God knows who them chilluns 'll marry. But this *is* rale purty paper," regretfully, putting her spectacles in place, "an' the beds is right well dressed, but I'd ruther hev a fire 'an all them frizzled papers a-setting in thet ole pitcher."

She looked about a little longer, then unbuttoned the ginger-colored skirt that had protected her during the long ride and shook out her frock. This frock was black, and a good piece of stuff, and the handkerchief about her throat was silk, and fastened with a large gold brooch, in which was set a ghastly picture of her husband. Her ear-rings had been put on before she left home, for she had not kept straws in the "bores" of her ears all these years for nothing. Her hair was screwed on top her head with a high comb brought from "North Calliny" by her mother. It had made her sunbonnet rather uncomfort-able, and the big hoop-earrings had felt very heavy, but she "hed to put on good clothes to down Minervy Budd." She smoothed her knit-ted mittens over her wrists, and extracting a large white handkerchief from her bundle, she folded it up as small as possible, and holding it tightly in her hands, began a stately descent on the lower regions.

"I wonder who's gethered," she muttered. "Thar's nothin' like a rale good sickness fur getherin' folks. I reckon Minervy Budd is got too much larnin' to hev anything to eat. I reckon she specks us to chaw newspapers. Hardy, Dave," she said to her nephew who stood in the barren, bleak hall that was checkered from end to end with a mosaic of red-clay foot tracks.

"Hardy, Aunt Tildy, is you well?"

"Well as common. Minervy looks as biggitty as a settin' hen," shaking hands carelessly, "how's youuns Par?"

"Dad's a-goin'. This do', Aunt Tildy," holding one open.

Mrs. Warren paused a moment, then entered with the dignity she thought due to herself, and saw that she made an impression. Mrs. Dave Durket saw it, too, and wondered, but stood aside, with her eyes cast down. Besides the sick skeleton propped up on the bed, there was quite a number of people sitting in the room, waiting, with solemn faces and folded hands, to see their friend die.

As Mrs. Warren had expected, the Budds were there; also Dr. Slocum, the family physician and his wife; and Mrs. Billingsly and her husband, Preacher Billingsly, who was a lawyer as well. He was a friend of long standing, and when Si returned on Sunday he had found Preacher Billingsly there, and from that time he had never left the sick man.

As Mrs. Warren entered, the preacher and the doctor rose. Oth-ers rose, too, and all watched the meeting.

"Hardy, brether Dave, does you know me?" approaching the bed and taking in hers the bony hand that lay on the quilt.

The hollow eyes opened. "Yes, Tildy," then drawing her down he whispered, "I've done right 'bout the lan', an' John Warren were mighty good never to make no fuss."

As Mrs. Warren had but one idea of right in regard to the land, this puzzled her, but she answered so as to be heard, "The Warrens hed plenty, Dave." Away from the Warrens she was loyal.

"An' as Hannah's a-goin' to tuck Si, she 'll git youun's shar', Tildy." Then his breath failed him, and the doctor put some whisky to his lips, while the spectators watched breathlessly, and none so breathless as Mrs. Dave. Si came in and leaned over his father, but the old man shook his head.

"Tildy, come close," he muttered, and again Mrs. Warren bent over him. "I keeps on a-seein' Dad, Tildy," he whispered. "He ain't never leff me since Sunday. He keeps on a-holdin' up hisn's han's like I wuz agoin' to knock him."

A pallor crept over Mrs. Warren's face, that seemed to spread to Si's as they looked at each other, and she whispered, "Did you do it, Dave?"

"Yes, oh, Lord! Yes!" he wailed, "won't my sins git no forgivenness?"

"Yes, yes! Brother Durket," struck in Preacher Billingsly, who had caught only this last wail, "jest hev faith, Brother Durket."

The hollow eyes seemed on fire. "But my ole Dad ain't *never* rested," he cried aloud, and the company shivered. "Day ner night, day ner night, he ain't never left me. He comes an' goes. I've seen him a-many a time a-peepin' in thet do' an' a-rockin' in the cheer by the fire an' a-cropin' up an' down the sta'rs an' *thar* he is! Go 'way, Dad! Go 'way! I've done jestice, jestice!" and while he stared and pointed he fell back dead.

The women screamed, but the men, looking in each other's eyes, were still. Mrs. Warren stood there for one moment, then turned and went out like one in a dream. Her brother *had* intimidated her father, had stolen her share of the property, and had been haunted! All these years her father had never rested, had roamed and wandered, following up the thief, had come even when his son lay dying. She paused in the hall, trembling and uncertain.

Si came up to her hurriedly with a glass of whisky he had been drinking and made her finish his potations. "Drink hit an' furgit all thet damned foolishness. Come git a bite," and taking her arm he led her into the long, low kitchen, where the family also ate. Jane Harner was serving, assisted by a friend, and their solemn greetings restored to Mrs. Warren some of her lost composure.

Si seated his aunt at the narrow table and helped her vigorously. Presently he went away, and when he returned, smelling more strongly of whisky, he was supporting Minerva, and followed by Dave. "Eat, Aunt Tildy, eat!" he cried. "Eat, Minervy. Hit were sickness made Dad crazy. Jane Harner, go call the folks, I'll sen' fur Hannah 'fore day, Aunt Tildy," helping himself. "She must git here 'fore the buryin'. Hit'll be ter-morrer evenin'. All's ready 'ceppen the grave, an' thet's easy dug now the ground is soft. Hit'll be over in the new graveyard whar Mar is buried, an' youun's Par, Aunt Tildy."

"Silas, my dear," snuffled Minerva, "graves is too much for my nerves. Will Cousin Hannah have a black dress, Aunt Warren?"

"Hannah Warren's got as much as you, Minervy Budd, an' she aint made skimpy, nuther," Mrs. Warren answered. Her spirit was returning. "*She* don't look like no pickled cucumber. She's got good hones' eyes thet don't wink an' blink liker sore-eye dog a-layin' in the sun, an' when she talks she says hit out like the best kinder folks is usin' to hear hit said, an' don't keep on a-whistlin' hit liker pattridge in the springtime."

"True as Scriptur!" Si cried.

"An' if I send her word or no, she mout not put on all she's got kase Hannah's got the Durket sperret if she *is* a Warren."

"She's got hit sho!" Si cried, and David blinked his foolish, big eyes and repeated, "Sho."

"I wants *too* see my Cousin Hannah," Minerva said. "I were away *too* cawlidge for so long a period, thet I hev not made her acquaintance, but, through Silas' speakin', I love her like a sister."

"Well, jest keep on," Mrs. Warren answered, "but don't look to see no fool from cawlidge. Hannah Warren's got good horse sense, an' don't need no cawlidge. God never made womens fur no cawlidge, an' jest so a woman kin wash, an' cook, an' sew, an' raise her chilluns, that's all the needcissity God is got fur her."

Minerva's little black eyes flashed, then were quickly cast down again. "I hope my Cousin Hannah 'll like me, anyhow," she said, with a toss of her head.

"She mout, an' she mout not," Mrs. Warren answered, "but Hannah don't like many folks, an' if Si wuz not a-stuffin' hisself, an' hisn's po' daddy a-bein' laid out, hed sesso."

"Hannah peddles to Sewanee, don't she?" Minerva asked.

There was a little flutter in the audience, then a deadly pause while Mrs. Warren eyed Mrs. Dave, who answered her enemy's gaze with malice in her eyes that did not waver until Mrs. Warren answered, with apparent frankness, "Yes, she did go a-peddlin', leastways, she tuck Lizer Wilson 'long to do the peddlin' an' lead the nag," looking about her with a smile. "An' Lizer never hed no better sense than to tuck Hannah to the back do', but Hannah knowed thet no Warren ner no Durket wornt made fur stannin' 'round back do's an' tradin' alonger niggers. So the nex' house whar Hannah knowed the woman, she sont Lizer to the kitchen, an' she went to the settin' room alonger Miss Agnes Wellin' an' Mr. Dudley, an' soon's he hearn her title he knowed her, an' were mightily pleased to git acquainted," nodding and smiling, while Minerva stared in astonishment. "An' Mr. Dudley an' Miss Wellin' is a-comin' down to see Hannah. Yes, she peddled, but thet's the way she done hit. An' you'd peddle day and night, Minervy Budd, to get to know them folks to Sewanee. But, Lord, them folks come from fur places, an' knows what's what, an' seen thet Hannah Warren air the right sort. An' talk 'bout book-larnin', mussy! Them folks never stirs 'thout books in they uns' han's, but fur all thet some is rale nice. I tole Hannah, says I, 'Jane Harner 'll surely tell hit thet you peddles,' says I. Says she, proud-like, 'A Warren or a Durket kin do anything,' says she. I tell you, Hannah Warren is got the Durket sperret."

Here the door opened and Brother Billingsly came in. "My dearly beloved friends," said he, "will you please to walk into where our departed brother is layin' at ease, his sins forgiven and his soul at peace." The company rose, then waited for Mrs. Warren and Minerva to lead the way. Minerva took her aunt's arm, and drooped her head lovingly on her shoulder. Mrs. Warren did not seem to observe her, for now the awful scene of the death rushed back on her, and she trembled and turned pale. Family pride made her glad that none but Si and herself had heard the confession, and though the whole company had heard the last pitiful cry, they would think, and truly, that the justice that had been done was to herself, for everyone knew that her brother had kept the whole property.

Arrayed in his best clothes, with a large white handkerchief over his face, the dead man lay, stiff and stark, in the coffin that rested on two chairs. On either side of the empty fireplace sat Si and Dave. Dr. Slocum was close by the coffin. The bed was 'fresh dressed,' lighted lamps and candles stood about, for the day, was closing, and a row of men were seated against the wall. As Mrs. Warren and Minerva approached the coffin, Dr. Slocum turned the handkerchief back with a gesture of resigned despair and looked away. Minerva fell on her knees and wailed aloud. Others began to groan and shake their heads with short, staccato grunts, but after one look Mrs. Warren walked away.

The doctor had told her that excitement was bad for her, and she was afraid. She left the room where the people were now crowding about the coffin, shaking their heads and groaning as if in the profoundest woe. Nobody really cared, but it showed a gratifying family influence that so many pretended. It was going to be a "good buryin'," but she had done enough for one day, and needed rest and a smoke.

She went to the kitchen, where Jane Harner and her friend were taking the first cups of the fresh coffee, made ostensibly for the 'watchers.' Jane had made it early in order to secure the grounds of former pots of coffee. If she waited, Mrs. Dave would herself secure the grounds. As cook, Jane had for two days provided with a lavish hand, and Mrs. Dave had not dared to watch or to object, for any shadow of carefulness on such an occasion would be the blackest disgrace. Jane's basket under the back steps had in it much cold pork, fried chicken, sausage, pies, cake, pickles, and sugar, and Jane now hoped to arrange for more sugar.

At the moment of Mrs. Warren's entrance Jane was saying that Mrs. Dave was so "skimpin'," that even scraps were scarce, for Minerva was not "a rale Durket who wuz free-handed." She said this very loudly as she saw Mrs. Warren.

Mrs. Warren nodded. "That's true, Jane," she said, "an' I wish you'd kindle a fire upstairs, and I don't much keer if you burns up them dratted papers in the fireplace."

This was a golden opportunity, and Jane whipped off a sugar dish, saying, as she went, "everybody knows the Budds."

Mrs. Warren drew her pipe and tobacco from her pocket and, pulling a chair close to the fire, sat down. She filled her pipe, lighting it with a coal, then tucking in her frock between her knees and ankles to keep it from scorching, she leaned forward, with her arms crossed on her knees, and smoked vigorously. She drove her thoughts from the present to the rearrangements that would come about when Si took possession, with Hannah as his wife and herself as general director. She saw Minerva vanishing. She saw Jane Harner installed as cook and general servant. She saw Hannah, very fine, rocking with idle hands, playing lady. She saw roaring fires, eternal cooking and company, she saw herself ruling all, the great woman of the county.

Suddenly she remembered the lonely old man across the mountain. She shook her shoulders. A young man was needed to work that place; Jim and his wife could come, and if the old man was such a fool as to prefer that "Warren hole" to this "Durket paradise," he could stay. She was tired of the "lonesomeness an' po'ness."

"Thar's a good Durket fire a-burnin', Mrs. Warren." Jane startled the old woman as she flourished in with the emptied and refilled sugar dish. "Hit's good and big, like youuns is usen to."

Mrs. Warren knocked out her pipe. "You're mighty right, Jane Harner," she said. "The Durkets is usen to plentifulness, but some folks will eat a hog down to hits yeers an' tail, Lord!" and she walked to the door followed by applauding giggles. At the door she paused. "Did Si tell thet nigger to go fur Hannah Warren?" she asked.

"Mussy, yes, tole him fust thing."

"An' whar's the nigger? I wanter send a word to Hannah."

Jane glanced at her companion, then said, "He's gone, Mrs. Warren, he tuck the nags to ole black Judy's," She hesitated, then blurted out, "he were feared; he said he dar'sent stay here kase o' the hant."

Mrs. Warren looked at her sternly. "Looker h'ar, Jane Harner, you is got mo' sense 'an to listen to sich foolishness. You know thet a dyin' man ain't 'sponsible fur all he says."

"Mussy, Miss Warren!" cried Jane, "I jest tole you what thet fool nigger said. Me an' Mincy never b'lieved nothin' like thet. But he *did* say that Si Durket couldn't git no nigger to stay, kase o' hisn's par a-dyin' so hard."

"Well, Si'll settle *thet* nigger," and Mrs. Warren left the room.

"Of different clay? Not so, but with a soul
Pure-fibered through and through."

~Unknown

X

When Hannah arrived, everybody who could be expected was at the Durkets. Eating and drinking were going on briskly in the kitchen, and Jane Harner and her friend Mincy had become so confidential as to assist each other in filling the baskets under the back steps. Mrs. Warren greeted Hannah affably, Minerva gushingly, and Si, though flushed and excited by the morning's potations, was a little timid in his welcome.

Minerva saw instantly that, as far as material went, Hannah's black frock surpassed her own, and, though strangely straight, it was not unbecoming to the tall, fair girl. She saw, too, that the brown hair rippled without any frizzing, that her skin was as smooth as ivory, and Minerva felt herself at a great disadvantage in the presence of this girl from "over the mountain." Nor could she account for the way in which people treated Hannah. Even Jane Harner, who had told scornful tales of the peddling, waited on her obsequiously, and when they entered the room where Brother Billingsly waited to "preach the funeral," Minerva saw that Hannah drew all eyes as she sat close beside her grandmother. Mrs. Warren saw it, too.

Preacher Billingsly did not make the sermon long, but he drew it very strong. He wound up with, "He was a dootiful son to his aged parents, a lovin' brother to his only sister, a devoted husband to his departed wife, a true father to his children. An' when his call came, his sins and justice was his cry. 'Justice, justice!' he cried. An', now havin' done justice, he is at rest a-playin' on his golden harp, wavin' his silver wings, an' a-singin' hallelujah! Not for him do we weep, but for his sister an' his niece a-settin' here, for his sons an' daughter-in-law a-standin' here, for his brother-in-law over in the Cove. For these we weep. Yea, we shed tears; yea, we mourn an' beat our breasts; yea, we cry and plead for help for these bereaved ones. Help me to cry, help me, help me!" Immediately moans and groans began, and Minerva fell down in hysterics.

Then, one by one, the family approached and took farewell of the corpse, all kissing it except Hannah. With folded hands she stood a moment, then moved away, and Si swore a silent, mighty oath that some day he would "break that sperret."

The people filed slowly round the coffin and out the door into the yard. The top was laid on the coffin, and the coffin put into a farm wagon. Dave drove, with Preacher Billingsly beside him. Si and Dr. Slocum took their seats on the coffin. Then the procession moved: Mrs. Warren and Mrs. Slocum in Dr. Slocum's lopsided old buggy; Minerva and Hannah following in the Durkets' equally old vehicle, whose back curtain, the top being down, hung almost to the ground; Mrs. Billingsly and Mrs. Budd in Preacher Billingsly's buggy, which had many points in common with the others. After that people came as best they could on foot, on horseback, and in wagons, winding down the muddy lane to where, on the edge of the woods, on the first swell of the mountains, was the new graveyard of the Durkets.

The coffin was put on two boards laid across the open grave, the top removed, and amid groans and cries the strange ceremony of the "last far'well" began. Minerva, Mrs. Budd and Jane Harner yelled; Mrs. Slocum and Mrs. Billingsly groaned and rocked; Mrs. Warren, being afraid of excitement, wiped her eyes and blew her nose, and scolded Hannah under her breath. "You kin holler jest as good as Minervy Budd," she said, "an' ain't a-doin' hit, hit's scannalous, jest scannalous!"

But Hannah stood unmoved. The drawn, dead face looking so

cold under the gray sky; the wind making strange noises in the bare trees as it swept down the mountain; the screams and cries all brought back her father's funeral, that had been terrible to her. She only shivered a little when her grandmother spoke.

The coffin lid was screwed on, and during this operation Hannah saw Si retire to the wagon and seek comfort in his bottle. After this she watched him with some anxiety. She knew what would come next, and longed to draw her shawl up over her face, but she was afraid of what might happen if she did not watch, so she only pulled her long bonnet on a little farther, and watched Si.

The lowering of the coffin into the grave, and the beginning of a hymn by Preacher Billingsly, were the signal for a general row. Si jumped down on the coffin, yelling like a maniac. Minerva fell on Dr. Slocum in hysterics, while Dave and Mrs. Billingsly and Mrs. Budd mingled their tears and groans. On rolled the hymn, and in was shoveled the earth until Si stood ankle deep; then the Budd brothers pulled him out and laid him in the wagon dead drunk. At last it was over. The crowd dispersed, save the Slocums and Billingslys and Budds, who went back for another night at the Durkets.

The next morning an early beginning was made. Mrs. Dave seemed to be in a state of suppressed excitement that made her silly, for at breakfast she asked Mrs. Warren how soon she would leave. It was a most unusual question. Mrs. Warren listened in contemptuous astonishment, then made answer to the company at large. "Minervy Budd had better larn her place."

Minerva giggled with what seemed pronounced insanity, and answered, "Too the best of my knowledge Durket farm *is* my place."

Si looked up angrily. "Mind youuns eye, Minervy," he said. Minerva giggled again, but, Preacher Billingsly shaking his head, she said no more.

After breakfast Mrs. Warren desired to know how things were left. Si said that Preacher Billingsly would read the will, he having drawn it up. They gathered about the fire with the will. It was soon read, and left everything to his son, Silas Durket. Mrs. Warren nodded, saying, "Hit's bad Dave ain't got a rich gal." Minerva smiled. Si looked expectant, but no one congratulated him, and Jane Harner in the background thought that things looked strange.

Presently Brother Billingsly cleared his throat and began an exhortation on the vanity of riches. Mrs. Budd and her sons, Mrs. Slocum and Mrs. Billingsly, moved their chairs, making a sort of circle about

Minerva and Dave. Mrs. Warren smoked. Si watched for a pause in which to go for another drink. Hannah longed to be gone. After a preamble, Brother Billingsly made the direct statement that Grandfather Durket had been unjust to his daughter, Sister Warren.

Mrs. Warren took her pipe from her lips and turned her face to the speaker, but Brother Billingsly was looking at Si. He went on to say that he had never held the old man responsible for the injustice; that he and many others had suspected that his son, Mr. David Durket, had compelled him to do this. On Sunday these suspicions had been verified, for Mr. Durket had confessed that he had used violence to compel his father to leave him the property, and that ever since he had been followed by his father's spirit, which could be proved by all who had witnessed his death.

Brother Billingsly paused to wipe his lips. Jane Harner drew nearer, Hannah leaned forward, Mrs. Warren's face grew stern, Si, rising, leaned against the mantelpiece with a terrible expression in his eyes, and Minerva's silly smile gave place to a look of apprehension. Brother Billingsly smoothed down his back hair, then proceeded with what seemed a narrative.

He had come over on Sunday, he said, to see Brother Durket concerning his spiritual condition. He had found Dr. Slocum, Mr. Reub and Sam Budd, and their mother. In the mercy of Providence it seemed to be arranged that these witnesses should be there. Before them all Brother Durket had confessed his sins, telling the means he had used to intimidate his old father and get all the property; that long ago he had repented, and now wanted justice done; that as his father had been treated so he had been treated, and driven by his son into making an unjust will; and that before it was too late, and while he was supported by these dear friends, who were not to reveal it, nor to leave him until he was buried, he would make a just will.

Reub Budd changed his position so as to be between Brother Billingsly and Si, and put his hand back under his coat.

Billingsly now produced a paper which he explained was a certified copy of the last will, which had been deposited with the Clerk of the County Court for safety. This will read that the tract of land known as Durket Farm was to be divided into two parts; the line to be drawn from the "big gum" that marked the limit on one side to the "milestone corner" which abutted on the public road; that this line leaving the buildings and the spring on one half, making it the most valuable half, his sons must draw lots for it. All stock and tools must be divided by arbitration. That he had not left anything to his sister, as she seemed satisfied and as her granddaughter, Hannah, marrying Si, would get her share.

There was a deadly pause, and Hannah, moving her chair, seemed to touch a spring. Everyone sprang up, and Mrs. Warren, dashing her pipe into the fire, said hoarsely, "Hit's a damned lie, Joe Billingsly, a lie, an' you know hit!"

"A lie, a lie!" Si screamed, and raised a chair, but Reub Budd covered him with a pistol, and the chair fell with a crash. Reub's action seemed to quiet things, and let Brother Billingsly's voice be heard insisting that they were Christians and this a Christian will, and the sooner the lots were drawn the better.

This suggestion relieved the tension. Si realized that half the farm was gone; still, he might draw the most valuable part, and if he could stay in the old house and kick the Budds out, he would not feel that he had fallen so far. He longed to begin the kicking, and agreed to draw lots immediately.

Two broom straws stuck in cracks of the wall would be the method and Jane Harner be the tool, she bein' uninterested. She was not allowed to approach the company, and received her orders from Dr. Slocum, who said, in a loud voice, "Break two straws from the broom, one long and one short; stick them in two cracks, one each side the fireplace in Brother Durket's room; then go out and slam the front door after you, and wait in the yard."

Jane, looking, half out of her wits, went her way, breaking up more than one straw on the journey. The awfulness of going alone into the room where the "hant" had rocked in the chairs, and where all day yesterday the corpse had lain, and the more mundane terror of having a hand in the division of the Durket property shook her being to its foundations, for the Durkets were fierce and reckless. Hurriedly she stuck the straws in cracks so far apart that if one projected a little more it could not be detected. Then she scurried out, giving the door a great jerk. What a hollow, reverberating, awful sound it was!

Si started with an oath. Why had he let them put the straws in his father's room? It was there he had struck his mother, it was there he had intimidated his old father. He shivered as he remembered. How could he have any luck in there?

All seemed spellbound until Dave rose. "I'm feared," he said.

This broke the spell, and they moved toward the door in a body. Along the narrow hall they jostled, none wanting to be first or last, and at the open door of the dead man's room they paused in silence.

Then Dave said, "I'm feared," and Minerva pushed him in.

Si pushed his way through the group and, following the reluctant David, marched up to the fireplace. He paused, he could not touch the straws; he asked Dave, "Which hand?" and Dave, being left-handed, held up that member, causing his wife to snarl, "Don't he know thet han's unlucky, don't he know nothin'?"

Si knew it, and turned quickly to the right. He put his fingers on the straw, but he did not draw it out until Dave did. One second Si stood still.

"Measure, measure!" came from the group in the doorway. Dave held up his straw, with a smile on his idiot face. It was at least three times as long as Si's.

Reub Budd strode into the room. From one to the other Si glanced, covered with Reub's pistol, then turned. He dashed his heavy heel against a window, driving out frame and glass. One wrench of the wreck with his hand, and he sprang through into the yard and was gone.

"The old heart sighs and waiteth patiently,
For Time is sure, and Truth is very strong."

~Unknown

XI

"If you had seen Si lip outer thet winder, Gramper, you'd a-been feared he'd kill hisself." Hannah was telling the story of the will, for Mrs. Warren had stated only the bare facts. She had watched Si's violent exit, then had ordered the horses. She had not said one word of farewell, nor had she spoken during the ride home. Arriving, she had given Mr. Warren an outline, had changed her dress, then sat knitting until supper, as silent as the dead.

The maltreatment of her father, and the defrauding of herself by her brother, were bad, but could be borne, because in her estimation they had aggrandized the Durkets. But that this evil should work for an enemy was intolerable.

When Hannah finished, Mr. Warren shook his head. "Si aint a-goin to kill hisself," he said, "ner do nothin' to nobody what kin hurt him, 'ceppen when he's drunk. Big talkin' don't make big doin'; hit's these still-tongue folks what's dangerous. An' now I know why Dave Durket ain't hed no luck. Mertildy's daddy were a hard man, but I never 'llowed Dave'd beat him when he got too weak to do nothin'. The Lord 'll wipe the Durkets out if they ain't keerful. I've seen a-many a name go out for the lack o' the Lord's blessin'. Peaceful folks what tries to do right don't make much stirrin', mebbe, but they spreads an' multiplies. But when folks gits biggitty an' tucks all they can git, then if you'll watch you'll see 'em fadin' outer the land. An' folks says mournful 'Thet's the last one'—they never 'llows thet God done hit kase the folks wornt wuth nothin' by hisn's count. If folks is fine, folks 'llows they oughter live."

"Minervy's mighty biggitty," Hannah said.

"But them Budds is mighty keerful; they allers cropes tell they're sure they kin walk. Now they've done crope inter Durket's farm, I reckon they'll start to stomp. But thar's no luck ner blessin' thar, an' I'm glad we ain't never hed a stick ner a straw frum thar."

Hannah looked up. "Si ain't got much now," she said, "won't Granny let me 'lone?"

"Thar ain't no tellin', Honey, Si's a Durket yit. Mertildy is a-steddyin' 'bout sumpen, a-settin' thar so still, but soon she can't hold hit, an' then I'll know. I never pesters her tell she gits done a-steddyin', then I 'grees tell I works her round. But sayin' no at fust settles her fur ever-and-ever, an' she'll grind tell she gits what she wants. She gits sorry, too, but she'll die 'fore she'll sesso. Po' Mertildy! I wonder whar Si is?" looking up as Mrs. Warren entered.

"I ain't pestered 'bout Si," she answered quickly, "an' if money an' Lawyer Blogs kin get them Budds outer Si's house, they'd better start, for I'll hev my rights now, sure."

"You didn't surely git youuns shar', Mertildy, but we hev plenty."

"John Warren," looking at her husband severely, "you knows I ain't greedy ner gredgin', but young Dave is a fool, an' no pusson gainsays hit; an' as fur Minervy Budd," slapping her hands together, "if I jest could box her ears oncest, she'd not chaw none fur a-while. Gosh!" And taking a piece of corncob and a knife from her pocket, she began to hollow out a pipe bowl. "An' them two fools *shent* hev the ole place."

"Ain't you got no pipe, Mertildy?"

"Pipe? I were that mad when Joe Billingsly, I ain't agoin' to call *him* 'preacher' ner brether, nuther, when he were a-readin' thet paper thet I busted my pipe 'ginst the chimbly back. Gosh! I wish I hed a-busted hit 'ginst Joe Billingsly's head. I wisht I hed! An' when I 'members how I jawed Hannah," looking down at the girl who kneeled in front of the fire, "kase she wouldn't holler at the buryin', I'm mad. If I'd a-knowed what my brether Dave hed wrote in thet paper, I'd never hev gone nighst the buryin', much less hollered." Screwing a piece of cane into the hole she had made for the pipe-stem, "But I will say thet Hannah Warren never put me to shame 'ceppen as a moaner, an' now I'm glad 'bout thet. An' when I seen Hannah a-stannin' 'longsider Minervy Budd, I says to Betty Slocum, says I, 'If hit ain't fur all the worl' liker horse an' a mule,' says I. But Betty knowed thet the mule were a-goin' in the horse's stable, an' she never said nothin'. But I'll git my shar' if I hes to gie hit to ole Blogs."

"Gie Durket land to a Blogs?" her husband said, in surprise.

"I'd ruther the Blogs hev hit as the Budds."

"But the Budds ain't got hit, hit b'longs to the Durkets yit, an' if you tuck hit, hit'll be Warren land or Blogs land one' but leff hit, an' hit's Durket land yit. An' if Si'll do what I say, he'll build him a nice house. If I 'members, thar's a good grove o' trees on Si's side o' the place."

"You 'members," Mrs. Warren answered, "but them trees is in the ole graveyard. A lot o' Si's land is in thet graveyard, an' thar's heaps o' onjestice in the line drawed across the farm."

"I 'grees to thet, Mertildy, but Dave might hev hed the bad side jest like Si done. An' then sperrets walks in the old house. Thet nigger what come to tuck the nags back, says Dave'll not git no niggers to stay on hisn's place."

Mrs. Warren was silent. Perhaps Minerva had not gained so much, after all.

"An' if Si'll jest do as I say," Mr. Warren went on, "he'll build him a house like them houses to Sewanee. Then thar'll be two Durket places."

Hannah rose. She had to go; this soothing method did not seem honest to her, and yet she saw the wisdom. A difficult point had been rounded, and Si reinstated, as it were. But did not her grandfather realize that if once Mrs. Warren undertook the uplifting of Si, she would insist on Hannah's marrying him? A new house, new furniture, and then a wife? She raised her hand in a silent vow.

Si did not kill himself, but appeared in Lost Cove the next day in a vile temper, and Mrs. Warren became so much interested in persuading him to a quiet course of action, that she forgot the lawsuit she had threatened. She built and furnished Si's new house several times that morning, while Mr. Warren showed Si that if he chose the arbitrators wisely, and let them hear no complaint, that they would give him every advantage in the division of the stock and movable stuff. People knew that Dave had more than his share, and public feeling would turn to Si. By dinner Si was quiet, and he and Mrs. Warren took Dock into their confidence; while from her grandfather Hannah heard the morning's talk, and found that his sympathies were stirred for Si. Her uncle's belated justice was working against her.

While gearing up the animals Dock watched her furtively, and, putting the lines into her hands, said, "Youuns Gramper seems like he thinks more o' Si, an' youuns Granny is a-goin' to stay in Si's fine new house. Will *you* go, Hannah?"

"*Thet* I won't."

"An' if youuns Gramper goes?"

The girl's face was white and set. "I'll hire out, or kill myself," she said.

Si went away pacified, and surprised Minerva so much by his quiet demeanor that she insisted on his returning to his old quarters. And Si speaking of his new house, Reub Budd said that Dr. Slocum had a book of plans, which he would get for Si. And the Budds, who had remained to keep the peace, rode away, feeling that things were safe. But Minerva's feelings were mixed. All the talk was for Si, all the plans were for Si, and she saw Hannah ruling over a much finer house, and Mrs. Warren playing the great lady. She began to think that she would rather have the new place.

The spring was turning out unusually bad. Rain and premature warmth that set all the fruit trees blooming. "Thar'll be no fruit this year," Mrs. Warren said, "kase thar's 'bleeged to be a late frost."

Hannah was troubled. Still she had been lucky of late. The hens were doing well, and there were two litters of pigs, and the calf born lately was a heifer so that there were some cheerful things. But the weather was bad, and she seemed to see the seed rotting in the ground.

Meanwhile Si came often. His house had been contracted for, and the lumber was on the spot near the old graveyard, where some trees had grown out of the burying limits, and made a pleasant shade.

Mrs. Warren had spent a night at Minerva's to look after Si's plans and the site, and when she came away she left Minerva feeling that the worst luck of her life was Dave's drawing the best half of the farm. The division of the movables and stock was now at hand, however, and Minerva determined to strike for her own advantage.

"I love thee with the breath,
Smiles, tears of all my life!—and if God choose,
I shall but love thee better after death."

~Sonnet 43, Elizabeth Barrett Browning

XII

It had been a desperate night, the rain coming down in straight, relentless streams, and the soft, cloudy morning did not promise much for clearing. Hannah looked after the young creatures to see that none had been drowned, looked hopelessly at the fields, and thought anxiously of the big spring. This was a strange formation in the side of the mountain. A steep path climbed up to it, then climbed down again into a great basin of rock where lay the pool. It had no inlet or outlet—an underground lake, and tradition said that it had no bottom.

This morning when Hannah went for water she climbed up as usual, and, as the path was slippery, made a long step to put her over the top of the basin. The day before she had to go down several feet to dip up the water, but today she grasped the rock to regain her balance for the water brimmed up to the top. She stood still in anxious astonishment. She had never seen it so high. She had heard her grandfather say that, once or twice, it had come over, the creek had backed up at the same time from the end of the Cove, the outlet not being large enough, and together they had flooded the little valley. Would there be a flood now?

There was not much hope in the soft, gray sky, and she filled her buckets quickly. She must get the pigs and calves to a safe place. She must get Dock to help her. It was early, and her grandmother was just stirring when she went to tell the news.

"Lord, Lord!" she heard her grandfather say, then groan as he realized his helplessness. She kindled the kitchen fire, and put on the kettle, then, mounting old Bess barebacked, she rode off to the Wilsons. Lizer stood in the door of the house, and Dock was at the woodpile.

"Dock!" she called, "Dock, come quick!" and, dropping the axe, Dock ran. Lizer came forward, too, but Hannah had already turned, and, with Dock trotting alongside, was on the way home.

"The spring's clean up to the top," she explained, "an' yisterday I went down an' seen that the creek was a-backin' up, an' I wants to git the stock to the mountain. Hit'll be awful. Dock."

"Mebbe hit won't, mebbe hit won't rain no mo'."

"But all what's done rained ain't riz yit," Hannah said, "an' the varmints 'll git the young pigs, sure."

"No, they won't," Dock answered, looking up, his kind face flushed with the quick time he was making, "kase I'll make a pen fur 'em an' kivver hit with rails, an' 'ginst night comes I'll build a fire nighst hit an' put my dog Buck in the pen, an' I reckon no varmints 'll come thar. An' we'll shet the calves in thar, too. Jest don't you fret, Hannah."

"I won't, an' we'll put the chickens in the loft an' the wood in the house, but the crap, Dock?"

"You've got mo' seed, an' 'twon't tuck long to plant agin, not long."

Hannah never forgot that day, gray and chilly, and raining at intervals. Fortunately it was not far they had to go to build the pen, and the part of the rail fence that was nearest the spot was quickly taken down and put into proper shape. Then Dock enticed the pigs and Hannah drove the calves, and, grunting and bleating, they were put away. The sitting hens were the next difficulty. To move one is almost fatal, and Hannah was tempted to take the risk of the water, but an extra shower made her change her mind, and in tubs and baskets, the hens, unmoved from their nests, were transported to the loft, and left covered until they should quiet down.

At last the day was done, and Hannah, kneeling in front of the fire, looked very tired. But she felt more hopeful. The rain might put out Dock's watch fire, but the dog was in the pen, and the evil from the water was sure, while the evil from varmints was only possible.

"Hit seems to be like I hearn the water a-pourin' over at the spring," Mrs. Warren said, coming in suddenly. "Hit's bad, an' Dock's gone to turn the stock out, so they kin find a high place. Hit's bad to be shet up in a hole."

Hannah went outside quickly to listen. She could hear Dock's voice and the stumbling footsteps of the cattle, and the calves, hearing their mothers, began to bleat.

The rain had ceased, and in the pause she listened. She heard a dim sound like falling water; she could not be sure it was the spring, for any stream would sound on a night like this. She looked for Dock's fire. It was a good thought putting it into that hollow gum trunk where the rain could not reach it. The trunk was big enough to burn all night, and if it fell it could not hurt anything. Dock was at the fire now, stirring it until a great cloud of red, wild sparks flurried about him, and silhouetted against the lurid light he looked double his real size.

The dog was barking with delight, and Hannah could see the cows passing in front of the fire. She drew her little shawl closer about her; it was not raining, and she remembered some wood they had not brought in. She found it quite easily, and, gathering up an armful, went back into the house. The next turn she let fall a log, and water splashed into her face. A rain pool, she thought. The third turn she made she met Dock. "I'm totin' in mo' wood," she said, and he turned to help her. This time she seemed to get into the water. She filled her arms and turned away, when an exclamation from Dock stopped her.

"Water! Hit's backed up, Hannah, an' don't come out no mo'."

Hannah's heart failed her. She staggered a little with her heavy load, then Dock came up.

"Hit's all right," he said cheerily, "hit'll soon clear up."

But Hannah walked beside him, silent. The darkness, the rising wind, the creeping water seemed living enemies. She was chilly, and her feet and clothes were wet, and there seemed nothing to do now and she went into the kitchen. Dock looked down on her for a moment as she sat, all drooped together, then, pushing up the fire in the stove, he went out, shutting the door.

Hannah did not move. She was tired out, and it seemed useless to fight any longer now the water had backed up. The kettle began to sing. Since dawn she had worked like a man, now she must work like a woman. If her father had lived, it would have been better. His patient face came up before her. She had never heard him complain. The kettle sang louder, and the steam shot from the spout. She got up slowly. "Po' daddy, hit's youuns work I'm doin'," she said, "an' I'll do hit tell I draps."

The dishes were soon put away, and she pulled down her sleeves, put out the fire, then paused to tell the old people that all was safe, saying nothing of the rising water.

She wondered if she needed to make a fire for herself; she was *so* tired. She saw a line of light under her door. She opened it. A bright fire burned in the chimney, the hearth was swept, and a pile of wood was in the corner.

"Dock done hit," she said, "an' him so wet and tired. I'd ruther been beat!" She shut the door softly and walked to the fire, while the slow tears filled her eyes. "He seen I were clean down, an' he done hit to hope me up an' me grumblin' in a good house an' everything handy. God knows I ain't no 'count. Po' Dock!"

And out on the hillside Dock minded the cattle, and at intervals stole down to watch the creeping water; quite happy through all the wild, wet night tending the fire and keeping guard. In the dim gray hour before day he went home and slipped into his little hut. Lizer must not know of his vigil nor must Hannah know.

"We wear out life, alas!
Distracted as a homeless wind,
In beating where we must not pass,
In seeking what we shall not find."

~*A Farewell*, Matthew Arnold

XIII

It was a dismal scene the next morning. The house was an island, and all things that could float—small coops, chips, brush—were bobbing up and down against the fences, and tapping like persistent ghosts against the house. The fowls that had gone to roost in the loft of the stable were making a great noise, and Hannah laughed as she heard them. "I'll git Dock to ride out an' feed 'em."

As she spoke she heard a cheerful "Git up, Bess," and a splashing as Dock rode up to the piazza.

The flood seemed to throw Mrs. Warren into a pleasant excitement. She pottered about sweeping out the chips, looking at the hens, and measuring the rise of the water, until Si's voice called from the highroad. Hannah's heart sank. She was not summoned, however, but when she took Mr. Warren's dinner in she saw that there was trouble. She nodded to Si, but he paid no heed, and he and Mrs. Warren went to dinner in silence.

"Si's been done powerful mean," Mr. Warren said, "they've gin him the po'res' heff o' ever'thing. The Budds done hit, They app'inted Reub Budd to choose fur Dave, an' Slocum for Si. Si says Slocum hed mostly first ch'ice, but tuck the wust every time. Si says Minervy hed Slocum paid. Thar is onjestice been done, an' trouble 'll come. Heaper Si's lan' is in thet ole graveyard, an' he says he's gwine to plow hit up kase thar's Budds an' Slocums buried thar."

Hannah looked at her grandfather in horror. "Who'd eat thet corn, Gramper? dead folk's corn!"

"Hit's awful, but Si's sot on doin' hit. Surely these is the last days, Hannah, an' folks ain't got no feelin's fur nothing, no insides o' any kind leff."

"Hev you hearn, Hannah?" Mrs. Warren asked when she and Si returned from the kitchen, "how they've cheated Si?"

"Yes, Granny, hit's bad. But them Budds don't look straight."

"If I jest live long enough," Si said, "I'll sp'ile Minervy. Thar's lots of ways to do hit. I'll ruin any pusson what goes aginst me," looking straight in Hannah's eyes.

All Mrs. Warren's excitement forsook her after this. The sun came out, Mr. Warren foretold good weather, and the water began to recede, but nothing roused her from her angry silence. The Durkets were being overrun by the Budds. The plowing up of the graveyard was rather awful, but anything else that Si could do for revenge would be justifiable, and the worse the better. She did not tell what Si had hinted in the way of retaliation. The trapping of rabbits to be turned into Minerva's garden, the rotten rails that Dave's own hogs could be persuaded to root away, and gain a night in the potatoes and corn; the mixture that would make the hogs seem to die of cholera. There was much that patience could accomplish, and if Dave put up corn, or "roughness," or meat that year it would be a surprisingly small quantity. All this had been outlined during dinner. Mrs. Warren brooded over it, but did not tell it, for she felt that her husband and Hannah were quite capable of warning Dave.

At supper Dock, who had been up to Sewanee that day, told some strange news to Mrs. Warren, reporting the talk about Si's house and the bad division of the things.

"He'll be hevin' a hant," Dock finished, "kase he's gwine to onderpin hisn's new house with the gravestones."

Mrs. Warren almost dropped her cup. "Surely that ain't true!"

"Thet's what they say," Dock answered, "an' all the folks is a-waitin' an' a-watchin' to see."

Build his house on piles of gravestones! Mrs. Warren did not sleep that night. For a time they did not hear any more of Si's plans. Meanwhile, the water subsided and things were replaced, but, of course, the crop was injured, the more so as there came a freeze while it was wet, and the apple and the peach trees looked as if they had been boiled. It was a very bad season, and Mr. Warren's rheumatism increased day by day.

It was hard on Hannah, and Lizer Wilson, returning from Sewanee, leaned over the fence to talk to the girl, who was milking, thinking to hear some complaints.

"Hit's a hard time we're a-goin' to hev," Lizer began. "Thar ain't much bo'ders come to Sewanee outside the students, an' tradin'll be sca'ce."

"Thet'll be hard on you, Lizer," Mrs. Warren said, coming out to the fence.

"Hit'll be hard on heapser folks," Lizer answered, "but if Hannah 'll keep Dock in work," with a leer in her eyes.

Mrs. Warren withered the leer with a glance. "Work'll be sca'ce, too," she said.

"An' they do say," Lizer went on quickly, "thet the flood over to Durket's were the wust thet ever was. Hit muster skeered the rabbits, kase Jane Harner says thet the sight o' them as were ketched in Dave's garden wornt never seen afore, an' hit were eat off clean as youuns han'."

"Thet's a jedg*ment* on Minervy Budd fur cheatin' Si," said Mrs. Warren.

"Hit looks thet a-way," Lizer assented. "An' thar ain't a nigger thet'll stay thar overnight kase o' the hant. An' t'other night they hearn a great miration in the chicken house, an' they ketched two critters eatin' jest ever'thing; thar wornt *no* nestesses leff."

"Thar hit is again," commented Mrs. Warren. "Hit's a judgment, an' if you'll watch, Lizer Wilson, you'll see thet Minervy Budd won't save nothin' *this* year."

"Hit do look thet a-way. Jane Harner says thet water never hurt Si, kase hit wasted hitself on Dave. An' Si's garden is good, an' some o' hisn's corn is s'prisin' high."

"Whar 'bouts?"

"In the, the best corn is in the ole graveyard."

"Who 'll want thet?" cried Hannah.

"Folks away won't know no difference," Lizer answered, "ner cattle at home."

"But no blessin' will come on Si," Hannah said. Mrs. Warren was silent.

"Jane says," Lizer went on, without comment, "thet Si made a good sale on the timber, an' tuck the stones to onderpin hisn's house, kase be says the Budds and Slocums is jest about fitten to onderpin hisn's house and top dress his land."

"And what do the Budds and Slocums say?"

"They're mad as fire, but they're fear'd, kase all the valley knows they done Si a onjestice."

Hannah shook her head. "Thet don't no-wise skuse Si," she said. "An' what's Minervy a-doin'?"

"They do say she's pestered to death. What with the niggers 'fusin' to stay thar, an' the chickens bein' eat up, an' the garden gone, an' the water a-washin' everything, she's too much to stand. Folks don't favor her much, nohow."

"She ain't nothin' to favor," struck in Mrs. Warren.

"Mighty nigh true," Lizer assented. "An' they do say Si's house is tastey, but he's skeerder what he's done, an' he's drinkin' hard, Jane says. You ought to go over thar, Mrs. Warren."

"You're right," was answered, with surprising mildness. "An' I'll try to git to go." Then Lizer went her way.

"Ain't you sorry, Granny?"

"Sorry, gal? Hit's done done, an I ain't a-goin' back on my own," Mrs. Warren answered, "an' I ain't afeared to go an' stay in Si's house. Gravestones or no gravestones, I'm a-goin'. An' I wants to see Minervy Budd pestered, pestered to death, please God."

Time wore on, and after a long absence, Lizer brought a message from Si that he was coming to fetch Mrs. Warren and Hannah. Lizer also told how the hogs had ruined Dave's potatoes, and that there was some strange disease among Dave's hogs. "An' the jedg*ment* is so sure that folks is skeered." Si, on the contrary, flourished, but people did not seek his company, and he wanted Mrs. Warren's aid in a social way.

"Si need not ax me," Hannah said, "I ain't a-goin' to no sich place."

When Si came, Hannah was on the front piazza. She declined firmly. "Do you mean hit, Hannah, mean that you ain't a-comin' to *my* house?" the pupils of his eyes contracting.

"Yes," she answered, "you have done a bad sin, plowin' up dead folks, an' I ain't a-comin'."

There was a moment's silence, then Si raised his hand to heaven.

"'Fore God, Hannah, I'll make you sorry," he said. He shook his finger in her face. "Thar's one mo' chance I'll gie you, an' if you 'fuses thet, the Lord 'll hev to he'p you fur the talk I'll raise."

"I don't want no mo' chance, Si, an' the Lord *will* he'p me." Then Mrs. Warren called, and Hannah went in.

Mrs. Warren was to spend two nights at Si's house. She went off with a brave front, but was much relieved to find that Jane Harner and her oldest daughter were to be there to do the work, and that Dave and Minerva were to receive her. This last bit of news pleased her, for she had come to enjoy Minerva's ill-luck quite as much as Si's house. Underneath all, however, was honest loyalty to the Durkets. She hoped that by staying in the house she could do away with the stories of "hants," and take from Hannah a strong argument against Si. If Hannah could adduce a "hant," all the world would support her against Si and the plowed graveyard and desecrated gravestones; whereas, great prosperity and genial freehandedness might obliterate all, if there were not a "hant" and an obstinate girl to remind people.

Mrs. Warren was delighted with everything. There was no sign of the old graveyard, instead, a field of the finest corn she had seen. She looked furtively at the foundations of the house, but the stones were so neatly built together that no one would think of gravestones in connection with them. The house was neatly finished, and painted, papered, and furnished with a gaudiness that enchanted Mrs. Warren. She and Si walked home with Dave and Minerva that afternoon, and while at the old house Mrs. Warren called attention to all the points of superiority in Si's house and farm. She sympathized cheerfully with Minerva's misfortunes, pointing out the judgment in it all so clearly that Minerva felt that for her the last great day had come and gone.

Si and Mrs. Warren sat late over the fire that night, and finishing with hot grog the old woman slept too heavily to be roused by "hants," but Jane Harner heard noises like fleeing footsteps and hushed oaths. She wrapped her head in the blanket—a "hant" that cursed and trampled like cattle was too awful!

Cows got into Dave's corn that night. Some of the top rails of the fence were old, and were broken where they jumped in. In the morning Dave was in despair, and Mrs. Warren and Si enjoyed his misfortune as only near relatives could. Many neighbors came in that day to see Mrs. Warren. She escorted them about gladly, calling on all to witness that she had slept soundly. Hot grog finished the second evening also, and though Mrs. Warren was tremulous when she reached home the next day, she could triumphantly deny the "hants," much to Hannah's discomfort.

Not long after this, on a fair fresh day, that made one glad to live, Si came over. Mr. Warren, whose rheumatism had gone, was in the garden, Hannah was at the washtub, and Mrs. Warren on the front piazza.

"I'm come to see Hannah," Si said. "The house is done, an if she's a-comin' I wants to know. This is the last chence I'm a-goin' to give her, an' thet's p'int-blank."

Mrs. Warren's eyes flashed. "If you wants the gal, Si Durket, thet ain't no way to talk, an' Hannah ain't gwine to tuck hit."

"She kin please herself," Si said doggedly, "but hit's her last chence."

"You're a fool," and, knocking the ashes from her pipe, Mrs. Warren rose. "I'll call her, an' I'll talk to her, but I ain't a-goin to hev no fits ner no 'sputin'. You must 'member, Si Durket, thet you ain't got but heff o' what you hed. Jest heff o' farm, an' piece o' thet graveyard. An' I wants you to know thet hit makes a difference to me, anyhow. Not to Hannah, kase she's sich a fool shed tuck you 'thout nothin', if so be she hed a favor to you. If you'll keep quiet, I'll keep on a-talkin' to her right stiddy 'bout hit an' bime by she mout tuck you."

Si's face grew more sullen. His aunt was right. He was worth only half as much as was expected, and had become, besides, a marked man.

Mrs. Warren waited; she knew that she had him at a great disadvantage. But Si made no acknowledgment of this; he brooded for a few moments, then repeated, "Hit's the last chence."

Mrs. Warren hesitated. Was he in earnest? Would it be wiser to persuade him or to call Hannah and let her teach his pride a lesson? She called, and the girl came reluctantly, wiping her hands on her apron. Greeting Si quietly, Hannah stood silent.

One moment the trio waited, then Si spoke, "I promised I'd come again, Hannah," he said, "an I'm come. What word is that fur me?"

"An' you'd better gie him a good word," Mrs. Warren struck in. "He'll gie you time to steddy 'bout hit, if you axes hit. I'm a-gittin' tired o' this foolishness, an' I aint a-goin' to hev hit. The nice new house a-waitin'," she urged, alarmed at the realization of the dangerous state of things, that the new house and furniture, that Minerva's complete defeat, that possibly the future of the Durkets, hung in the balance. "An' ever'thing so handy, an' Minerva nigh dead kase hit ain't hern.

Now mind what you say, gal, an' gie youuns cousin a good word, fur God knows what we'll do 'ginst the winter."

Hannah glanced apprehensively at her grandmother, but as the old woman went on, half cajoling, half threatening, she turned her face away and looked down the little valley.

"I ain't never hed but one word fur Si," she said, still looking far away, "an' he knows thet word, an' you knows thet word, an' I'll set my life 'gainst the winter."

Si turned on his heel and walked away with a look in his eyes that startled the old woman. Would he kill the girl some time when she was away from the house?

"Si!" she called, "Si!" but he paid no heed, and mounting his horse, dashed straight up the hillside. Then Mrs. Warren turned on Hannah, and for the first time in her life Hannah realized what awful things words could be. Abused, taunted, cursed, insulted, lashed past endurance by the vulgar fury of the old woman's tongue, she turned a white face and blazing eyes on her persecutor.

"Thet's enough," she said in a low tone. "Youuns words hev set me free, an' I'm a-goin'."

"Hannah!" and old Mr. Warren laid his hand on her shoulder. "Tuck thet back, chile!"

"I can't, Gramper," and, trembling with excitement, she went back to her work. Mrs. Warren's words burned in her ears; dreadful words she had never heard before. If her grandmother could say such things, what could not Si say? And he had threatened her. Her one thought was to get away from them. She would go to Sewanee and get work. She was sorry to leave her grandfather, but she could not stay where such things were said to her.

While she worked through the long day with feverish nervousness she matured her plans, and a determination once reached, she felt happier, even though her pillow was wet with tears when she fell asleep.

XIV

Mrs. Warren would not speak to Hannah the next morning, and ignored the preparations for going to Sewanee. She saw no bundle, only the butter and eggs that always went for coffee and sugar, and she drew the rash conclusion that Hannah had repented. When all was ready, Hannah led the horse to the big gate. Mr. Warren stood there, waiting.

"You're comin' back today?" he asked wistfully.

"Yes, Gramper," then looking down, "Ax Granny what she said to me."

"I hearn, but furgit an' furgive, or mebbe God 'll furgit an' not furgive."

"You only hearn some, Gramper." Then she rode away.

Once more she found Agnes and Max Dudley at the gate.

"Where have you been all this time?" Agnes asked.

"Home, workin'."

"You look overworked," Max said.

"Hit ain't work thet hurts," Hannah answered, "but everything hev gone against me. I've come to hire out," looking wistfully at Agnes.

"Hire? You?" Max questioned. "Will your people allow it?"

"I wont ax. Granny's done said words what set me free. I'll send 'em all the money, but I won't live thar any mo'. I can't."

"If you are in earnest," Agnes said, "I want a girl. Can you wait on table?"

Hannah looked puzzled. "You mean set a table? I dunno if I knows youuns ways, but I kin larn."

"Come in, then, and we will talk about it."

Max lifted his cap. "I will see you later, Miss Agnes," he said. Then to Hannah, "I think I will go to Lost Cove this very day."

Old Mr. Warren and his son had impressed Max, when he met them, as being so thoroughly good. And the handsome face of the son was the saddest he had ever seen. That his daughter should offer herself as a servant was an unknown thing in her grade of life. Sometimes a native would go into service, but never of Hannah's class. He wondered what had driven her to it.

The girl and her story interested him, and he decided to go to Lost Cove and solve the little mystery. It was a charming day for the walk, and he might do some good.

Meanwhile Hannah and Agnes had settled terms, and Hannah was to come the next day. But their relations seemed to have changed, and without being told Hannah went out by the back door. Miss Welling had been very clear and decided in the statement of Hannah's duties, but her voice had been kind, and her terms liberal, and afterward she had smiled pleasantly and hoped that Hannah would like her new home. What had made Hannah for the first time leave the house by the back door? The girl puzzled over this question as she rode.

The level road being done, Hannah gathered up the bridle for the rough descent, and saw Max Dudley.

"You have caught me," he said, "I am glad, for your grandmother might not be pleased to see me."

"I reckon she will; she mostly likes comp'ny."

Max laid his hand on her bridle, and they journeyed on together. "Do you think you will like being a servant?"

"I dunno."

"You won't be free, you know, and your place will be in the kitchen. Have you thought of all this?"

"I dunno, Mr. Dudley." Hannah's heart grew cold, and the sure things of life seemed to be slipping away. "I don't know how hit'll be, but it can't be no harder than Granny."

"What made her so angry?"

"Kase I won't marry my cousin, Si Durket." The color rushed into the girl's face. "I can't do that, no, sir. I'll be a nigger fust."

"And your grandfather?"

"Gramper don't favor Si."

They had come down the mountain quite rapidly while they talked, and were now at the Warrens' gate, where Lizer Wilson leaned, talking to Mrs. Warren. The conversation ceased as Hannah and Dudley appeared, and Lizer smiled as Max helped the girl off the horse, instead of leading the horse to the fence and allowing her to climb down, as was the valley custom. Mrs. Warren looked pleased, but Lizer, knowing the differences that obtained at Sewanee, smiled a smile that vocalized itself while Dock ate his dinner.

"What kin you say fur youuns great Hannah Warren," she began, "a-comin' down the mountain longer University boy, an' him a-leadin' ole Bess like Hannah couldn't ride a nag. An' a-heppin' her off like she were hisn's woman, an' a mile o' fence right thar whar any right kinder gal woulder clum down. An' ole Mrs. Warren so proud, like Hannah hed done met up alonger her ekals. An' him, Dudley's his name, takin' off hisn's hat, an' bowin' an' shuckin' han's like he does up to the University womens. Gosh! But he jest nods hisn's head to me. I knows mor'n he thinks I knows 'bout him, a-keepin' comp'ny alonger that Agnes Wellin' up yander. She holds herself mighty high, an' if she do tuck Hannah to the parlor, an' sen's me to the kitchen, taint kase she 'lows Hannah's her ekal. Gosh, but Hannah Warren 'll be as low down as Lizer Wilson soon."

"I'll kill her fust!" Dock's face had grown very white under Lizer's fire of innuendo. He had not spoken, for that would have made things worse, but his anger broke bounds at last, and it was with infinite scorn that he looked on his father's wife and said, "I'll kill her fust."

Lizer rose, too, her low face contracting with fury. "You'll kill her fust, will you? 'Fore God, I'll make hit so you'll want to. I knows how to hurt you, Dock Wilson, an' I'll do hit or die. Jest wait, wait!" and she shook her fist in his face.

Walking up the mountain in the red afternoon light, Max Dudley remembered Hannah Warren in many different poses. She had shown to great advantage in her own sphere. He would call on Agnes Welling and tell her of the flood as Hannah had described it, making it quite an idyl. He wondered how the girl would bear being a servant, as servants were held by the educated classes. It would take character to stand such a test, and in his heart he added, "blood." There was no telling about American blood, and Mr. Warren's blood might have been very blue in ages past. Hannah might have hereditary right to her simple dignity and beauty.

And Hannah, waiting at the gate for the cows, asked her grandfather, with a hopeless ring in her voice, "What's the diffrunce, Gramper, 'twixt me an' Miss Agnes? An' Mr. Dudley don't look like he's the same kinder creetur as Si Durket."

"Thet's true," Mr. Warren answered. "An' steddyin' 'bout hit, hit seems like folks an' cattle favors one another. All cattle is got fo' legs, an' yeers, an' tails, but hit takes more'n yeers, an' tails, an' legs, to make a Jersey cow. Jim Blount, up yander, is got a cow liker pictur. Hit's a cow, but hit's no mo' like ourn cows 'an Mr. Dudley's like Si Durket. Thar *is* a diffrunce, and I've been a steddyin' 'bout hit, an' to save my life I can't see nothin' in hit but wittles, an' shelter, an' seein' fur."

"Well, thet beats me," Hannah said.

"So hit do tell you steddies 'bout hit. Now a man what plows must hev bacon an' cornbread, an' heapser hit, an' when hisn's day's work's done he's so tired thet he don't steddy 'bout hisn's shelter. But them folks to Sewanee, they don't to say work, an' they eats mostly chickens an' light bread, an' when they gits done a-settin' aroun' all day readin' books, they ain't to say clean wore out, an' ever'thing's got to be mighty nice 'fore they kin sleep. An' their pars, an' all their gran'pars done the like afore 'em, tell they come to look an' to be mighty diffrunt from folks what's a-been plowin' since Adam. An' they looks at weuns like Jim Blount's cow would look at ourn cow, an' they'd die to live like weuns live."

"But Granny don't 'llow thar's no difference."

Mr. Warren chuckled. "Granny's eyes ain't been let to see nothin' but Durkets," he said, "an', anyhow, some folks don't see fur. Now thar were Pete and Joshaway; Pete were furever findin' sumpen— pickin' up buttons, an' nails, an' the like; an' Joshaway, a-drappin' ever'thing. An' when I come to steddy 'bout them boys, I seen thet Pete were allers a-lookin' down, an' Joshaway allers a-lookin' up. An Pete traded Joshaway outer ever'thing. But Joshaway didn't keer. If he could set by the branch an' watch the water, or lay on hisn's back a-watchin' the clouds, he were satisfy to let Pete tuck ever'thing. An' Pete went out to Texas to make money, an' Joshaway stayed home an' died a-workin' fur ole folks what couldn't do him no good. An' settin' by the fire a po' cripple, I've steddied a heap, an' if Joshaway coulder had book larnin' he'd abeen like them folks at Sewanee, kase he never eat much nohow. But Joshaway an' them folks to Sewanee seen fur, seen further than money. But Granny don't. She never knows the blossoms is a-blowin', ner she never hears the rain a-talkin', she never b'lieves in no sperret 'ceppen the Durket sperret. But she don't mean no harm. An' folks what seen fur tuck to fine wittles, an' folks what never seen fur was satisfy alonger bacon. But I dunno which gits the most satisfaxion, an' hit seems they gits mixed somehow, kase you an' Joshaway oughter been to Sewanee, an' not in no kitchen nuther."

The girl's face grew hard. "If hit gits mixed, hit gits mixed," she said, "an' I'm a bad mistake, kase I'll heffter be satisfy in the kitchen, to Sewanee."

For a moment Mr. Warren put his hand over his eyes, then he lifted his head. "The fust time I seen Jim Blount's fine cow, she were in a mighty po' stall," he said, "but thet didn't hurt her, no, sir, she set the old stall off, she did."

"What I aspired to be,
And was not, comforts me:
A brute I might have been,
but would not sink i' the scale."

~*Rabbi Ben Ezra*, Robert Browning

XV

The life at Sewanee was a revelation to Hannah. "You never seen the like, Gramper," Hannah said, on her first visit home. "They eats the soup, then all *them* dishes hev to be tuck offen the table; then they hes meat, an' taters, an' sich; then all them dishes hev to be tuck offen the table; then they has raw greens, an' all them dishes hev to be tuck offen the table; then I gits a silver trowel an' scrape that table to get the crumbs offen hit; then they hes sweet mixtry's they calls 'zert; an' cawfee. An' when hits done thar ain't one o' them, 'Fesser Wellin', ner Miss Agnes, ner her leetle nevvy, hev eat a good meal—they picks."

"Hit seems to me like hit's a heap o' foolishness," Mrs. Warren said, "an' I don't see whar you gits time fur youuns dinner."

Hannah flushed hotly. "Oh, I gits time; I eats in the pantry."

"Alonger the niggers?"

"No, the niggers eats in the kitchen."

"Too good for the niggers, an' not good enough for white folks," Mr. Warren pushed his chair back. "Is you satisfy, gal?" he asked.

"Hit's bettern some things I knows on," Hannah answered. Then a silence fell while Mr. Warren walked to the gate and back. When he resumed his seat Mrs. Warren asked, "Does you set down while youuns white folks is a-eatin' ?"

"No, Miss Agnes don't want me to set down."

"Do she let you talk?"

"No, she don't."

Mr. Warren looked at the girl curiously. "Thet's *wussern* a nigger."

Hannah was silent. Her cheeks would always burn with the memory of Agnes' words: "A servant must always stand in the presence of a master or mistress, Hannah, and never speak unless spoken to." Those words made her remember how the apple blossoms had looked after the frost.

"Hev theyuns got ary dorg?" Mrs. Warren asked at last, "kase if thar ain't none, sposen you gits down an' be a dorg?"

Hannah rose. "I must be a-startin'," she said.

"I'll git Bess an' the mule," Mr. Warren answered, "you shent go back like a nigger, nohow."

Dock, who was regularly hired now, had been sitting on the step listening; and the admission wrung from the girl hurt him. Being even *his* wife would be better. He had never dared to lift his eyes to Hannah, and he did not now, except in a sort of dream.

In parting with her grandfather at the Wellings' gate, Hannah said, "I ain't a-comin' home fur a long time, Gramper. Long as I'm up har hit don't seem bad, kase I sees the difference 'twixt me an' Miss Agnes so p'int blank thet hit seems right fur me to tuck orders; but when Granny talks it seems awful. Far'well."

Max Dudley watched Hannah with much interest, and Cartright with amusement. "It is ruination," Cartright said, "to lower that 'wild child of the forest' to civilization."

"On the contrary," Agnes answered, "she is being elevated."

"She looks cast down," Max rejoined.

"Of course; she is now realizing that she is not the highest, but that is necessary. We must see the heights before we can scale them."

"Are you sure civilization is a height?"

"Yes, Mr. Dudley, and I say, Rise at any cost. The girl is a different creature already. You remember when you dined with us yesterday, she became so absorbed in the conversation that she forgot her duties?"

"Yes," Max answered. He remembered uncomfortably the pained

interest on the girl's face as Professor Welling discussed caste and the dense ignorance of the "Covites," their lack of ambition, and his hopelessness as to their future. The look of wondering pain in the girl's eyes had made Max contradict as flatly as he might the Professor's position. How pitiful that she did not stay in her own sphere.

He looked back to where Hannah followed them, carrying Miss Welling's books. They were on their way to a mission Sunday school, where, twice during the week, Agnes went to impart secular knowledge. Hannah went with her always. As Max looked back now, there was a lack of spirit in the girl's whole bearing that was pathetic. "Are you tired, Hannah?" he called, almost involuntarily. Agnes and Cartright turned, too, and Hannah looked up quickly.

"No, sir, no, I ain't tired."

"You see I have been a guest in her house," Max explained in a lower voice to his companions, "and I do not think she understands the 'accident of birth.' To her equality is a fact, not a theory."

"I do not agree with you," Agnes answered, "Hannah quite understands that there is a difference, for she asked the cause."

"And your answer?"

Agnes smiled. "To my surprise I was rather puzzled how to answer. She told me that her grandfather thought it was due to 'shelter, an' wittles, an' seein' fur.'"

"Good!" Cartright exclaimed. "Environment, and 'seeing far' will stand for the survival of the fittest. Good."

"And Mr. Dudley's sympathy is wasted," Agnes went on, "for you see they discuss this thing." And they moved aside to let a horseman pass. He gave a surly "Evenin'," and Agnes thought she had never seen a more evil face. Hearing a rude laugh, she turned. "He speaks to Hannah," she said.

"Some rustic lover," and Cartright moved on.

"No, we will wait for her. See, she has stepped quite into the bushes. Call her, Mr. Dudley."

"We are waiting, Hannah!" Max called, and walked a few steps toward her. Then Si, for it was he, rode on.

Hannah had been horrified when startled from her dreams by Si's voice, and had drawn aside to let him pass, but he stopped. "I'm a-goin' to the Cove," he said, "what shall I say?"

"Nothin', 'ceppen I'm well," she answered.

"An' whar's you a-goin'?"

"To school."

"Po' folks' school! I've hearn 'bout 'em. Larnin' the po' Covites fur nothin'. An' you walks behind an' totes youuns missus' books. Lord!" and he laughed. "Won't I tell Aunt Tildy, an' she'll bile over."

Here Max's call interrupted them, and Hannah started forward.

"Youuns marster's a-callin'; go on, Nigger," jeered Si, in a low voice, and Hannah made no answer.

"Is it all right, Hannah?" Max asked as she neared them.

"Yes, sir," looking up with flashing eyes and scarlet cheeks. "Hit were my cousin, sir, Si Durket."

"Oh!" and Max resumed his place by Agnes' side.

"That small, small, imperceptible
Small talk, which cuts like powdered glass
Ground in Tophana."

~*Broken Dreams*, Celia Emmeline Gardner

XVI

Often after this, Si met the school party. He had ascertained the days on which they went out, and that during the week Hannah and Miss Welling went alone, but that many times Max Dudley walked out to meet them. On Sunday Dudley and Cartright always went. Much of Si's information came from Lizer Wilson, who had told him also of Dudley's escorting Hannah down the mountain. And Si had seen Dudley give his umbrella to Hannah once. A sudden summer shower, and the girl was unprotected at the station. Max handed her his umbrella and joined Cartright.

Cartright had smiled, saying, "She is very handsome, but fancy giving one's umbrella to a servant."

"She is a woman, and, in many ways, an unprotected one," Max answered.

"And so you draw attention to her?"

Max looked at his companion curiously. "I do not quite understand you."

Cartright laughed. "I understand you, however." A third student joined them, and the subject was dropped.

But it all sifted down to the valley, where it spread and crept up to the station again, then to the University. Dudley had been chaffed by Cartright for giving Miss Welling's maid his umbrella. The laugh grew. Some laughed at the devotion that could reach from mistress to maid, some because the maid was so handsome, but all laughed in a quiet way.

So the summer waxed and waned, and Hannah, not wanting to be disturbed, did not go home at all. At first she got home news from Dock, but gradually Dock's visits ceased, and Hannah feared that he had heard the talk, which her grandmother had hurled at her that last day. At last, in September, she grew anxious, and decided to go down. She asked for a day, but a guest was expected, and Agnes promised her several days later on. The guest was a Miss Vernon, and after the first week she often embarrassed Hannah by her cool and amused stare.

Miss Vernon accompanied the party to the mission Sunday school one day, ridiculing it at every step. Merrily they squabbled, Miss Vernon and Cartright against Max Dudley and Agnes, and Hannah, trudging on behind, wondered at the bright badinage and laughter. How narrow, and dark, and empty her world had been! How could she go back? Agnes had done much for her, teaching her many things outside her work, and the eager mind had grown rapidly.

During the afternoon a storm came up that settled into a steady downpour. Only two umbrellas were in the party of five, and there was a discussion. A number of the people were going to wait, and as some had to come far on the road to Sewanee, it was decided that Hannah should wait, in hope of the weather clearing. Hannah pleaded that she preferred a wetting, but Agnes was firm, and Hannah was left. Presently the party met the negro man sent by Professor Welling with cloaks and umbrellas.

"If only we had waited," Agnes said.

"Let me go back for Hannah," suggested Max, taking the extra shawl and umbrella. "We have not come far, and it would not do to leave her to Peter," he added, in a lower tone. "He regards her only as a servant, you know."

"You are very kind," and Agnes looked up gratefully.

Then Max turned back, and Cartright pulled his mustache to hide a smile. "I suppose Dudley is living up to the lesson I heard him impressing this afternoon," he said. "Duty to one's neighbor. He is *such* a crank; I really believe he tries to do it."

"Take care, Mr. Cartright," and though Agnes smiled, there was a flash in her eyes. "I am . . ."

"I know," and Cartright helped her over a little stream. "But Dudley goes too far. At the station the other day he gave that girl his umbrella. It is foolish, and causes remark." And he drew Agnes' cloak more closely about her, looking straight down into her eyes, "After all, the girl is a servant."

"Mr. Dudley *is* queer, but, then, Hannah is uncommonly handsome," said Miss Vernon.

A horseman passed them, and Agnes recognized Si Durket, of whom Hannah had told her.

Hannah stood alone in the schoolhouse doorway. The young people who giggled together regarded her as "sot up," and avoided her. Presently she saw Max Dudley returning. The young people giggled more than ever, and the old people, who wisely kept a "great gulf fixed" between their class and the university men, looked disapprovingly. They had heard talk about Hannah Warren, and seeing Max return in the rain for her, the vague reports took shape. When Max entered the room there was a dead silence.

"Miss Agnes sent this shawl, Hannah," he said. "We met the servant just a little way from here. If we walk fast we can catch them."

Hannah pulled her bonnet farther over her face, and wrapping the shawl hastily about her, stepped out into the rain before Max.

"Wait for the umbrella!" he called, but Hannah did not heed. Harder and harder came the driving rain and wind, but Hannah hurried on. With her bonnet drawn down and the shawl held close about her, she seemed not to know that Max was with her, and now and then helped her over bad places. On they went, with the umbrella well down in front. Suddenly they heard a shout, and found a horseman nearly on them, the horse starting wildly at the umbrella. Hannah sprang aside, and, looking up, faced Si Durket. There was a moment's pause, even in the storm, the girl thought, and, righting the umbrella, Max stepped again to Hannah's side. With a laugh, Si rode on.

"Your cousin?"

"Yes, sir." Yes, it was Si, and those people at the schoolhouse had laughed, and Lizer Wilson had hinted many times at her not being able to guide her horse down the mountain. There would be talk. But her grandmother's talk about Dock was worse. Would not one piece of talk kill another? And where would her character be when all was said?

"How quick you have been!" Agnes said, glancing at Cartright.

"Yes, Hannah raced." Then to Cartright, "What is the joke?"

"My dear Dudley, I am only pleased to have some assistance with the umbrellas," Cartright answered.

Plodding on behind, Hannah wondered why Si could not have met them after they had joined the party.

"Art thou a dumb, wronged thing that would be righted
Entrusting thus thy cause to me? Forbear!
No tongue can mend such pleadings; faith requited
With falsehood—love, at last aware
Of scorn—hopes, early blighted."

XVII

Behind her back Agnes' friends were laughing at her and blaming her; varying their remarks with wonderings as to whether she would marry Cartright or Dudley. Cartright had money, but Dudley agreed with her in all her fads, especially as to these country people and her own maid. Meanwhile, Cartright kept Miss Welling in something of a temper about Dudley. Hannah had not had her holiday yet, and for some time had had no word. She was vaguely uneasy, when late one afternoon Dock came to the back door looking very miserable. "Kin I see you, Hannah?"

Hannah came out hastily. "Is Gramper sick, Dock?"

No, nothin' don't ail nobody. I jest come to git the word 'bout you. Is you well? Is all a-goin' well? Is you satisfy, Hannah?"

"Yes, Dock," the misery on his face creeping into her heart. "An' what ails you?"

"Nothin', nothin.' Jest youuns Granny couldn't sleep last night kase an owl come thar and hollered all night long. I couldn't sleep nuther, an' I jest come to make sure 'bout you, thet's all. Far'well." He went away, and Hannah's heart sank. Something was wrong and Dock could not help her.

Things were quiet after this, but somehow Hannah could not please her mistress. Could Miss Agnes be sick? Then one morning Dock came to say that Hannah was wanted at home, and Mr. Warren would come for her that afternoon. And Dock could explain nothing and escaped as soon as possible.

Very slowly Hannah went to find Agnes; very slowly, for she was weak and cold and trembling. She paused in the dining room to gain composure, and heard voices in the drawing room. It was the high, sharp voice of Mrs. Skinner. "Indeed, for her own sake I would not keep her a moment longer," she said. "Good or bad, I should send her home. I have always thought her much too handsome for a servant." Then the voices were lost in the hall as Agnes conducted her visitor to the door.

Hannah leaned against the wall. It was she they were talking about, for the cook was black, she who must be sent home. Agnes returned through the hall, and Miss Vernon with her, laughing. "You are as solemn as in owl, Agnes. I would not let the stupid talk bother me. Send the girl home. I heard when I first came that they were laughing at Mr. Dudley about Hannah."

"And you did not tell me?" Agnes asked quickly.

"Why should I? You have eyes and ears, and as Mr. Cartright is the coming man, why should you care if Mr. Dudley makes a fool of himself? And he seems to have done it thoroughly."

"I do *not* care," Agnes answered, but she shivered a little. The color flashed into Hannah's face, and her drooping figure straightened. A fire seemed lighted in her brain. Her grandfather had heard all this; all Sewanee had been talking, and of course the valley. She was to be sent away; her name was a byword! And Miss Agnes did not care. She went into the drawing room and found Agnes and Miss Vernon at the window, watching the approach of Mr. Cartright. "What is it?" and Agnes turned her head.

"Gramper is sent for me," her eyes were full of ineffable sadness, "says he'll come this evenin'."

Agnes' delicate color faded a little. "Very well," she said. "Your money will be ready. And," she paused, then added, "as the term is nearly over, you need not return."

"Yes, Miss Agnes," the dark eyes not wavering, "shall I set the dinner table?"

"Yes, and let Mr. Cartright in." Cartright met the eyes of the girl as she held the door open, 'like a dumb animal,' he thought, and hurried past.

"I am only a thing," Hannah thought. "A stick or a stone 'thout no feelin's." Great God! She knew her own class thoroughly. She had done nothing, and they knew it, but they would be glad to humble Mrs. Warren who "held her head so high," and herself, who had kept aloof. They would pretend to scorn her, would whisper when she came near, would laugh and make coarse jokes on her. A great wave of bitterness swept over her. Miss Agnes, who knew the truth, had turned from her. Who would speak a word for her good name? Good name? It was already a byword. The glass she was polishing fell from her hands with a crash. She looked down, one of the best tumblers. The shock restored her and changed her train of thought.

"We kin stan' up tell we draps," Dock had said. She must stand up, as far as the world could see.

She finished her work and went to her room to arrange her clothes. Her wardrobe had greatly increased and her things made two bundles. But all the things that Agnes had given her she put aside. She could not take them. Just as she finished she saw her grandfather at the gate, with old Bess and the mule. He looked older, and his head was bent, as if he could look no man in the face. *Why* did he not face the world and cry out to all that Si had done it! Why did he not kill Si?

She went down hastily with the two bundles. "Hardy, Gramper," looking at him wistfully. "Here's my things."

The old man lifted his eyes, but not his head, and sighed.

"Si done hit, Gramper." She went on hurriedly, "You knows hit's all lies?"

"Lies or no lies, everybody is a-talkin' an' Hannah Warren's name is in the dirt. Thar's no use a-tryin' to hide thet; we must hide you."

For a moment Hannah leaned against the horse. Si *had* ruined her.

"What is this, Hannah, going home?" Max Dudley stood behind her. "Ah, how are you, Mr. Warren?" to the old man.

"Yes, sir," Hannah answered, shocked into strength once more. "I'm goin' home. I'll be back in a minute, Gramper," and she turned to the house just as young Melville came up hurriedly, saying, "Come, Dudley, come, I have something to tell you." She knew what he meant.

Up to her room she crept, sitting down one moment to regain her strength, then she folded each ribbon and frill that Agnes had given her—the collars, the simple brooch. She would put them in Agnes' room. They would speak and say, "Covites have feelings." Would anyone ever love Agnes as she had done?

She pinned her little shawl about her, and, taking the little fineries and her bonnet, went to Agnes' room. In the doorway she paused; it was so pretty. Suppose she had lived in a place like this, would she have grown careless of people's feelings? Did fineness make people hard? A dry sob broke the stillness. She moved hastily to put down the things.

Not on the dressing table, nor on the table, the sofa? *That* was lower. She turned the things over in her hands; they looked to be very poor when brought into this room. She laid them on the rug, near the fireplace. Miss Agnes would see them when she came, a humble little pile, then she went out, closing the door.

In the hall below she met Agnes with some money in her hands. Her eyes shone and two spots of color were on her cheeks. "Your money," she said, "you have done remarkably well as waitress."

"Yes, Miss Agnes," but Hannah did not touch the money. "I broke one o' the good tumblers, Miss Agnes, an' please tuck it out."

"That is nothing," Agnes said quickly, "I *never* count such things."

"But I does, Miss Agnes," and Hannah's hands remained folded.

Agnes paused, too provoked to speak, then put the money on a table near by. "There is your money," she said, "Goodbye," and she walked away.

Hannah watched her a second, then took all the money save one half-dollar and went out. She mounted the horse in silence, and as they rode off, asked quietly, "What did Mr. Dudley say, Gramper?"

"Nothin' much. He axed me what made you go, an' I tole him, an' they turned round and gone, lookin' like the dead."

"An' all fur Si's lies," Hannah said.

"Lies or no lies," the old man answered, as before, "hit's done done, an' youuns name is ruined. Youuns Granny laughs one minute, an' cusses the next. Thar's nothin' fur me to say, kase when the women folks of a fambly goes down, hit's done fur. An' Lizer Wilson grins, an Si, well, Si says he's willin' to kivver youuns shame. Si says thet, an' hit's all we kin do."

Hannah clenched her teeth. Si, whose vile lies had brought her to this, offering to screen her from the world! Did they forget that death was left her still?

When they were out of the station limits Mr. Warren spoke again.

"Hit's a good offer, to kivver youuns name. Thar's mighty few'd be willin' to pick a gal up outen the mud."

"Gramper, Si's throwed the mud on me to git me," Hannah said sternly. "I ain't done nothin', an' I ain't a-goin' to tuck Si, like I'm glad to git shed o' my name. I ain't shamed, an' I'll die 'fore I'll tuck Si."

"Hesh, gal! youuns life ain't yourn. Mertildy says hit all comes o' you bein' so biggity, an' hit's true. Weuns is got to git outen this trouble, and Si's the best chance."

Hannah wheeled old Bess across the road, and stopped the mule. "If you says thet agin', Gramper, I'll ride straight on an' never come back no more." Her eyes burned like fire.

A groan broke from Mr. Warren's lips. "God hev mercy!" he said. Hannah waited a moment, then turned the horse and rode on. Presently Mr. Warren's mutterings began again. "Whar *is* he'p to come from? Mr. Dudley 'll not make no motion. He kep' on a-sayin' 'Thar's nothin' in hit. God knows thar's nothin' in hit.' An' he looked like death. An' t'other feller says, 'Come, Dudley, come, hit's all damned nonsense.' 'Damned nonsense,' says I, 'yes, but *my* name is in the dirt, and *my* gal is done ruined. Who'll b'lieve hit's damned nonsense?' Thet's what I said, an' Dudley looked like death."

Hannah's head dropped. Shame on shame. Agnes had turned from her, and Max Dudley . . . He had been so good to her, she knew it hurt him. The old man muttered on, but she did not listen. Her thoughts went back and forth, and pain seemed everywhere.

Down the rugged road they went in silence; then the green valley and the old home. The cows were waiting outside the fence, the chickens were scratching in a perfunctory way before going to roost, the pigs in their favorite mud holes looked pictures of content, and the blue smoke curling from the kitchen stovepipe showed the approach of supper. The mountain tops still gleamed with sunlight, but the shadows were thick in the little valley.

Hannah saw her grandmother in the lobby, and longed to turn and flee, but her horse followed the mule and the bent old man through the gate that Dock, with averted face, held open. Mrs. Warren went into her room, and shut the door. What did it matter? When even Dock Wilson turned his face away, the limit was reached. Hannah went quietly to her room, but though Mr. Warren followed he did not put down the bundles, and to Hannah the room looked strange. Harness and tools were against the walls, and the clothes hanging about were men's clothes. Mr. Warren watched her. She asked no questions, but moved to take the bundles.

"Not yit," he said. "Dock stays in har, an' Si, when he's over. Youuns Granny 'llowed the loft would do fur you."

A blow from the old man would not have been so cruel a shock. "Yes, hit 'll do," she answered.

"Youuns Granny 'llowed Dock'd run the place on shar's, an' you'd tuck Si an' go," Mr. Warren said, as he followed up the steep steps, and, putting, aside the bundles, sat down on the low bed, made of boards laid on boxes, and looked at the girl, who had gone to the end window.

Presently she turned, and said, "The loft, or the cow house, or the pigpen is good enough fur me, if so Granny likes, but Si ain't good enough. If hit's to choose 'twixt rags, an' starvin', an' p'intin' fingers, or Si, I'll tuck hit all, but I'll *never* tuck Si!"

Mr. Warren climbed down the ladder slowly.

"Stronger than woe is will; that which was Good
Doth pass to Better—Best."

~Edwin Arnold

XVIII

Only one end of the loft had been made habitable, but on its improvement someone had spent great energy. The bed was neatly
made, and by it was the bit of rag carpet that had been in Hannah's
room, downstairs. There was no way of making a fire, for the chimneys went through in solid columns, but a bolt had been put on the
trapdoor that shut the loft from the lower world and air, and the largest cracks in the roof were stuffed carefully with straw. A shelf had
been put near the window, and on it was Hannah's little looking glass.
On a box in one corner stood a tin basin and a piece of yellow soap, a
rough-dried towel hung from a nail in the roof, and a bucket of fresh
water was near.

"Dock done hit," she said, "if he turned his head away or no,
Dock done hit," and, at this first sign of sympathy, the tears sprang to
her eyes. Tears were not for her now, and, brushing them aside, she
untied her bundles. She took out her finest apron and best kerchief
and, after rearranging her hair, put them on. She was quite conscious

of the improvement in her wardrobe and in herself, and was determined to appear at her best. She needed every possible help now.

If her grandfather had stood by her, if her grandmother had not shown her contempt by putting her in the loft, shown it to Dock and Si, and so to the countryside, she might have left her cause to others and broken down, but this treatment, as of one absolutely unworthy, roused her. The experience of a lifetime had swept over her since morning. She had to fight, and she descended to her grandmother's room as if she were an honored guest. She even went so far as to smile as she crossed the lobby, thinking, "Hit's the Durket sperret."

She did not heed that, after the first glance on her entrance, her grandmother turned her head away, but walked to the fire, and, drawing a chair forward, sat down. Mr. Warren stared. How changed, how grand she was. What had happened? And he looked across at his wife doubtfully.

But there was no doubt in Hannah's manner as she smoothed her white apron, and folded her hands, as she had seen Agnes do; then began quietly to speak words that froze Mr. Warren's blood, almost.

"Granny," looking at the old woman, "couldn't you have stopped Si's lies? You knew hit was lies, kase you knew me. Hit don't look natteral for you to let 'em do me this bad to skeer me into tuckin' Si, an' you a-knowin' that I ain't skeery?"

Mrs. Warren was knitting, but at the girl's first words her hands began to tremble, then she dropped them and her work in her lap, but did not turn or speak.

"You said some hard words to me afore I went away," Hannah went on, "words thet no decent gal hed no 'casion to hear, but I never 'llowed you'd let outside folks talk 'bout youuns own flesh and blood. An' I never 'llowed thet you b'lieved hit till you put me up loft."

Mrs. Warren trembled. Had the last day come that she should be dared like this! She was boiling with fury, but she remembered the third fit, and controlled herself. Her hands were gripped together, her eyes were flashing, her lips were quivering, but when she spoke her voice was quiet.

"I would have stopped it, Hannah Warren, if I hed hearn hit start, but hit were all through the country 'fore I hearn hit. An' I knowed p'int-blank that a-many a ole debt o' mine were patched on to hit, an' I were a-bein' paid off. An' I put you up loft kase hit's good enough for you. An' I hev cussed you, yes, an' all the Warrens, an' I hev cussed Si, yes, cussed him with a blight an' a blain, an' the sufferin' o' death 'thout death!" and rising she left the room.

There was silence until Mr. Warren spoke. "Si's a-stoppin' har," he said.

"Si!"

"That's hit, youuns Granny kep' him har fur you."

Hannah rose. Through the window she saw Si comin, then Dock spoke to him, and he turned toward the kitchen.

"Minervy an' Dave's nigh ruined," Mr. Warren went on, "an' Si hev done hit. He tole hit when he were drunk."

"An' Si thinks to ruin me."

"An' he hev done thet," Mr. Warren rejoined, "through all the country he hev done thet. Jim Blount tole me so, an' Bill Cole tole me so, an' Lizer Wilson an' Jane Harner tole me so. Yes, hit's done done!" clasping his hands as he looked into the fire. "My Joshaway's gal's ruined! I let you talk youuns Granny down, but thar ain't no stoppin' the world, gal, lessen you gits married. An' thar ain't no man but what 'll stop befo' he'll stoop to Hannah Warren, my Joshaway's gal!"

Hannah stood with one hand on the mantelpiece and listened. It was true. She had felt it that morning in Agnes' manner, in the ride through the village, where everyone stared, and no one spoke, felt it in Dock's averted face, in her grandfather's despair, in the very atmosphere, this disgrace so unmerited, so dreadful.

"Si makes a mighty good offer," Mr. Warren went on, "he says he'll settle hisn's farm on you, if I'll settle this place on youuns chilluns. I tole him I'd done settled hit on you a'ready, an' he 'llowed thet Dave's shar'd come in to you, too, kase Dave hedn't no chilluns, an' hedn't no right to leff the land outen the fambly. Hit looks to me like hit'd be the upbuildin' o' both famblies. An' Si," looking away from the unwavering eyes of the girl, "Si, drinkin' like he does, ain't a-goin to live much longer."

There was a pause, then Hannah turned toward the door. "To tuck a man an' watch to see him die o' drink is wussern all that hes been said 'bout me."

"Hannah!" The despair in the cry stopped her with her hand on the latch. "I've been a-bearin' so much!" raising his clasped hands. "Thar were the talk 'bout you an' Dock, the talk youuns Granny tole you, then come the talk 'bout you an' Dudley. An' every day I hearn hit a-grindin', an' a-grindin', tell I knowed thar worn't no wusser hell. An' when the talk settled an' I poured hit off, the dregs was jest this a-

way: Dock wouldn't never dar' to ax you an' Dudley ain't a-goin' to
steddy 'bout you an' Si jest come in 'twixt the two," putting his hands
over his face, "an' I 'llowed hit would not be sicher a long trial, an' a-
many a woman hev stood sich. Oh, God forgive me!"

Hannah crossed the room swiftly, and kneeled by the old man's
chair. "Gramper, I kin live the lies down . . . or go."

"If you goes, the lies will grow like weeds of a rainy summer, an'
I can't live 'em down. Hit 'll kill me."

Hannah rose. She had no answer for these bitter truths.

At supper she talked a little to Dock, for neither Mrs. Warren nor
Si would speak, and Mr. Warren refused all food. Her help in all work
being declined, she went outside where the cows were. When Dock
came to turn them out he said as he passed, "'Pend on me, Hannah,
an' don't be skeered into nothin'. I couldn't kill Lizer, she's a woman,
but I kin kill Si!" Then Mrs. Warren calling Hannah, he hurried away.

"You called me Granny?" Hannah asked when she reached the
old woman. Then she saw that Si stood just within the doorway. Mr.
Warren sat bent over the fire. "You called?"

"Yes," Mrs. Warren answered, "but I ain't a-wantin' you. Si is the
fool."

"I'm axin' fur the last time, Hannah," and Si half closed his light
eyes as he looked at her. "An' mighty few would ax you now."

"Mighty few, Si," Hannah answered, "but I won't be beholden to
none."

"What 'll you do? Hope an' pray fur Dudley?" The scorn of the
girl's eyes made him look away. Mrs. Warren's clasped hands grew
rigid, and the old man lifted up his bowed head. Almost he could
have killed the villain!

"Whatever I hopes an' prays fur," Hannah said quietly, "thar is
this fur *you* to 'member, Si Durket. I kin be druv down to the lowest,
but never druv down to tuckin' you, never!" And she smiled as she
saw that Lizer Wilson had come in and had heard. "An' I hope you'll
tell hit, Lizer Wilson," she added.

Mrs. Warren started, and reeled a little, then went to her place by
the fire. Si looked at the door, but Hannah stood there. She saw his
wish, and smiled. "You've hed enough?" she said. "Your jedg*ment* is
jest a-startin', soon this won't seem like nothin'. 'Twont be long 'fore
all youuns wickedness comes home, not long," then she went to her
loft.

"It is nonsense," Melville said. He and Max had been walking up and down the road for some time. "To dismiss the girl was foolish," he went on, "for that gave the affair tone and color, but I cannot see where you have any duty or blame in the matter. As for Cartright, he is scheming for his own ends."

Many, many times Melville had covered this ground, but Dudley came back always to the starting point—Hannah's misery.

"You do not understand," he answered in a voice that had lost all life, "what an awful thing it is for the girl. Blount says that the stories grow worse at every turn."

"Damn Blount!" Melville interrupted.

"Suppose we do? That does not help my position. Just consider *my* position."

"I have gone over it a hundred times, and you have to thank Cartright's envy and Mrs. Skinner's folly for it. Come, it is bedtime."

"You go. I will come presently." Once alone, Dudley walked into the forest and sat down on a fallen tree. He felt dazed still. When he had met Hannah at the gate that afternoon, and heard the old man's story, he was shocked and angry, and alone with Melville had called him a fool for taking the girl away. Melville betrayed, unwittingly, the extent of the talk, and Cartright joining them, fresh from the Wellings, revealed that Agnes had dismissed the girl. Max walked straight to Blount's shop, and Blount's words appalled him. "The girl is ruined, and as nice a girl as ever stepped. It is a shame, but it is done."

Then with Melville by his side, raging and swearing, he returned to the University in a sort of a mist.

How had it happened? Who had done it? What was his duty?

For a year his name had been coupled with the name of Agnes Welling. He was Professor Welling's assistant and most intimate in the house. He had only waited to finish his course before speaking to Agnes.

Melville said that Cartright had influenced Agnes into dismissing Hannah; it was this that had ruined the girl. Cartright's influence was a new thing. If he should go to Agnes and say, "This talk is all false, you know that I love you, will you marry me?" Could she say "Yes," and hear the world say, as Cartright reported it to have said already, that her rival was her maid, who had been sent away? His ideal Agnes would have stood by Hannah.

He sprang to his feet, *still* she was his ideal! He had loved her so long, so truly, he could not let her go.

In reality it was Agnes who had disgraced Hannah, and must he pay for her mistake by righting the girl before the world? A servant? A "Covite!" A woman. As a gentleman and a Christian, what was his duty to this fellow creature?

The moonlight seemed to fade, and the darkness to fold about him hopelessly. The night was waning; he would go home.

For a little while the next morning things seemed confused again, but he lay still until he collected his thoughts and laid fresh hold on his determinations. After twelve o'clock he would be free, and would go to Lost Cove.

Poor Melville could find out nothing. He followed Dudley until twelve o'clock, when Dudley said, "I have an engagement," and Cartright joining them, Melville could find out nothing, and went away. Dudley walked on, with Cartright beside him, until Dudley turned off.

"Going to the station?" Cartright asked.

"No, to Lost Cove."

"Good Heavens, man! In the face of all this talk?"

"Because of all this talk."

Had the autumn woods been ever as beautiful or the sky as blue or life as full of charm and possibility as on this day? Would it ever be thus again? But he must not think. He must bend all his being to this duty; there would be time enough afterward for thinking.

It might be that he could yet lay his case before Agnes. His ideal Agnes would uphold him. But the real Agnes, Agnes as Cartright seemed to know her, would she laugh at him for his pains?

"If you loved only what were worth your love,
Love were clear gain, and wholly well for you:
Make the low nature better by your throes!
Give earth yourself, go up for gain above!"

~James Lee's Wife, Robert Browning

XIX

Dinner was over, and Lizer Wilson was heating irons in Mrs. Warren's room, where the old man sat over the fire. Mrs. Warren was busy in the kitchen, Dock in the yard, while Hannah, not being allowed to help, had wandered off. She had gone to the spring, and sat on the edge of the basin. On one side, through the thick growth of slim young poplars and maples, she could see the valley and fields, and the mountains that shut all in. On the other she looked down to the mysterious pool. It was dark and still, and people said it had no bottom. At Sewanee she had heard this idea laughed at.

Sewanee! She bowed her head on her hands. Her grandmother did not want her; need she stay here? The talk would grow in the valleys, but at Sewanee it would soon die, then Miss Agnes could marry Mr. Dudley, and all would be well. She would be left desolate, but she was only one. Trampled in the dust, left for dead. Who cared?

A noise startled her, and she rose quickly, to find Dock standing before her. "Does Granny want me?" she asked.

Dock stood silent, with one hand grasping a young maple until it shivered and dropped its scarlet leaves about him, while the girl watched and trembled as the young maple did. At last Dock raised his head, and his eyes were full of pain and fire.

"Lizer says thet you need not a-been so biggity last night to Si, kase Si only done what he done kase youuns Granny axed him to do hit to save the two famblies. An' there worn't no other man would tuck youuns now." A fresh shower of scarlet leaves fluttered down about him. "I didn't knock her, kase I ain't never knocked a woman yit. I told her she were a-lyin', an' she knowed hit, an' I were one man thet would lay down an' be chopped to pieces fur you, body an' soul. An' hit's true, Hannah," and his eyes were filled with a light that would have glorified any face on earth. "Hit's God' truth, but I never would have told hit, 'ceppen fur everybody a-turning 'gainst you. I ain't nobody, an' I knows hit, an' I don't 'llow thet you hev come down to me, thar ain't no sich foolishness in me. But all is a talkin', Hannah," shaking his head sadly, "an' I kin give you a honest name, an' I kin work fur you, and shoot fur you, an' I *would*. An' no pusson would dar' to tuck Hannah Wilson's name 'twixt tongue an' teeth to spit hit out, kase I'd kill 'em. An' if you wants to go 'way, I'll go, an' if you wants to stay, I'll stay. An' I'll never cast nothin' in youuns teeth, ner sot up to be no ekal o' yourn. Don't gimme no word now," he added, swaying the little maple tree back and forth, "but keep it in youuns mind fur sumpen to hold on to." Then he went away.

Nothing could have shown Hannah the depth of her fall as completely as this offer did. Nothing could have proved as cruelly the hopelessness of her position. That *Dock Wilson* should dare such a proposition! She sat down again, casting her apron over her head, and rocking herself back and forth. The strength of the man's love had not touched her yet. Hannah Wilson! He had coupled the names. Hannah Wilson! What better than Lizer Wilson? To Agnes Welling and her friends, all were "Covites" together. *Was* there a true difference? Between herself and Agnes Welling there was a wide difference, but between herself and Dock? And between Dock and the much admired Si Durket? This last difference was plain enough, and Dock's kind face, glorified by his love, rose up before her. Soul and body he would die for her, he would work and fight for her, and never think she had descended to his level. She remembered how he had worked for her and watched over her in the spring, asking no return.

The swaying motion ceased, and her apron fell from over her

face. Now he offered to stand between her and the world, and he knew that Si, who made the talk, would keep it alive.

What was the difference between her and Dock? Somehow or other he seemed above her now. Marry Dock, then Miss Agnes would know that the talk was not true, and would marry Mr. Dudley. With the thought of Sewanee there came a vision of her leaden-lined future.

Suddenly the sound of the horn came to her. She looked at the sun; it was not suppertime. What could it mean? Again the sound, and this time more sharp, and someone was waving to her down in the field. Quickly she went, and saw her grandfather beckoning. Before she reached him she heard the words, "Mr. Dudley's to the house," and her heart seemed to stop. Had Agnes sent for her to come back, and give the talk the lie? She laid hold on the old man's arm to steady herself. The joy shook her as no pain had done.

"Mr. Dudley?"

"Thet's hit. He's come to tuck you away, chile, an' stop the talk. Mertildy's in a mighty takin', an' Lizer Wilson looks like she's been frostbit. Lord, gal, you are done saved, and nobody 'll dar' to talk no mo'. An' thar'll not be no mo' kitchen fur you to Sewanee."

"Gramper," she staggered a little, stopping him with a sudden gasp. "What is you a-sayin'?"

The old man hurried her on, and his voice was a little less tremulous as he repeated his words.

"Come fur me?" the girl whispered. "Mr. Dudley," and she flung up her hands as one who is mortally wounded. How low, how low she had fallen. She clung to a post of the back piazza, unable to go farther. Dudley came for *her*, then all thought the worst of her. And Agnes!

"Come on, gal, come on. Mr. Dudley's a-waitin' fur you, an' youuns Granny's a-waitin'. I reckon she's right sorry she put you up loft. An' Lizer Wilson is a-scorchin' all the clothes she's a-tryin' to iron. Don't you smell 'em? An' yander she is a-peepin' at you."

Hannah straightened herself up, and the shivering ceased. She stepped quickly through the lobby, where Lizer was ironing, to the front piazza, where Max Dudley and Mrs. Warren were waiting.

Max leaned against one of the posts, holding his Oxford cap by the long tassel; and behind him, through the purple mist, the gorgeous, autumn-tinted mountain-side. Standing there, be looked so lonely, so apart, as if some magic line had been drawn between him and his kind, while an atmosphere of deathlike stillness seemed to hem him in. And watching him curiously, with anxious, flickering eyes, old Mrs. Warren waited.

For weeks the old woman had been under a great strain, struggling with all her strength against the many warring passions that tore her and cried for utterance. All this morning she had hurried from one thing to another, to keep from an outburst of some sort, until now the supreme excitement of Max Dudley's coming seemed to have weakened her beyond movement, save for the nervous rocking of her chair.

He had made his offer calmly and quietly in the presence of all, and for a moment things had grown dim before Mrs. Warren's vision, then cleared as she looked proudly into the astonished eyes of Lizer Wilson, and into the sad face of Dock, who had come up while they talked.

People might say what they pleased now, but no girl in any valley had ever had a chance like this. And Si! How Si would rage to think of what his talk had accomplished. Hannah could stand with the best now, and the Warrens be acknowledged as the equals of all.

She started when Hannah's quick step sounded in the lobby, and Max lifted his head and drew himself away from the support of the post. His tired eyes dilated, and his pale face grew whiter as the girl approached. And Lizer paused, with uplifted iron, and Dock drew a step nearer.

"You wanted me, Mr. Dudley?" and Hannah paused in front of him, with her hands clasped and two crimson spots on her cheeks.

"Yes, Hannah." His voice was very low, and the girl realized, by a subtle instinct, all that he suffered, saw clearly the marks of despair on his face, and wondered why she did not die of shame. "Yes, Hannah," then he paused, as if to steady his voice. "I have come to ask you to marry me, and help me to stop this talk. Your grandfather and grandmother have given their consent, and the matter lies with you. We know that there is no truth in anything that has been said, and everyone who knows you, Hannah, knows you to be a good, true woman, and as such I have come to offer you the protection of my name." His voice was very low, but Hannah thought she had never heard anything sound so sweet before. All bitterness passed from out her heart, all doubts, and the great humiliation of her life seemed turned to glory. Then his voice ceased, and in the tense stillness Mrs. Warren rose, with a strained look in her eyes. What was it she saw in Hannah's face? Dock leaned forward, Mr. Warren drew a step nearer, and Lizer forgot the heavy iron she still held poised.

"I'm obleeged to you, Mr. Dudley, fur the true words you hev said this day," Hannah began, "an' fur stannin' up fur me thet couldn't do nothin' fur myself. An' I knows what hit means, Mr. Dudley, for you to say the words you have said this day, an' I prays the Lord will bless you for hit." And while she spoke soul looked into soul, the distance between them was bridged, and the strength of her beauty struck Max as it had never done before. She was superb. "You hev been mighty good to me, Mr. Dudley," she went on, "but thar's a fur way 'twixt you an' me, thar's a diffrunce as wide as all this valley," with a little, sweeping gesture. "An' you ain't fur folks like me. But thar's one o' my own folks, Mr. Dudley, hev offered me his honest name, an' please God all will hap out right. But all the same, God bless you, Mr. Dudley."

"Hannah! Gal!" a sharp voice cried, and all turned quickly, "Is you crazy, crazy? Si 'll never come agin, never!"

There was a moment's pause, and Hannah looked down into the old woman's face pityingly. How gray and drawn it looked, and she said soothingly, "Num mine, Granny, hit's all right, hit's a better man 'an Si Durket, Granny."

"True, Hannah?" And Max laid his hand on Hannah's shoulder.

"As true as God's daylight, Mr. Dudley," turning her beautiful face up to his. "An' yander he stands—Dock Wilson."

There was a low moan, and the old woman reeled forward heavily.

> "The high that proved too high,
> the heroic for earth too hard,
> The passion that left the ground,
> to lose itself in the sky,
> Are music sent up to God
> by the lover and the bard,
> Enough that he heard it once;
> we shall hear it by and by."

~*Abe Vogler*, Robert Browning

XX

It was cold, but Melville waited patiently at the top of the mountain for Dudley. He would not go farther, for fear of missing him in the dusk, and he had much to tell him. It was a long way he had come to meet his friend, but what he had to say was not for others to hear, and the long walk back would give Dudley time to recover himself.

Presently he heard him coming, and Melville shrank from the task he had set himself. How could he tell Dudley? But Max was upon him by this, and started, as if from a dream. "What has happened?" he asked, and laid his hand on Melville's shoulder.

"I was anxious," Melville faltered. "What has happened to you?"

"Nothing. The girl refused me. A princess could not have done it more grandly, and the old grandmother died in a fit. But what ails you?"

"Cartright . . ."

"Well, Cartright?" and leaning against a tree, Dudley took off his cap and passed his hand wearily across his brow and eyes. The scenes in the Cove had tired him more than he had realized until now, and now he felt almost too weary to go farther. "What about Cartright? He knew where I was gone; has he posted me for a fool?"

"Worse than that."

Dudley started forward, taking hold of Melville. "What has he *dared* to say?"

"About you? Nothing. It is, it is Miss Welling." The grasp on Melville's shoulder became almost unbearable. "Oh, Dudley, Cartright is engaged to Miss Welling! Asked her at noon, announced it at once, and Mrs. Skinner says that Professor Welling is 'immensely pleased.' I told you Cartright was working for his own ends, and I thought that you would like to have a walk after hearing. So I slipped away, nobody knows I am come."

There was a moment's silence, then Dudley turned homeward, walking slowly.

This story of an attempted sexual assault
by a black man which ends with his
imprisonment rather than a lynching
appeared in the February 1898 issue of
Harper's Magazine. It was published in the
short story collection *An Incident and Other
Happenings* by Harper & Brothers in 1899.

AN INCIDENT

IT WAS AN ORDINARY FRAME HOUSE standing on brick legs, and situated on a barren knoll, which, because of the dead level of marsh and swamp and deserted fields from which it rose, seemed to achieve the loneliness of a real height. The south and west sides of the house looked out on marsh and swamp; the north and east sides on a wide stretch of old fields grown up in broom grass. Beyond the marsh rolled a river, now quite beyond its banks with a freshet. Beyond the swamp, which was a cypress swamp, rose a railway embankment leading to a bridge that crossed the river. On the other two sides the old fields ended in a solid black wall of pine barren. A roadway led from the house through the broom grass to the barren, and at the beginning of this road stood an outhouse, also on brick legs, which, save for a small stable, was the sole outbuilding.

One end of this house was a kitchen; the other was divided into two rooms for servants. There were some shattered remnants of oak trees out in the field, and some chimneys overgrown with vines, showing where in happier times the real homestead had stood.

It was towards the end of February, a clear afternoon drawing towards sunset, and all the flat, sad country was covered with a drifting red glow that turned the field of broom grass into a sea of gold; that lighted up the black wall of pine barren, and shot, here and there, long shafts of light into the somber depths of the cypress swamp. There was no sign of life about the dwelling house, though the doors and windows stood open, but every now and then a negro woman came out of the kitchen and looked about, while within a dog whined.

Shading her eyes with her hand, this woman would gaze across the field towards the ruin, then down the road, then, descending the steps, she would walk a little way towards the swamp and look along the dam that, ending the yard on this side, led out between the marsh and the swamp to the river. The overfull river had backed up into the yard, however, and the line of the dam could now only be guessed by the wall of solemn cypress trees that edged the swamp. Still, the woman looked in this direction many times, and also towards the railway embankment, from which a path led towards the house, crossing the head of the swamp by a bridge made of two felled trees.

But look as she would, she evidently did not find what she sought, and muttering "Lawd, Lawd," she returned to the kitchen, shook the tied dog into silence, and seating herself near the fire gazed somberly into its depths. A covered pot hung from the crane over the blaze, making a thick bubbling noise, as if what it contained had boiled itself almost dry, and a coffee pot on the hearth gave forth a pleasant smell. The woman from time to time turned the spit of a tin kitchen wherein a fowl was roasting, and moved about the coals on the top of a Dutch oven at one side. She had made preparation for a comfortable supper, and evidently for others than herself.

She went again to the open door and looked about, the dog springing up and following to the end of his cord. The sun was nearer the horizon now, and the red glow was brighter. She looked towards the ruin, looked along the road, came down the steps and looked towards the swamp and the railway path. This time she took a few steps in the direction of the house, looked up at its open windows, at the front door standing ajar, at a pair of gloves and a branch from the vine at the ruin, that lay on the top step of the piazza, as if in passing one had put them there, intending to return in a moment. While she looked, the distant whistle of a locomotive was heard echoing back and forth about the empty land, and the rumble of an approaching train. She turned a little to listen, then went hurriedly back to the kitchen.

The rumbling sound increased, although the speed was lessened as the river was neared. Very slowly the train was moving, and the woman, peeping from the window, watched a gentleman get off and begin the descent of the path.

"Mass Johnnie!" she said. "Lawd, Lawd," and again seated herself by the fire until the rapid, firm footstep having passed, she went to the door, and standing well in the shadow, watched.

Up the steps the gentleman ran, pausing to pick up the gloves and the bit of vine. The negro groaned. Then in at the open door, "Nellie!" he called, "Nellie!"

The woman heard the call, and going back quickly to her seat by the fire, threw her apron over her head.

"Abram!" was the next call, then, "Aggie!"

She sat quite still, and the master, running up the kitchen steps and coming in at the door, found her so.

"Aggie?"

"Yes, suh."

"Why didn't you answer me?"

The veiled figure rocked a little from side to side.

"What the mischief is the matter?" walking up to the woman and pulling the apron from over her face. "Where is your Miss Nellie?"

"I dun'no', suh, but yo' supper is ready, Mass Johnnie."

"Has your mistress driven anywhere?"

"De horse in de stable, suh." The woman now rose as if to meet a climax, but her eyes were still on the fire.

"Did she go out walking?"

"Dis mawnin', suh."

"This morning!" he repeated, slowly, wonderingly, "and has not come back yet?"

The woman began to tremble, and her eyes, shining and terrified, glanced furtively at her master.

"Where is Abram?"

"I dun'no', suh." It was a gasping whisper.

The master gripped her shoulder, and with a maddened roar he cried her name, "Aggie!"

The woman sank down. Perhaps his grasp forced her down. "'Fo' Gawd!" she cried, "'fo' Gawd, Mass Johnnie, I dun'no'!" holding up beseeching hands between herself and the awful glare of his eyes. "I'll tell you, suh, Mass Johnnie, I'll tell you," crouching away from him. "Miss Nellie gimme out dinner en supper, den she put on she hat en gone to de ole chimbly en git some de brier what grow dey. Den she come back en tell Abram fuh git a bresh broom en sweep de ya'd. Lemme go, Mass Johnnie, please, suh, en I tell you better, suh. En Abram teck de hatchet en gone to'des de railroad fuh cut de bresh. 'Fo' Gawd, Mass Johnnie, it's de trute, suh! Den I tell Miss Nellie say de chicken is all git out de coop, en she say I muss ketch one fuh unner supper, suh; en I teck de dawg en gone in de fiel' fuh look fuh de chicken. En I see Miss Nellie put 'e glub en de brier on de step, en walk to'des de swamp, like 'e was goin' on de dam, 'kase de water ent rise ober de dam den, en den I gone in de broom grass en I run de chicken, en I ent ketch one tay I git clean ober to de woods. En when I come back de glub is layin' on de step, en de brier, des like Miss Nellie leff um." She stopped and her master straightened himself.

"Well," he said, and his voice was strained and weak.

The servant once more flung her apron over her head, and broke into violent crying. "Dat's all, Mass Johnnie, dat's all! I dun'no' wey Abram is gone; I dun'no' what Abram is do! Nobody ent been on de place dis day, dis day but me, but me! Oh, Lawd, oh,LawdenGawd!"

The master stood as if dazed. His face was drawn and gray, and his breath came in awful gasps. A moment he stood so, then he strode out of the house. With a howl the dog sprang forward, snapping the cord, and rushed after his master.

The woman's cries ceased, and without moving from her crouching position she listened with straining ears to the sounds that reached her from the stable. In a moment the clatter of horses' hoofs going at a furious pace swept by, then a dead silence fell. The intense quiet seemed to rouse her, and going to the door, she looked out. The glow had faded, and the gray mist was gathering in distinct strata above the marsh and the river. She went out and looked about her as she had done so many times during that long day. She gazed at the water that was still rising, she peered cautiously behind the stable and under the houses, she approached the woodpile as if under protest, gathered some logs into her arms and an axe that was lying there; then turning towards the kitchen, she hastened her steps, looking back over her shoulder now and again, as if fearing pursuit. Once in the kitchen she threw down the wood and barred the door, she shut the boarded window shutter, fastening it with an iron hook; then leaning the axe against the chimney, she sat down by the fire, muttering, "If dat nigger come sneakin' back yer now, I'll split 'e haid open, *sho*."

Recovering a little from her panic, she was once more a cook, and swung the crane from over the fire, brushed the coals from the top of the Dutch oven, and pushed the tin kitchen farther from the blaze. "Mass Johnnie 'll want sump'h'n to eat some time dis night," she said, then, after a pause, "en I gwine eat *now*." She got a plate and cup, and helped herself to hominy out of the pot, and to a roll out of the oven, but though she looked at the fowl she did not touch it, helping herself instead to a goodly cup of coffee. So she ate and drank with the axe close beside her, now and then pausing to groan and mutter, "Po' Mass Johnnie, po' Mass Johnnie, Lawd, Lawd, if Miss Nellie had er sen' Abram atter dat chicken, like I tell um, Lawd" shaking her head the while.

Through the gathering dusk John Morris galloped at the top speed of his horse. Reaching the little railway station, he sprang off, throwing the reins over a post, and strode in.

"Write this telegram for me, Green," he said, "my hand trembles:

"To Sam Partin, Sheriff, Pineville:

"My wife missing since morning. Negro, Abram Washington, disappeared. Bring men and dogs. Get off night train this side of bridge. Will be fire on the path to mark the place. John Morris."

"Great God," the operator said, in a low voice. "I'll come too, Mr. Morris."

"Thank you," John Morris answered. "I am going to get the Wilson boys, and Rountree and Mitchell," and for the first time the men's eyes met. Determined, deadly, sombre, was the look exchanged, then Morris went away.

None of the men whom Morris summoned said much, nor did they take long to arm themselves, saddle, and mount, and by nine o'clock Aggie heard them come galloping across the field, then her master's voice calling her. There was little time in which to make the signal fire on the railroad embankment, and to cut lightwood into torches, even though there were many hands to do the work. John Morris's dog followed him a part of the way to the woodpile, then turned aside to where the water had crept up from the swamp into the yard. Aggie saw the dog, and spoke to Mr. Morris. "Dat's de way dat dawg do dis mawnin', Mass Johnnie, an' when I gone to ketch de chicken, Miss Nellie was walkin' to'des dat berry place."

An irresistible shudder went over John Morris, and one of the gentlemen standing near asked if he had a boat.

"The bateau was tied to that stake this morning," Mr. Morris answered, pointing to a stake some distance out in the water, "but I have another boat in the top of the stable." Every man turned to go for it, showing the direction of their fears, and launched it where the log bridge crossed the head of the swamp, and where now the water was quite deep.

The whistle was heard at the station, and the rumble of the oncoming train. The fire flared high, lighting up the group of men standing about it, booted and belted with ammunition belts, quiet, and white, and determined.

Many curious heads looked out as the sheriff and his men, six men besides Green from the station, got off, then the train rumbled away in the darkness towards the surging, turbulent river, and the crowd moved towards the house.

Mr. Morris told of his absence in town on business. That Abram had been hired first as a fieldhand, and that later, after his marriage, he had taken Abram from the field to look after his horse and to do the heavier work about the house and yard.

"And the woman Aggie is trustworthy?"

"I am sure of it, she used to belong to us."

"Abram is a strange negro?"

"Yes."

Then Aggie was called in to tell her story. Abram had taken the hatchet and had gone towards the railroad for brush to make a broom. She had taken the dog and gone into the broom grass to catch a fowl, and the last she had seen of her mistress she was walking towards the dam, which was then above the water.

"How long were you gone after the chicken?"

"I dun'no', suh, but I run um clean to the woods 'fo' I ketch um, en I walked back slow 'kase I tired."

"Were you gone an hour?"

"I spec so, suh, 'kase when I done ketch de chicken I stop fuh pick up some lightwood I see wey Abram been cuttin wood yistiddy."

"And your mistress was not here when you came back, nor Abram?"

"No, suh, nobody, en 'e wuz so lonesome I come en look in dis house fuh Miss Nellie, but 'e ent deyyer, en I look in de bush fuh Abram, but I ent see um nudder. En de dawg run to de water en howl en ba'k en ba'k tay I tie um up in de kitchen."

"And was the boat tied to the stake this morning?"

"Yes, suh, en when I been home long time en git scare, den I look en see de boat gone."

"You don't think that your mistress got in the boat and drifted away by accident?"

"No, suh, nebber, suh. Miss Nellie 'fraid de water lessen Mass Johnnie is wid um."

"Is Abram a good boy?"

"I dunno', suh, I dun'no' nuttin' 'tall 'bout Abram, suh; Abram is strange nigger to we."

"Did he take his things out of his room?"

"Abram t'ings? Ki! Abram ent hab nuttin' ceppen what Miss Nellie en Mass Johnnie gi'um. No, suh, dat nigger ent hab nuttin' but de close on 'e back when 'e come to we."

The sheriff paused a moment. "I think, Mr. Morris," he said, at last, "that we'd better separate. You, with Mr. Mitchell and Mr. Rountree, had better take your boat and hunt in the swamp and marsh, and along the riverbank. Let Mr. Wilson, his brothers, and Green take your dog and search in the pine barren. I'll take my men and my dogs and cross the railroad. The signal of any discovery will be three shots fired in quick succession. The gathering place 'll be this house, where a member of the discovering party 'll meet the other parties and bring 'em to the discovery. And I beg that you'll refrain from violence, at least until we can reach each other. We've no proof of anything . . ."

"Damn proof!"

"An' our only clue," the sheriff went on, "the missing boat, points to Mrs. Morris's safety." A little consultation ensued, then agreeing to the sheriff's distribution of forces, they left the house.

The sheriff's dogs, the lean, small hounds used on such occasions, were tied and he held the ropes. There was an anxious look on his face, and he kept his dogs near the house until the party for the barren had mounted and ridden away, and the party in the boat had pushed off into the blackness of the swamp, a torch fastened at the prow casting weird, uncertain shadows. Then ordering his six men to mount and to lead his horse, he went to the room of the negro Abram and got an old shirt. The two lean little dogs were restless, but they made no sound as he led them across the railway. Once on the other side, he let them smell the shirt, and loosed them, and was about to mount, when, in the flash of a torch, he saw something in the grass.

"A hatchet," he said to his companions, picking it up, "and clean, thank God!"

The men looked at each other, then one said, slowly, "He coulder drowned her?"

The sheriff did not answer, but followed the dogs that had trotted away with their noses to the ground.

"I'm sure the nigger came this way," the sheriff said, after a while. "Those others may find the poor young lady, but I feel sure of the nigger."

One of the men stopped short. "That nigger's got to die," he said.

"Of course," the sheriff answered, "but not by Judge Lynch's court. This circuit's got a judge that'll hang him lawfully."

"I b'lieve Judge More will," the recalcitrant admitted, and rode on. "But," he added, "if I know Mr. John Morris, that nigger's safe to die one way or another."

They rode more rapidly now, as the dogs had quickened their pace. The moon had risen, and the riding, for men who hunted recklessly, was not bad. Through woods and across fields, over fences and streams, down bypaths and old roads, they followed the little dogs.

"We're makin' straight for the next county," the sheriff said.

"We're makin' straight for the old Powis settlement," was answered. "Nothin' but niggers have lived there since the war, an' that nigger's there, I'll bet."

"That's so," the sheriff said. "About how many niggers live there?"

"There ain't more than half a dozen cabins left now. We can easy manage that many."

It was a long rough ride, and in spite of their rapid pace it was some time after midnight before they saw the clearing where clustered the few cabins left of the plantation quarters of a well known place, which in its day had yielded wealth to its owners. The moon was very bright, and, save for the sound of the horses' feet, the silence was intense.

"Look sharp," the sheriff said, "that nigger ain't sleepin' much if he's here, and he might try to slip off."

The dogs were going faster now, and yelping a little.

"Keep up, boys!" and the sheriff spurred his horse.

In a few minutes they thundered into the little settlement, where the dogs were already barking and leaping against a close-shut door. Frightened black faces began to peer out. Low exclamations and guttural ejaculations were heard as the armed men scattered, one to each cabin, while the sheriff hammered at the door where the dogs were jumping.

"It's the sheriff!" he called, "come to get Abram Washington. Bring him out and you kin go back to your beds. We're all armed, and nobody need to try runnin'."

The door opened cautiously, and an old negro looked out. "Abram's my son, Mr. Partin," he said, "an' 'fo' Gawd he ent yer."

"No lyin', old man; the dogs brought us straight here. Don't make me burn the house down; open the door."

The door was closing when the sheriff, springing from his horse, forced it steadily back. A shot came from within, but it ranged wild, and in an instant the sheriff's pistol covered the one room, where a smoldering fire gave light. Two of the men followed him, and one, making for the fire, pushed it into a blaze, which revealed a group of negroes—an old man, a young woman, some children, and a young man crouching behind with a gun in his hand. The sheriff walked straight up to the young man, whose teeth were chattering.

"I arrest you," he said, "come on."

"That's the feller," confirmed one of the guard. "I've seen him at Mr. Morris's place."

"Tie him," the sheriff ordered, "while I get that gun. Give it to me, old man, or I'll take you to jail, too." It was yielded up, an old-time rifle, and the sheriff smashed it against the side of the chimney, throwing the remnants into the fire. "Lead on," he said, and the young negro was taken outside. Quickly he was lifted on to a horse and tied there, while the former rider mounted behind one of his companions, and they rode out of the settlement into the woods.

"Git into the shadows," one said, "they might be fools enough to shoot."

Once in the road, the sheriff called a halt. "One of you must ride back to Mr. Morris's place and collect the other search parties, while we make for Pineville jail. Now, Abram, come on."

"I ent done nuttin', Mr. Partin, suh," the negro urged. "I ent hot Mis' Morris."

"Who said anything 'bout Mrs. Morris?" was asked, sharply.

The negro groaned.

"You're hanging yourself, boy," the sheriff said, "but since you know, where is Mrs. Morris?"

"I dun'no', suh."

"Why did you run away?"

"'Kase I 'fraid Mr. Morris."

"What were you 'fraid of?"

"'Kase Mis' Morris gone."

They were riding rapidly now, and the talk was jolted out.

"Where?"

"I dun'no', suh, but I ent tech um."

"You're a damned liar."

"No, suh, I ent tech um; I des look at um."

"I'd like to gouge your eyes out!" cried one of the men, and struck him.

"None o' that!" ordered the sheriff. "And you keep your mouth shut, Abram, you'll have time to talk on your trial."

"Blast a trial!" growled the crowd.

"The rope's round his neck now," suggested one, "and I see good trees at every step."

"Please, suh, gentlemen," pleaded the shaking negro, "I ent done nuttin'."

"Shut your mouth," ordered the sheriff again, "and ride faster. Day 'll soon break."

"You're 'fraid Mr. Morris 'll ketch us 'fore we reach the jail," laughed one of the guard. And the sheriff did not answer.

The eastern sky was gray when the party rode into Pineville, a small, straggling country town, and clattered through its one street to the jail. To the negro, at least, it was a welcome moment, for, with his feet tied under the horse, his hands tied behind his back, and a rope with a slipknot round his neck, he had not found the ride a pleasant one. A misstep of his horse would surely have precipitated his hanging, and he knew well that such an accident would have given much satisfaction to his captors. So he uttered a fervent "Teng Gawd," as he was hustled into the jail gate and heard it close behind him.

Early as it was, most of the town was up and excited. Betting had been high as to whether the sheriff would get the prisoner safe into the jail, and even the winners seemed disappointed that he had accomplished this feat, although they praised his skillful management. But the sheriff knew that if the lady's body was found, that if Mr. Morris could find any proof against the negro, that if Mr. Morris even expressed a wish that the negro should hang, the whole town would side with him instantly, and the sheriff knew, further, that in such an emergency he would be the negro's only defender, and that the jail could easily be carried by the mob.

All these thoughts had been with him during the long night, and though he himself was quite willing to hang the negro, being fully persuaded of his guilt, he was determined to do his official duty, and to save the prisoner's life until sentence was lawfully passed on him. But how? If he could quiet the town before the day brightened, he had a plan, but to accomplish this seemed well nigh impossible.

He handcuffed the prisoner and locked him into a cell, then advised his escort to go and get food, as before the day was done—indeed, just as soon as Mr. Morris should reach the town—he would probably need them to help him defend the jail.

They nodded among themselves, and winked, and laughed a little, and one said, "Right good play actin'," and watching, the sheriff knew that he could depend on only one man, his own brother, to help him. But he sent him off along with the others, and was glad to see that the crowd of townspeople went with his guard, listening eagerly to the details of the suspected tragedy and the subsequent hunt. This was his only chance, and he went at once to the negro's cell.

"Now, Abram," he said, "if you don't want to be a dead man in an hour's time, you'd better do exactly what I tell you."

"Yes, suh, please Gawd."

"Put on this old hat," handing him one, "and pull it down over your eyes, and follow me. When we get outside, you walk along with me like any ordinary nigger going to his work, and remember, if you stir hand or foot more than to walk, you are a dead man. Come on."

There was a back way out of the jail, and to this the sheriff went. Once outside, he walked briskly, the negro keeping step with him diligently. They did not meet any one, and before very long they reached the sheriff's house, which stood on the outskirts of the town. Being a widower, he knocked peremptorily on the door, and when it was opened by his son, he marched his prisoner in without explanation.

"Shut the door, Willie," he said, "and load the Winchester."

"Please, suh," interjected the negro.

For answer, the sheriff took a key from the shelf, and led him out of the back door to where, down a few steps, there was another door leading into an underground cellar.

"Now, Abram," he said, "you're to keep quiet in here till I can take you to the city jail. There is no use your trying to escape, because my two boys 'll be about here all day with their repeating rifles, and they can shoot."

"Yes, suh."

"And whoever unlocks this door and tells you to come out, you do it, and do it quick."

"Yes, suh."

Locking the door, the sheriff turned to his son. "You and Charlie must watch that door all day, Willie," he said, "but you mustn't seem to watch it, and keep your guns handy, and if that nigger tries to get away, kill him, don't hesitate. I must go back to the jail and make out like he's there. And tell Charlie to feed the horse and hitch him to the buggy, and let him stand ready in the stable, for when I'll want him, I'll want him quick. Above all things, don't let anybody know that the nigger's here. But keep the cellar key in your pocket, and shoot if he tries to run. If your uncle Jim comes, do whatever he tells you, but nobody else, lessen they bring a note from me. Now remember. I'm trusting you, boy, and don't you make any mistake about killing the nigger if he tries to escape."

"All right," the boy answered, cheerfully, and the father went away. He almost ran to the jail, and, entering once more by the back door, found things undisturbed. Presently his brother called to him, and the gates and doors being opened, came in, bringing a waiter of hot food and coffee.

"I told Jinnie you'd not like to leave the jail," he said, "an' she fixed this up."

"Jinnie's mighty good," the sheriff answered, "and sometimes a woman's mighty handy to have about, sometimes, but I'd not leave one out in the country like Mr. Morris did, no, sir, not in these days. We could do it before the war and during the war, but not now. The old niggers were taught some decency, but these young ones, God help us, for I don't see any safety for this country 'cept Judge Lynch. And I'll tell you this is my first an' last term as sheriff. The work's too dirty."

"Buck Thomas was a boss sheriff," his brother answered, "he found the niggers all right, but the niggers never found the jail, and the niggers were 'fraid to death of him."

"Maybe Buck was right," the sheriff said, "and 'twas heap the easiest way, but here comes the town."

The two men went to the window and saw a crowd of people advancing down the road, led by Mr. Morris and his friends on horse-back.

"I b'lieve you're the only man in this town that 'll stand by me, Jim," the sheriff said. "I swore in six last night, and I see 'em all in that crowd. Poor Mr. Morris. In his place I'd do just what he's doin'. Blest if yonder ain't Doty Buxton comin' to help me. I'll let him in, but see here, Jim, I'm going to send Doty to telegraph to the city for Judge More, and I want you to slip out the back way right now, and run to my house, and tell Willie to give you the buggy and the nigger, and you drive that nigger into the city. Of course you'll kill him if he tries to escape."

"The nigger ain't here?"

"I'm no fool, Jim. And I'll hold this jail, me and Doty, as long as possible, and you drive like hell! You see?"

"I didn't know you really wanted to save the nigger," his brother remonstrated, "nobody b'lieves that."

"I don't, as a nigger. But you go on now, and I'll send Doty with the telegram, and make time by talkin' to Mr. Morris. I don't think they've found anything; if they had, they'd have come a - galloping, and the devil himself couldn't have stopped 'em. Gosh, but its awful! Who knows what that nigger's done. When I look at Mr. Morris, I wish you fellers had overpowered me last night, and had fixed things."

He let his brother out at the back, then went round to the front gate, where he met the man whom he had called Doty Buxton.

"Go telegraph Judge More the facts of the case," he said, "an' ask him to come. I don't believe I'll need any men if he'll come, and besides, he and Mr. Morris are friends."

As the man turned away, one of the horsemen rode up to the sheriff.

"We demand that negro," he said.

"I supposed that was what you'd come for, Mr. Mitchell," the sheriff answered, "but you know, sir, that as much as I'd like to oblige you, I'm bound to protect the man. He swears that he's never touched Mrs. Morris."

"Great God, sheriff, how can you mention the thing quietly? You know . . ."

"Yes, I know, and I know that I'll never do the dirty work of a sheriff a day after my terms up. But we haven't any proof against this nigger except that he ran away . . ."

"Isn't that enough when the lady can't be found, nor a trace of her?"

"I found the hatchet."

"And . . ."

"It was clean, thank God!"

Mr. Mitchell jerked the reins so violently that his horse, tired as he was, reared and plunged.

"Mr. Morris declines to speak with you," he went on, when the horse had quieted down, "but he's determined that the negro shall not escape, and the whole county 'll back him."

"I know that," the sheriff answered, patiently, "and in his place I'd do the same thing, but in my place I must do my official duty. I'll not let the nigger escape, you may be sure of that, and I've telegraphed for Judge More to come out here. I've telegraphed the whole case. Surely Mr. Morris 'll trust Judge More?"

Mitchell dragged at his mustache. "Poor Morris is nearly dead," he said.

"Of course; won't he go and eat and rest till Judge More comes? Every house in the town 'll be open to him."

"No, he'll not wait nor rest, and we're determined to hang that negro."

"It 'll be mighty hard to shed our blood, friends and neighbors," remonstrated the sheriff, "and all over a worthless nigger."

"That's your lookout," Mr. Mitchell answered. "A trial and a big funeral is glory for a negro, and the penitentiary means nothing to them but free board and clothes. I tell you, sheriff, lynching is the only thing that affects them."

"You won't wait even until I get an answer from Judge More?"

"Well, to please you, I'll ask." And Mitchell rode back to his companions.

The conference between the leaders was longer than the sheriff had hoped, and before he was again approached, Doty Buxton had returned, saying that Judge More's answer would be sent to the jail just as soon as it came.

"You'll stand by me, Doty?" the sheriff asked.

"'Cause I like you, Mr. Partin," Doty answered, slowly, "not 'cause I want to save the nigger. I b'lieve in my soul he's done drownded the po' lady's body."

"All right, you go inside and be ready to chain the gate if I am run in." Then he waited for the return of the envoy.

John Morris sat on his horse quite apart even from his own friends, and after a few words with him, Mitchell had gone to the group of horsemen about whom the townsmen were gathered. The sheriff did not know what this portended, but he waited patiently, leaning against the wall of the jail and whittling a stick. He knew quite well that all these men were friendly to him, that they understood his position perfectly, and that they expected him to pretend to do his duty to a reasonable extent, and so far their good nature would last, but he knew equally well that in their eyes the negro had put himself beyond the pale of the law, that they were determined to hang him, and would do it at any cost, and that the only mercy which the culprit could expect from this upper class to which Mr. Morris belonged was that his death would be quick and quiet. He knew also that if they found out that he was in earnest in defending the prisoner he himself would be in danger, not only from Mr. Morris and his friends, but from the townsmen as well. Of course all this could be avoided by showing them that the jail was empty, but to do this would be at this stage to insure the fugitive's capture and death. To save the negro he must hold the jail as long as possible, and if he had to shoot, shoot into the ground. All this was quite clear to him; what was not clear was what these men would do when they found that he had saved the negro and they had stormed an empty jail.

He was an old soldier, and had been in many battles; he had fought hardest when he knew that things were most hopeless; he had risked his life recklessly, and death had been as nothing to him when he had thought that he would die for his country. But now, now to risk his life for a negro, for a worthless creature whom he thought deserved hanging, was this his duty? Why not say, "I have sent the negro to the city"? How quickly those fierce horsemen would dash away down the road. Well, why not? He drew himself up. He was not going to turn coward at this late day. His duty lay very plain before him, and he would not flinch. And he fixed his eyes once more on the little stick he was cutting, and waited.

Presently he saw a movement in the crowd, and the thought flashed across him that they might capture him suddenly while he stood there alone and unarmed. He stepped quickly to the gate, where Doty Buxton waited, and standing in the opening, asked the crowd to stand back and to send Mr. Mitchell to tell him what the decision was. There was a moment's pause, then Mitchell rode forward.

"Mr. Morris says that Judge More cannot help matters. The negro must die, and at once. We don't want to hurt you, and we don't want to destroy public property, but we are going to have that wretch if we have to burn the jail down. Will you stop all this by delivering the prisoner to us?"

The sheriff shook his head. "I can't do that, sir. But one thing I do ask, that you'll give me warning before you set fire to the jail."

"If that 'll make you give up, we'll set fire now."

"I didn't say it'd make me surrender, but only that I'd like to throw a few things out, like Doty Buxton, for instance," smiling a little.

"All right, when we stop trying to break in, we'll be making ready to smoke you out. The jail's empty but for this negro, I hear."

"Yes, the jail's empty, but don't you think you oughter give me a little time to weigh matters?"

"Is there any chance of your surrendering?"

"To be perfectly honest," the sheriff answered, "there isn't." Then, seeing the crowd approaching, he slipped inside the heavy gate, and Doty Buxton chained it. "Now, Doty," he said, "we'll peep through these auger holes and watch 'em, and when you see 'em coming near, you must shoot through these lower holes. Shoot into the ground just in front of 'em. It's nasty to have the dirt jumpin' up right where you've got to walk. I know how it feels. I always wanted to hold up both feet at once. I reckon they've gone to get a log to batter down the gate. They can do it, but I'll make 'em take as long as I can. We mustn't hurt anybody, Doty, but we must protect the State property as far as we're able. Here they come. Keep the dirt dancin', Doty. See that? They don't like it. I told you they'd want to take up both feet at once. When bullets are flying round your head, you can't help yourself, but it's hard to put your feet down right where the nasty little things are peckin' about. Here they come again. Keep it up, Doty. See that? They've stopped again. They ain't real mad with me yet, the boys ain't, only Mr. Morris and his friends are mad. The boys think I'm just pretending to do my duty for the looks of it, but I ain't. Gosh! Now they've fixed it. With Mr. Morris at the front end of that log, there's no hope of scare. He'd walk over dynamite to get that nigger. Poor feller. Here they come at a run. Don't hurt anybody, Doty. Bang! Wait, I'll call a halt by knocking on the gate; it 'll gain us a little more time."

"What do you want?" came in answer to the sheriff's taps.

"I'll arrest every man of you for destroying State property," the sheriff answered.

"All right, come do it quick," was the response. "We're waitin', but we won't wait long."

"I reckon we'll have to go inside, Doty," the sheriff said, then to the attacking party, "If you'll wait till Judge More comes, I promise you the nigger 'll hang."

For answer there was another blow on the gate.

"Remember, I've warned you!" the sheriff called.

"Hush that rot!" was the answer, followed by a third blow.

The sheriff and Doty retreated to the jail, and the attack went on. It was a two-story building of wood, but very strongly built, and unless they tried fire the sheriff hoped to keep the besiegers at bay for a little while yet. He stationed Doty at one window, and himself took position at another, each with loaded pistols, which were only to be used as before—to make "the dirt jump."

"To tell you the truth, Doty," the sheriff said, "if you boys had had any sense you'd have overpowered me last night, and we'd not have had all this trouble."

"We wanted to," Doty answered, "but you're new at the business, an' you talked so big we didn't like to make you feel little."

"Here they come," the sheriff went on, as the stout gate swayed inward. "One more good lick an' it's down. That's it. Now keep the dirt dancin', Doty, but don't hurt anybody."

Mr. Morris was in the lead, and apparently did not see the "dancin' dirt," for he approached the jail at a run.

"It's no use, Doty," the sheriff said, "all we can do is to wait till they get in, for I'm not going to shoot anybody. It may be wrong to lynch, but in a case like this it's the rightest wrong that ever was." So the sheriff sat there thinking, while Doty watched the attack from the window.

According to his calculations of time and distance, the sheriff thought that the prisoner was now so far on his way as to be almost out of danger by pursuit, and his mind was busy with the other question as to what would happen when the jail was found to be empty. He had not heard from Judge More, but the answer could not have reached him after the attack began. He felt sure that the judge would come, and come by the earliest train, which was now nearly due.

"The old man 'll come if he can," he said to himself, "and he'll help me if he comes, and I wish the train would hurry."

He felt glad when he remembered that he had given the keys of the cells to his brother, for though he would try to save further destruction of property by telling the mob that the jail was empty, he felt quite sure that they would not believe him, and in default of keys, would break open every door in the building, which obstinacy would grant him more time in which to hope for Judge More and arbitration. That it was possible for him to slip out once the besiegers had broken in never occurred to him; his only thought was to stay where he was until the end came, whatever that might be. They were taking longer than he had expected, and every moment was a gain.

Doty Buxton came in from the hall, where he had gone to watch operations. "The do' is givin'," he said, "what 'll you do?"

"Nothin'," the sheriff answered, slowly.

"Won't you give 'em the keys?"

"I haven't got 'em."

"Gosh!" and Doty's eyes got big as saucers.

Very soon the outer door was down, and the crowd came trooping in, all save John Morris, who stopped in the hallway. He seemed to be unable even to look at the sheriff, and the sheriff felt the averted face more than he would have felt a blow.

"We want the keys," Mitchell said.

The sheriff, who had risen, stood with his hands in his pockets, and his eyes, filled with sympathy, fastened on Mr. Morris, standing looking blankly down the empty hall.

"I haven't got the keys, Mr. Mitchell," he answered.

"Oh, come off!" cried one of the townsmen.

"Rocky!" cried another.

"Yo' granny's hat!" came from a third, while Doty Buxton said, gravely, "Give up, Partin, we've humored this duty business long enough."

"Do I understand you to say that you won't give up the keys?" Mitchell demanded, scornfully.

"No," the sheriff retorted, a little hotly, "you don't understand anything of the kind. I said that I didn't have the keys, and further," he added, after a moment's pause, "I say that this jail is empty."

There was silence for a moment, while the men looked at each other incredulously, then the jeering began again.

"There is nothing to do but to break open the cells," Morris said, sharply, but without turning his head. "We trusted the sheriff last night, and he outwitted us; we must not trust him again."

The sheriff's eyes flashed, and the blood sprang to his face. The crowd stood eagerly silent, but after a second the sheriff answered, quietly, "You may say what you please to me, Mr. Morris, and I'll not resent it under these circumstances, but I'll swear the jail's empty."

For answer Morris drove an axe furiously against the nearest cell door, and the crowd followed suit. There were not many cells, and as he looked from a window the sheriff counted the doors as they fell in, and listened for the whistle of the train that he hoped would bring Judge More. The doors were going down rapidly, and as each yielded the sheriff could hear cries and demonstrations. What would they do when the last one fell?

Presently Doty Buxton, who had been making observations, came in, pale and excited. "You'd better git yo' pistols," he said, "an' I'll git mine, for they're gittin' madder an' madder every time he ain't there."

"Well," the sheriff answered, "I want you to witness that I ain't armed. My pistols are over there on the table, unloaded. Thank the good Lord!" he exclaimed, suddenly, "there's the train, an' Judge More! I hope he'll come right along."

"An' there goes the last do'," said Doty, as, after a crash and a momentary silence, oaths and ejaculations filled the air. He drew near the sheriff, but the sheriff moved away.

"Stand back," he said, "you've got little children."

In an instant the crowd rushed in, headed by Morris, whose burning eyes seemed to be starting from his drawn white face. Like a flash Doty sprang forward and wrenched an axe from the infuriated man, crying out, "Partin ain't armed!"

For answer a blow from Morris's fist dropped the sheriff like a dead man. A sudden silence fell, and Morris, standing over his fallen foe, looked about him as if dazed. For an instant he stood so, then with a violent movement he pushed back the crowding men, and lifting the sheriff, dragged him towards the open window.

"Give him air," he ordered, "and go for the doctor, and for cold water!" He laid Partin flat and dragged open his collar. "He's not dead, see there; I struck him on the temple; under the ear would have killed him, but not this, not this! Give me that water, and plenty of it, and move back. He's not dead, no, and I didn't mean to kill him, but he has worked against me all night, and I didn't think a white man would do it."

"He's comin' round, Mr. Morris," said Doty, who knelt on the other side of the sheriff, "an' he didn't bear no malice against you, don't fret, but it's a good thing I jerked that axe outer yo' hand! See, he's ketchin' his breath, it's all right," as Partin opened his eyes slowly and looked about him.

A sound like a sigh came from the crowd; then a voice said, "Here comes Judge More."

Morris was still holding his wet handkerchief on the sheriff's head when the old judge came in. "My dear boy," he said, laying his hand on John Morris's shoulder. But Morris shook his head.

"Let's talk business, Judge More," he said, "and let's get Partin into a chair, where he can rest; I've just knocked him over."

Then Morris left the room, and Mitchell with him, going to the far side of the jailyard, where they walked up and down in silence. It was not long before Judge More and the sheriff joined them.

"The evidence was too slight for lynching," the judge said, looking straight into John Morris's eyes.

"Great God!" Morris cried, and struck his hands together.

"What more do you want?" Mitchell demanded, angrily. "His wife has disappeared, and the negro ran away."

"True, and I'll see to the case myself, but I'm glad that you did not hang the negro."

A boy came up with a telegram.

"From Jim, I reckon," the sheriff said, taking it. "No, it's for you, Mr. Morris."

It was torn open hastily, then Morris looked from one to the other with a blank, scared face, while the paper fluttered from his hold.

Mitchell caught it and read aloud slowly, as if he did not believe his eyes, "Am safe. Will be out on the ten o'clock train."

Morris stood there, shaking, and sobbing hard, dry sobs.

"It 'll kill him!" the sheriff said. "Quick, some whiskey!"

A flask was forced between the blue, trembling lips.

"Drink, old fellow," and Mitchell put his arm about Morris's shoulders. "It's all right now, thank God!"

Morris was leaning against his friend, sobbing like a woman. The sheriff drew his coat sleeve across his eyes, and shook his head.

"What made the nigger run away?" he said, slowly, adding, as if to himself, "God help us."

A vehicle was borrowed, and the judge and the sheriff drove with John Morris over to the station to meet the ten o'clock train. The sheriff and the judge remained in the little carriage, and the station agent did his best to leave the whole platform to John Morris. As the moments went by the look of anxious agony grew deeper on the face of the waiting man. The sheriff's ominous words, falling like a pall over the first flash of his happiness, had filled his mind with wordless terrors. He could scarcely breathe or move, and could not speak when his wife stepped off and put her hands in his. She looked up, and without a query, without a word of explanation, answered the anguished questioning of his eyes, whispering, "He did not touch me."

Morris staggered a little, then drawing her hand through his arm, he led her to the carriage. She shrank back when she saw the judge and the sheriff on the front seat, but Morris saying, "They must hear your story, dear," she stepped in.

"We are very thankful to see you, Mrs. Morris," the judge said, without turning his head, when the sheriff had touched up the horse and they moved away, "and if you feel able to tell us how it all happened, it 'll save time and ease your mind. This is Mr. Partin, the sheriff."

Mrs. Morris looked at the backs of the men in front of her; at their heads that were so studiously held in position that they could not even have glanced at each other; then up at her husband, appealingly.

"Tell it," he said, quietly, and laid his hand on hers that were wrung together in her lap. "You sent Aggie to catch the chickens, and the dog went with her?"

"Yes," fixing her eyes on his, "and I sent," she stopped with a shiver, and her husband said, "Abram."

"To cut some bushes to make a broom," she went on. "I had been for a walk to the old house, and as I came back I laid my gloves and a bit of vine on the steps, intending to return at once, but I wished to see if the boat was safe, for the water was rising so rapidly." She paused, as if to catch her breath, then, with her eyes still fixed on her husband, she went on, "I did not think that it was safe, and I untied the rope and picked up the paddle that was lying on the dam, intending to drag the boat farther up and tie it to a tree." She stopped again. Her husband put his arm about her.

"And then?" he said.

"And then, something, I don't know what, not a sound, but something, something made me turn, and I saw him, saw him coming, saw him stealing up behind me, with the hatchet in his hand, and a look, a look," closing her eyes as if in horror, "such an awful, awful look! And everybody gone. Oh, John!" she gasped, and clinging to her husband, she broke into hysterical sobs, while the judge gripped his walking stick and cleared his throat, and the sheriff swore fiercely under his breath.

"I was paralyzed," she went on, recovering herself, "and when he saw me looking he stopped. The next moment he threw the hatchet at me, and began to run towards me. The hatchet struck my foot, and the blow roused me, and I sprang into the boat. There were no trees just there, and jumping in, I pushed the boat off into the deep water. He picked up the hatchet and shook it at me, but the water was too deep for him to reach me, and he ran back along the dam and turned towards the railroad embankment. I was so terrified I could scarcely breathe; I pushed frantically in and out between the trees, farther and farther into the swamp. I was afraid that he would go round to the bridge and come down the bank to where the outlet from the swamp is and catch me there, but in a little while I saw where the rising water had broken the dam, and the current was rushing through and out to the river. The current caught the boat and swept it through the break. Oh, I was so glad! I am so afraid of water, but not then. I used the paddle as a rudder, and to push floating timber away. My foot was hurting me, and I looked at last and saw that it was cut."

A groan came from the judge, and the sheriff's head drooped.

"All day I drifted, and all night. I was so thirsty, and I grew so weak. At daylight this morning I found myself in a wide sheet of water, with marshes all round, and I saw a steamboat coming. I tied my handkerchief to the paddle and waved it, and they picked me up. And, John, I did not tell them anything except that the freshet had swept me away. They were kind to me, and a friendly woman bound up my foot. We got to town this morning early, and the captain lent me five dollars, John—Captain Meakin—so I telegraphed you, and took a carriage to the station and came out. Have, have you caught him? And, oh, but I am afraid, afraid!" And again she broke into hysterical sobs.

She asked no explanation. The negro's guilt was so burned in on her mind that she was sure that all knew it as well as she.

"You need have no further fears," her husband comforted. And the judge shook his head, and the sheriff swore again.

A white-haired woman in rusty black stood talking to a negro convict. It was in a stockade prison camp in the hill country. She had been a slave owner once, long ago, and now for her mission work taught on Sundays in the stockade, trying to better the negroes penned there.

This was a new prisoner, and she was asking him of himself.

"How long are you in for?" she asked.

"Fuhrebber, ma'am; fuh des es long es I lib," the negro answered, looking down to where he was making marks on the ground with his toes.

"And how did you get such a dreadful sentence?"

"I ent do much, ma'm, I des scare a white lady."

A wave of revulsion swept over the teacher, and involuntarily she stepped back. The negro looked up and grinned.

"De hatchet des cut 'e foot little bit, but I trow de hatchet. I ent tech um, no, ma'm. Den atterwards 'e baby daid; den dey say I muss stay yer fuhrebber. I ent sorry, 'kase I know say I hab to wuck anywheys I is; if I stay yer, if I go 'way, I hab to wuck. En I know say if I git outer dis place Mr. Morris 'll kill me sho, des sho. So I like fuh stay yer berry well."

And the teacher went away, wondering if her work, if any work, would avail; and what answer the future would have for this awful problem.

Sarah B. Elliott Bibliography

Short Fiction

"After long years." *Youth's Companion* 77 (April 23, 1903), 197-198.

"As a Little Child." *Independent* 39 (December 8, 1887), 26-28.

"Baldy." *Harper's Magazine* 98 (February 1899), 416-422.

"Beside Still Waters." *Youth's Companion* 72 (August 9, 1900), 385-386.

"An Ex-Brigadier." *Harper's Magazine* 80 (May 1890), 888-898.

"Faith and Faithfulness." *Harper's Magazine* 93 (October, 1896), 791-797.

"Florentine Idyl." *Independent* 40 (February 2, 1888), 26-29.

"Hands All Round." *Book News* 17 (September 1898), 1-6.

"Hybrid Roses." *Harper's Magazine* 113 (August 1906), 434-449.

"An Idle Man." *Independent* 39 (June 9, 1887), 26-28.

"An Incident." *Harper's Magazine* 96 (February 1898), 458-472.

"Jack Watson—A Character Study." *Current* 6 (September 11, 1886), 164-167.

"Jim's Victory." *Book News* 16 (October 1897), 47-53.

"The Last Flash." *Scribner's Magazine* 57 (June 1915), 692-695.

"A Little Child Shall Lead Them." *Youth's Companion* 76 (December 18, 1902), 649-650.

"Miss Ann's Victory." *Harper's Bazar* 31 (April 9, 1898), 317-318.

"Miss Eliza." *Independent* 39 (March 24, 1887), 26-27.

"Miss Maria's Revival." *Harper's Magazine* 93 (August 1896), 461-467.

"Mrs. Gallyhaw's Candy-stew." *Louisville Courier-Journal* (January - February 1887). This was a short story published in five weekly installments from January 30-February 27, 1887).

"Old Mrs. Dally's Lesson." *Youth's Companion* 78 (December 29, 1904)., 660-661.

"The Opening of the Southwestern Door." *Youth's Companion* 81 (February 28, 1907), 100-101.

"Progress." *McClure's Magazine* 14 (November 1899), 40-47.

"Readjustments." *Harper's Magazine* 120 (May 1910), 824-832.

"Some Data." *From Dixie*. Edited by Mrs. K.P. Minor. Richmond: West, Johnson & Co., 1893.

"Some Remnants." *Youth's Companion* 75 (April 18, 1901), 198-199.

"Squire Kayley's Conclusions." *Scribner's Magazine* 22 (December 1897), 758-769.

"Stephen's Margaret." *Independent* 40 (July 5, 1888), 26-28.

"Study of Song in Florence." *Harper's Magazine* 36 (March 1902), 215-222.

"What Polly Knew." *Smart Set* 9 (February 1903), 121-123.

"Without the Courts." *Harper's Magazine* 98 (March 1899), 575-579.

"The Wreck." *Youth's Companion* 81 (December 19, 1907), 637-639.

Essays and Other Short Non-fiction

"Ibsen." *Sewanee Review* 15 (January 1907), 75-99.

"A Race That Lives in Mountain Coves." *Ladies' Home Journal* 15 (September 1898), 11-12.

"Spirit of the Ninteenth Century in Fiction." *Outlook 67* (January 19, 1901), 153-158.

"A Study of Woman and Civilization." *Forensic Quarterly Review 1* (February 1910), 90-101.

Travel Writings

On her 1887 trip to the Holy Land and Europe, Sarah Barnwell Elliott wrote under contract to the *Louisvillle Courier-Journal* a series of writings from her trip which ran January 9-August 28, 1887. The stories were: "Loitering in Paris" (January 9, 1887), p. 16; "From Paris to Pisa" (January 23, 1887), p. 14; "Rome" (February 13, 1887), p. 1; "Across the Way" (March 20, 1887), p. 14; "The Land of Ham" (March 21, 1887), p. 4; "Sights in Egypt" (April 20, 1887), p. 2; "Jerusalem" (April 29, 1887), p. 2; "Jerusalem the Holy" (May 8, 1887), p. 19; "The City of Flowers" (May 12, 1887), p. 3; "Florence" (June 5, 1887), p. 16; "Etruscan Gods" (June 18, 1887), p. 4; "Siena, Italy" (July 3, 1887), p. 14; "In the Tyrol" (July 19, 1887), p. 4; "Merry England" (August 14, 1887), p. 14; "Oxford, England" (August 16, 1887), p. 2; "Old England" (August 28, 1887), p. 16.

Novels

The Durket Sperret. New York: Henry Holt & Co., 1898.

The Felmeres. New York: D. Appleton Co., 1879. Published by Henry Holt & Co., 1895.

Jerry. New York: Henry Holt & Co., 1891.

John Paget. New York: Henry Holt & Co., 1893.

The Making of Jane. New York: Henry Holt & Co., 1901. Reprinted 1912.

A Simple Heart. New York: John Ireland Co., 1887.

Non-Fiction

Sam Houston. The Beacon Biographies of Eminent Americans. Edited by M.A. De Wolfe Howe. Boston: Small Maynard & Co., 1900.

Play

Master of the King's Company. Written in collaboration with Maud Hosford. Copyright 1902. Produced at the Imperial Theater in London, October 6, 1904 as *His Majesty's Servant.*

QUESTIONS FOR DISCUSSION

1. The judicial system was a less used form of addressing matters between two grieved parties, as is made clear in both "Squire Kayley's Conclusions," "Without the Courts," and even "An Incident." How has this changed in the past century? In what ways have Americans become more litiguous? Are we better off for these differences?

2. In "Miss Maria's Revival" the staid Episcopal gentlewoman experiences a private conversion of heart even as her town goes through the throws of revival. The author's father, Bishop Stephen Elliott, changed his life following the Beaufort, South Carolina, revival of 1831, which is referenced in the short story. What might the author seek to reveal by showing us this private conversion in the midst of townspeople making public affirmations of faith? Is one preferable over the other?

3. In "Faith and Faithfulness" the once enslaved maid Kizzy seeks to care for Miss Maria as they live in reduced circumstances. In what

ways are "faith" and "faithfulness" shown by these two women? Where do you see faith? Where do you find faithfulness?

4. "An Ex-Brigadier" shows fault lines have occured in the old gentility and some niceities can no longer be afforded. The Ex-Brigadier spent years lying in order to get by, why does he convince young Willoughby to tell the truth?

5. Old Mrs. Warren spoke of the 'versity folk as "darn fools settin' round with books in their hands" who she saw as strangely lacking because they bought everything and saved nothing. How do the new arrivals to the Cumberland Plateau seem as you see them through the eyes of the Covites?

6. Mrs. Warren views the Durkets and Warrens as aristocratic lines, among the "upper ten" among the mountain folk. How might these distinctions be viewed by the University folk?

7. There is a "great gulf" fixed between the old folk of the coves and University men. How does Hannah Warren's crossing between these two worlds upset the boundaries? What assumptions are made about her relationships because she crosses this divide?

8. How do you feel about Hannah's choice to refuse Max Dudley's proposal in favor of Dock Wilson?

9. In "An Incident" the Sheriff is determined not to let "Judge Lynch" resolve the case. In time it is revealed that Mrs. Morris is still alive. What point might the author be making with this story?

10. In the very last line of "An Incident" the question of education is raised. Some reviewers have seen this sentence as the point of the short story. Do you agree? What answer does this ending provide? What questions does it raise?

11. After reading this sampling of Sarah Barnwell Elliott's writings about the Old South coming to terms with the changed circumstances of life following the American Civil War, how did she view the South through the eyes of others?

12. What was your favorite story of this collection? Why?